MIGHTY, MIGHTY

◆ ◆ ◆

MIGHTY, MIGHTY

WALLY RUDOLPH

SOFT SKULL PRESS

This book is a work of fiction. Names, characters, places, and incidents either are products of the author's imagination or are used fictitiously. Any resemblance to actual events or locales or persons, living or dead, is entirely coincidental.

Library of Congress Cataloging-in-Publication Data Is Available

Cover design by Jarrod Taylor
Interior design by Tabitha Lahr

ISBN 978-1-59376-623-8

Soft Skull Press
New York, NY
www.softskull.com

Printed in the United States of America

For Duke

❝ Violence is the American version of love. **❞**
—Roger Reeves

Today had been an anomaly, a damned aberration from the start.

Norman had woken up late, been trying to catch up all morning. He stomped on the tiles as he washed his face in the kitchen sink and shouted at his yellowed coffeemaker to drip while he dried his face with two takeout napkins that turned into molding mud on his cheeks as soon as they touched wet. For no reason at all, he'd woken up just past 6 AM and, just like that, he'd put his nearly sixteen weeks of flawless attendance at Old St. Pat's 7 AM mass at risk. He could stand being late. For Christ's sake, things come up. But for no reason—*no reason at all?* That drove him crazy, made his 'roids flare. He hated rushing on the toilet. He hated leaving his kitchen and front hallway a mess. He hated speeding in his truck. He hated slamming his hand on the top of his steering wheel till the rubber got hot enough that he could twist it. On days like this, he felt older than his sixty years. His heart slammed, pressed against his rib cage until his crisp arteries cracked, collapsed, and spread against bone. The pressure built and built in his ears until all he heard was the knock of blood trudging through his veins. His head became a throbbing beacon of anxiety, and in response—out of habit—his hands closed into fists.

Norman closed his eyes, took a deep breath, and tried in vain to still his mind as he exited off the Dan Ryan into downtown. After thirty-six years with the Chicago police, his retirement was going into its sixth year, and he'd be the first to tell you it wasn't getting any easier. He missed the work, missed the laughs. He missed waking up in the middle of the night and tearing across the city like its harpy prince, another monster from the lake. Just a blue dash flasher and high beams—that's how he always liked it. A lot of the other detectives liked to chirp in on a body with their sirens wailing, jackets off, showing off their new leather shoulder braces like a bunch of trashy skanks parading their one and only hundred-dollar bra.

Norman never needed much. He didn't like to impress. Esteem, obedience, the way the young uniformed officers cleared the way when he arrived—that's what Norman wanted. A clean suit, a white—a glowing white—starched collar, a nice tie, nails trimmed, hair combed, his cheeks, chin, and neck clean and freshly shaved, everything soft to the touch and smelling like the small of a ritzy girl's thigh. That's how you got what you wanted. Present yourself professionally. Walk like you know how to use your gun. Keep your rings shined, pointed to the sun, and never pull a punch. Or more simply: *Do the work.* He could count how many cops worth their salt he'd met over his whole career on one hand. The rest were just counting days to their retirement. Calendars and markers were practically department issue after your fifteenth year. Something that—for the life of him—Norman couldn't understand now that he was retired.

The days dragged on and on. He'd watched his fingers get fat and, more and more, caught his jaw hanging loose sucking air. Oh, there'd been plans. An indoor shooting range in Evanston close to the house. His only son, Georgie, who himself was turning forty-five, could run the place. Then, briefly, Norman considered applying for a contractor license. He enjoyed installing things, putting together furniture, and Georgie—with a little instruction, some strict guidance—could take some of the extra work, earn some honest walk-around money. Then there was the boat. His old partner, Paul Colsky, had come up with the idea: Norman could run fishing tours, tell some of his best detective yarns—the clean ones, anyway—to out-of-work out-of-towners in hip waders and Gilligan hats while Georgie, of course, manned the wheel. Norman had liked that idea the most, and he even went as far as picking up a *Boat Trader* at a gas station and examined the small black-and-white photographs of every private sale in Illinois through his gold-rimmed bifocals while he filled up his Ford Explorer with unleaded plus.

But in the end, Norman fucked off the ideas—every single one. They all smelled of schemes or even worse—*desperation*. He did what he knew: He prayed. He picked up his worship, started anew. At the beginning of summer—a hot day in late May—Georgie stood him up once again, and in a daze Norman found himself speeding through the city just like now. Windows down, eyes filled with trembling tears, he didn't know where he was going, how far it'd be. He let his truck drive itself, and it was on that day he changed parishes, left the bush leagues of St. Mary's in Evanston and found himself batting with the heavy hitters, the fucking *di maiores*, down at Old St. Pat's in the city.

He should've done it years ago.

At St. Pat's, he met Father Healy. It was Father Healy who suggested that Norman start taking better care of himself. "So you retire and let it all go to shit?" he had poignantly asked the first time they met. Father Healy recommended Norman come to church more—daily, even—until Norman learned how to cope with his new life in Chicago. Norman had lost his wife, his job, and still faced the continual battles with Georgie, his divinely conceived son.

"Pray till your knees hurt, Norman," said the father. "Then take a break, and start again."

And Norman had. And it worked. By the end of June, he'd dropped ten pounds, and for the first time that he could remember he could easily run three times around his block. In August, he went to check his levels, and every one—*every single one*—came in on the mark. His LDL's were down to 68. His blood pressure was going strong at 140/90—but he'd always run a little high. He was a spirited man who'd rediscovered his spirit, and nothing said that more than his pillow-soft prostate. Since the start of September, he'd not gone one morning without Louisville Slugger–type wood. He could put a hole in a wall if he was sleepwalking. A few nights, he even glazed his sheets like a teenager, rolled over into a puddle of cold dick grease the size of Heidecke Lake. Those mornings, he wished his wife, Eileen, were still alive. They could've laughed about it—the irony. Back when they wanted kids, he could barely wet a napkin, and the little he shot could barely kiss her eggs. His father had been the same way, and Georgie, unfortunately, too. Three generations of Quinn men blessed with broad shoulders that could toss kegs like they were made of egg carton but couldn't get their wives pregnant no matter how hard they tried. Georgie—just like Norman—had been a miracle of modern kitchen science. The result of months and months of attempts with a Dixie cup of Norman's grease loaded into a stainless-steel turkey baster at their doctor's office. Norman remembered the day he knew Eileen was pregnant. It was well before she told him—maybe it was the years of working homicide—but he could smell that her scent had changed. And when she finally told him two weeks later, he only smiled. He let her run around the house, jabber on the phone for hours. He went to work that day, brought an extra cigar for Paul, and parked their unmarked cruiser just off Michigan and smoked their shift away while the suckers fought traffic.

He didn't know it then, but the peace and happiness he felt that day was the grace of God, and he'd been chasing it ever since. Norman parked his truck in a handicapped space and jogged to St. Pat's front door. He splashed his head with holy water and knelt down in the first pew at the back of the church as Father Healy finished the morning mass. The Holy Ghost, a beautiful blonde-haired woman, flew in front of a fiery sun in the last stained-glass panel overlooking the church. In the light, the powerful angel looked twice her size and, at once—as he stared at her—Norman felt his heart finally calm, and his breath slowly reduced back to its slow, grating, belly-filling pace. He hated being old. He hated being alone. He hated that up until that very moment it had taken all of him, every bit of his will and strength to barely make it to the only place that he wanted to be. He'd missed the first and second readings, the Gospel, the homily, the consecration of the

Eucharist, and most importantly, Communion—the whole point of the God-damned trip—and now, even though he hadn't even finished confessing his hate to the Lord Jesus Christ, he would have to push himself back onto the pew and force his old watery thighs to stand him up before Father Healy saw him kneeling out of turn as he exited the church.

Quickly, Norman shut his eyes, silenced his black-coffee-juiced mind, and looked inward past his St. Christopher medallion on his chest, his bristled white chest hairs, through his few fattened moles into his leathery skin behind the first layer of thick congealed fat, and begged with all of his bruised heart to be freed from his anger, frustration, and the constant images of the thousands of dead bodies he'd seen as a homicide detective, the boiling wall of black paint he woke up to every single night, and the sound of Georgie when he was a child screaming, demanding that Norman save his life.

He rose.

"Mandy, you up?" Pap whispered at her door.

Amanda shivered, pulled the sheet up to her chin. A cold draft blew across her naked body. The window was wide open in her room. Cigarette ash scattered across the floor. Chance lay next to her naked, his brow furrowed in his sleep. Her face was sticky with spilled beer and sex, and her throat burned deep into her chest. She put on Chance's T-shirt from the floor, tiptoed to the door, and cracked it open.

"You okay in there?"

Amanda could barely see her grandfather's worried eyes, but his aftershave came on strong and clean—he had already showered and dressed.

"I'm fine," said Amanda. "What time is it?"

Pap pulled up his sleeve, pressed the light on his digital watch.

"Just past one."

"Oh, God—I'm sorry, Pap. I'll come out."

"How's that boy?" asked Pap.

Amanda swallowed hard, trying to choke down her embarrassment.

"He's . . . He's fine."

"I heard him getting sick last night. Don't worry about breakfast. I had my coffee."

Amanda didn't know what to say. Pap ran the back of his hand down her cheek and smiled.

"Close that window. I'll turn the heat on. Guess it's fall already, huh?"

He turned, started down the apartment's short hallway to the living room.

"Pap, don't forget—"

"I know where my pills are, Mandy."

Amanda shut the door, wiped the sleep from her eyes. On her windowsill, cigarette butts floated in a glass of water she hadn't poured. She remembered Chance holding her cheeks, kissing her over and over. She couldn't remember where, what bar they'd left. Towering yellow light had lit up the empty street. The pavement looked wet and black even though there'd been no rain. She remembered running her hand over his buzzed hair, pulling him into her face as she kissed him back. He grabbed at her through her jean jacket, somehow got his freezing hand under her sweater, squeezed at her tits before he gripped her bare hip and pulled her close enough that she could feel him hard.

No one was supposed to know.

Chance didn't care, but she did. She was supposed to be getting her life together, making positive changes, not getting drunk and screwing the strange boy who'd rolled into town from God knows here. He'd appeared three months ago at Ghost Town, the tattoo shop where her sister, Stefy, worked. At first, he was just helping out—emptying the trash, running and buying bourbon, beer, plastic wrap, and surgical tape for the owner, Lee. Amanda wasn't even aware of him. For two months, "Chance" was just another name she heard in the background. When she saw him, he was just another pink face moving through her life in a blur. Since her last relationship—if you can call it that—she didn't see men, and more important, she didn't want them to see her. After three years of trading saliva and speedballs, moon-rocked pipes and death-valley rushes that hit like steel bats with her ex-lover, Georgie Quinn, she wanted nothing more than to disappear. She grew her hair long, covered up, and everywhere she went dropped her shoulders and caved her chest like she was descending a never-ending set of stairs.

But then, predictably after a night of swimming in well liquor and charity beers from her sister, she saw Chance or more importantly saw that he saw her. And then all of a sudden he was apparent, everywhere smiling. Walking her to the market, finding time to escort her to the train. And while part of her doubted the sincerity of his cute half-lip-turned smirk, another part of her—her heart—sparked in his company. Because—despite herself—when she was with him, she felt safe. She laughed; he was part antidote, part distraction, a living, breathing square-shouldered remedy that she could hold on to while her life ripped and bucked like a cursed paper ox.

The problem was he was falling for her, and she for him. She knew because she'd only felt it once before, almost a decade ago, and it had struck her the same silly pathetic way. Maybe it was because she was turning thirty this year—officially leaving her twenties—but the idea of walking down the street holding hands, eating food together in some restaurant neither of them could afford before they got black-out drunk on two-dollar polyurethane shots at some bar where they both sucked face with strangers a million times before, and then fucking in the street or—like last night, for the first time—in her bedroom in her grandfather's apartment seemed like a bad episode of a lousy show created to titillate lonely teenage girls but surprisingly empowered recently divorced middle-aged women who needed another average-looking body—no one too hot, but no fucking trolls—with a vagina to hoist onto their personal flags as they tried to reclaim their lives that they'd misspent like a bag of foreign change at a carnival arcade.

Fuck that, thought Amanda as she took an old magazine, bent down, and swept the cigarette ash onto it with her hand. *Go fuck Oprah.*

She wasn't ready. She didn't have the time. Her days were filled with taking care of Pap, keeping their life together, avoiding thinking about what she would do if he succumbed to the cancer that appeared and disappeared in his organs like a wild fungus that grew stronger with the weather.

"Sorry about the smokes. You said it was alright last night."

Chance sat up in her bed, blinked his eyes trying to wake up.

"Pap—my granddad—said you got sick," said Amanda.

"Fucking tequila."

"Literally," said Amanda, smiling.

Chance laughed, and Amanda's heart jumped. Spending time with him was like a drug. Every moment a fleeting cure to her crippling pangs of self-doubt, insecurity, and the unnerving feeling that she carried around everywhere that she was—like she knew everyone thought she was—just a fuck-up drunk. Chance held her, touched her, cared for her how she always wanted. He never grabbed at her like an animal. He didn't slam inside her like he was trying to throttle her through the bed. He just kissed her, and after that, it always felt like just one long dance—everything making sense, his hands and lips never an annoyance, always exactly where they needed to be.

"We forgot about these again," said Chance, holding up a string of condoms.

"It's okay," said Amanda.

"How you figure that?" he asked.

"'Cause I can't get pregnant."

"Oh . . . I'm sorry."

"It's not your fault. It's me."

Amanda took off his shirt, went to her closet. The floor creaked as Chance put his feet on the floor. Suddenly, his arms wrapped around her waist. He kissed her on the neck.

"You left the window open, by the way," she said.

"Actually, that was you."

She turned around, pressed her cheek to his chest, heard his lungs filling with air, his heart beating steady in dull warm knocks.

"Put on some clothes. I want you to meet someone."

Amanda opened the door, took Chance's hand, and together they walked down the hallway to the living room. Pap wearing his favorite moth-nibbled gray sweater was seated in his recliner. His fine silver hair was slicked back with pomade, and behind his thick-framed glasses his eyes didn't move from the redheaded news anchor on TV. Her lips were wet with gloss, and her blue pupils sparkled like two blue plastic gems. Beneath her, BREAK-ING NEWS flashed in red before a casualty count began scrolling slowly across the bottom of the screen.

"You sounded like a mare in heat, son," said Pap, squinting his eyes to read the names.

"Sorry if I woke you, sir," said Chance.

Amanda let go of Chance's hand, went into the kitchen, and pulled two mugs from the cupboard. She filled them with coffee and carried one out to Chance, who was standing still, scared to open his mouth. Pap eyed him up and down and then cleared his throat in a long scraping hock before he spoke.

"How old are you, Chance?"

"Thirty-four."

Pap dropped his glasses to the end of his nose and peered over them, trying his best to appear intimidating. "Do you have a vocation? Can you do anything with your hands?"

"I worked some shipping barges back home, sir, but I don't consider myself a sailor or—"

"What are you then?!"

Pap shot out the question loud. Chance twitched in his seat. The apartment went quiet as Pap—pleased that he'd startled a man half his age—folded his hands across his belly and waited for an answer.

"Guess I'm just alive at this point," said Chance, getting up to leave. "Good morning."

Pap's eyes softened. He grabbed Chance's hand, patted it over and over as he pulled him back onto the couch.

"Stay," he said. "Drink your coffee."

On the television, the local weatherman waved his hand across an animated map of Illinois. Bouncing suns turned into waltzing storm clouds from Waukegan to Lansing. Pap's eyes drifted just above their heads to three framed family photographs lined up on the wall. There was Wayne and Caroline, Amanda's parents, on their wedding day in the backyard of their first house—the one Pap had given to his son as a wedding present—in Maryland. Wayne in his olive dress uniform, his army service hat tucked under his right arm, stood with Caroline in her cream satin wedding dress, her waist barely pregnant—just showing Amanda inside her body. With tired smiles on their faces, the young couple stood by a chain-link fence looking cold and uncomfortable. Weeds and dark green grass grew tall at their feet. The cuffs of Wayne's dress slacks were soaked wet, and the short train of Caroline's dress was spotted with mud.

The second picture was of the girls: Stefy—no older than four—clutching a small two-year-old Amanda wrapped in a red crocheted blanket on the front steps of the same home. Stefy, her brown hair a curled mess, smiled big, squinting her entire face against the sun, while Amanda's eyes were purposefully closed as if in that moment the entire world was exploding and she couldn't bear the sight.

The last photo was a black-and-white portrait of Pap's dead wife, Grandma Sara. She was young, beautiful. Her head was cocked and poised; her blonde hair rested on her shoulders in a shining ocean of curls. She leaned gently towards the camera—happy but not thrilled—content but not satisfied. The photographer had done his job—captured the life in her young eyes—because no matter where you stood, Grandma Sara looked past you, like someone she sorely needed had just entered the room behind your back. Pap closed his eyes, touched the fingers of his left hand to his lips.

"I'm not as active as I once was," Pap said. "I watch the news on TV. I listen to broadcasts on the radio. Sometimes, I turn the volume up on the both of them when Mandy's not here. The neighbors slam on the wall and the floor. I don't care. The noise helps me think. I speak to my wife about it—"

"Pap, you okay?" asked Amanda.

"I'm fine, fine . . . Where's your family from, Chance?"

"Caruthersville, Missouri."

"I know Caruthersville," said Pap. "On the Mississip'."

"That's the one," said Chance.

"I've passed through Caruthersville. I like to think parts of this country are in my heart. Mandy, can you get me some water?"

"You need to lie down, Pap. We should leave," said Amanda.

Pap's watch alarm began beeping. He pressed at it, turning it off.

"Don't be silly. I just need to take my horse pills or I start whining."

Amanda went to the kitchen and filled a glass with cloudy water from the sink. She set it down on the counter and counted out Pap's medication from his three prescription bottles. He'd taken two doses of oxycodone since yesterday and only had four doses of Xeloda and Decadron left. Amanda swept one of each of the pills into her hand and put an extra oxycodone in her pocket. She turned to leave, but heard Pap's lowered voice in the living room.

"Mandy doesn't like to hear about this, but her mother—Caroline's side of the family—was from Missouri. North, though, by Kansas City. She was a good woman. Nice family. I was thrilled when my son brought her home."

Amanda carried out the water and pills and handed them to Pap.

"Here you go," she said.

"I was just telling Chance about your mom—"

"Why?" asked Amanda.

"Because it's good to know where people are from. Isn't it, Chance?"

Pap winked, dropped all the pills into his mouth. He closed his eyes and swallowed hard as he drank from the glass.

"You don't know where you're going, unless you know where you're from," said Chance.

"Now, that's some fucking truth right there!" shouted Pap, slapping his knee. "I'm a third-generation Beaumont from the great state of Maryland. My granddad, Mandy's great-great-grandfather, came off the boat in 1908—"

"Here we go," said Amanda.

"This is important shit, Mandy. I'll be dead soon, and you'll need to know."

"Pap, don't say that."

"I'm serious. What is it, Chance? Say it again—'You don't know yourself unless you know where you're from,' right?"

"Close enough," said Chance.

"Alright, that's enough," said Amanda. "Chance has to go, Pap."

"He can stay."

"No, I really should be going."

"And you need to lie down," said Amanda.

"Well, fuck me then. I'm being put to bed by my granddaughter. We've seen it all, haven't we, Chance?"

Before Chance could answer, Amanda took him by the hand and walked him to the front door. They held hands down the stairs, and when they reached the front gate to the building they stared at each other, waiting for the other to lean in and say good-bye.

"Stefy and I are going to Delilah's tonight," said Amanda. "It's dollar-beer Monday—want to come?"

"So we're going public with our romance?"

"I didn't say that. I'm just asking if you want to drink crap beer with me and my sister."

Chance pulled her close, ran his hand down her face, and kissed her. Amanda's cheeks flushed.

"I'll be there."

When it was cold, the trains were louder. After living in Chicago for fourteen years, Stefy swore she could tell when the seasons were changing just by the mash of metal on the tracks. At the end of winter— just before the weeklong joke of a spring—the tracks thawed, warmed. The metal softened and by the first week of June—as sweat started to steam the entire city—the train reduced to a reliable thumping. Like sweet guitar buzzing inside a pair of tuned mufflers, the train kept the entire city company through summer. It didn't matter what line you were on or what side of the city, if you were in earshot of the L, it felt like you were one stop away from home. But now at the end of the summer—just before winter returned like some forgotten drunk uncle swinging freezing punches and pissing black ice—the trains turned back into barreling, shrieking monsters. Even the buses got loud, angry like all the ghosts of the baddest rotten Brahma bulls rose from the ashes of the stockyards and possessed the engines of the red, white, and blue machines.

As a Blue Line train tore overhead, Stefy covered her ears, brought her knees to her chest, and stared out the shaking front windows of Ghost Town Tattoo. Chrome truck bumpers rattled on the shop's purple walls, and the black-and-silver life-size stenciled skeletons seemed to dance relishing the noise. Business was slow. Stefy curled up in her old cracked red-leather barber chair and prayed onto Damen Avenue that someone would come in besides the ex-convicts looking for Lee's freebie cover-ups. A young white couple bundled in matching blue-and-orange puffy jackets jogged by pushing their matching cream-colored baby in a blue-and-orange stroller down the street. They looked like they'd escaped from a catalog. With their buttoned noses and wind-cherried skin, they bounded in natural strides like the sidewalk was made of magic rubber, and each step brimmed their bodies with hope. It was people like this that made it hard to believe the stories Lee told her. How Damen Avenue used to belong to the drunks—wandering, dying bodies that washed the pavement in puke and blood when he bought the faded brick building in 1968.

It was a humid July afternoon when Lee—just twenty-two years old at the time—and a tall, sharp-boned Vice Lord named Samuel "Cupid" Calloway met to do business. The two men had decided that $40,000 in stolen gold would be the price for the building. Lee, then a citywide-known crook, handed Cupid his life's work—a shoebox filled with busted chains and broken watches, and Cupid, an aged founding member of the Almighty Vice Lords street gang, tossed him the building's waterlogged title. Two days later, Cupid's body turned up with five others in a junkie shack across town. A needle sticking out of his neck, his heart and lungs dead asleep from some casper chink smack that had just come across the lake from the north. That same year, Lee got locked up in Joliet for seven years on a botched snatch-and-grab. When he got out, he opened up Ghost Town and decorated the place with salvaged car parts, discounted purple paint, and anything old, brass, and iron.

Stefy had never touched a tattoo needle before she worked at Ghost Town. There were no shops in Ellicott City, Maryland, where she and Amanda had grown up. Amanda, barely seventeen, was Stefy's first client. Stefy inked a space symbol on the top of her sister's right shoulder while Lee watched, dribbling drunk, threatening advice. At the time, Stefy was reading William Cooper and believed the two black concentric circles suggested galactic enlightenment. In five long hours, Stefy rendered the circles with a tattoo pistol made of Walkman parts, a sewing needle, and a drugstore bottle of India ink—the same machine Lee had learned on in prison. The tattoo blurred more every year, but Amanda was never embarrassed by it and neither was Stefy. She was a sought-after artist now, and the two shambled circles were her first work. They were valuable like her grandfather, Pap, and the fading memories of their family's life in Maryland.

A chain of silver spoons and forks jingled as another battered man pulled open Ghost Town's front door. Stefy recognized this one; Lee once said he was a kind murderer. He'd been in at least four times before. He had an unlucky brown face and carried it accordingly—heavy, tucked between thickened shoulders that looked like they could still crush stone.

"Lee here?" he asked, quietly.

Stefy didn't answer. She looked past him just over his ear so he'd know she wasn't scared even though she was. She nervously scratched her nose, brushed back her dyed cherry hair, and called out loud,

"Lee, client here!"

"Okay, put him in my chair," a rough husky voice shot back.

"Over there," said Stefy, pointing to Lee's empty barber chair at his station.

"Thanks," said the man, nodding his huge shaved head like he was close to collapse.

She'd asked Lee a hundred times why he did this—gave away free cover-up tattoos. Once—just once—she'd looked at the books and stopped counting his free hours after she'd crossed what amounted to $76,000 in three months. He was giving away a fortune. Lee was always back-booked at least six months, but most of the time he struggled to keep the lights on in the place, and with no mortgage, it didn't make any sense. Stefy had begged him many times—when the shop was so cold her clients' skin was pulled too tight to take ink—to just give it a rest for a while, maybe only do the freebies on Mondays or in the mornings when most people didn't come in. And every time Lee said he would consider it, until one or two guys walked in—a lot of them came in pairs—and asked to speak to Lee. And after their standard ten-minute greeting of hard stares and barely audible grunts, sweaters and shirts would come off, and tears would start flowing as the men showed Lee their prison tattoos that until that moment were their personal curses, living evil in their skin.

Just like now, Lee would put on his reading glasses, nod his bearded head, snap on a pair of black surgical gloves, and start blacking out the man's laughing doves or another's giant swastikas, crude BGF tattoos, or five-point crowns. Tears turned into stars or crosses around their eyes, and the majority of skulls into blooming flowers. When the work was completed, they all left with some version of the same tattoo somewhere on their body: The mighty, mighty dagger splitting the rose was Lee's only requirement for payment. And by the end, after they had spent what amounted to weeks in painful three-hour sessions with Lee, all the men wanted the image. They had earned it along with Lee's friendship. Even though Stefy rolled her eyes when Lee told her—her reflex to anything that made her nervous, hit close to her heart—she knew the dagger really did mean the world to these particular men, that it wasn't in the same class of tattoo as her specialty gypsy girls and walk-in panthers. She longed to ink art with the same tear-jerking significance. Watching Lee, she saw she could change people's lives. That every time she stretched a client's skin tight between her index finger and thumb, lowered her tattoo gun, and sowed ink into their skin, it was a chance to start a powerful new beginning or provide a sorely needed doting reminder. She hated that he gave them away, but then maybe that was the point. If Lee charged for his beautiful daggers, maybe they wouldn't guard these men so well, maybe they wouldn't prevent them from falling back into their former life of raze, rape, and ruin.

eorgie chewed the garlic clove, watched the sun diminish with the city out the window. It took all day to get home. Three buses. Three trains. The city turned from ash black to lily white to greasy brown and then white again the farther he got north. Sirens melted into cell phone rings. Colored weaves straightened into perfumed blonde hair. Burglar bars disappeared. Cops smiled at people eating on the train. And there was a stretch of stops—from Fullerton to Howard—that the train was a rolling Dunkin' Donuts. He swore someone was brewing fresh coffee near the back, and then three college girls got on that smelled so sweet, he stood up, got close, closed his eyes, and enjoyed pictures of them kissing, slapping, squatting together in his fairy-tale wood.

He got off at Dempster, pissed behind an apartment building, and started making his way west. When the garlic mashed into a pulp, he spit it out, pulled another clove from his pocket, and popped it in his mouth. Out the corner of his eye, his reflection walked with him in the passing storefront windows. He was scared to look. The man looked taller than him, heavier, like a fat-faced, fat-assed version of himself that he'd never met. He sucked in his gut, pulled back his long black hair, and stomped faster trying to outrun the pock-faced giant to his left. His faded black jeans scratched at his legs; his crotch started to sweat, and he wondered if his twin was wearing underwear and that's how was able to keep up. After Ashbury, he lost him. He crossed the street into his old neighborhood and left the sack of shit in the stained-glass window of a free synagogue.

This is why he didn't like coming home during the day.

He preferred the morning—early morning. The robbing hour from two twenty to four forty-six on the dot. Everyone is asleep then. And if you're awake, you can only blame yourself if you get got. When he got to the house, he didn't bother with the front, went straight to the back door knowing that even though he'd told his father a thousand times to replace that silly-ass brass knob with a double cylinder dead bolt—*You're begging to get murdered*, he'd said—his old man had kept the same damn worthless lock. He smiled as he flipped out his buck blade, farted as he swiped the lock. His stomach hurt, mouth still got wet when he broke into homes. It was something that he never got over. When he was younger, he'd sweat like a pig going through jewelry cabinets, run from the house vomiting, speed away in that crap Mustang with his stomach doing somersaults. It got so bad he told his father. He was desperate, out of options, and was embarrassed to tell a doctor that as a grown man, he regularly messed his pants. His father didn't laugh like he thought he would. He listened, patted him on the knee, and made him a sandwich for lunch. When they were done, they went to the backyard. His father showed him part of the roof that had been leaking, made him climb up on a ladder, and then when he was near the top—the rain gutter at his eye—his father kicked the ladder out and watched him slam onto the ground.

He remembered orange and black—sunlight—warming his closed eyelids as he lay on the ground. He smelled the jasmine bush, his dead mother's favorite, that he had planted as a child with her watching, smoking her second and last cigarette of the day. The soft damp ground cradled him, and he remembered thanking the city that it was summer not winter, and in that moment—with his head throbbing, shin bleeding, and a finger broken—he was sure there were angels, but still remained undecided about God.

He should've died.

He'd seen men fall from less, suffer more. Broken hips, fractured skulls. He was where his father had been standing when his friend—trying to steal a worthless satellite dish—fell from three feet off the ground and died, his head hitting the ground like a rotten peach—ripping, splitting open like it never had bone. As he rolled side to side and took stock of the pain that was buzzing across his body, he felt his father rubbing his shoulder then picking him up, whispering,

"You okay? You okay there? You okay?"

He smiled because he understood. His pants were dry front and back, not a drop of piss or shit. He laughed, took his father in his arms, and the two huge men hugged. After a couple of hours, a case of Old Style, and a large pizza, his father gave up his secret: He'd mashed garlic into their sandwiches at lunch. The garlic calmed his belly, eased his cramps, and even after the fall from the roof temporarily cured him from his gambling colon. Since then, he carried a head of garlic with him at all times. He sucked on them like lozenges, craved them like Diet Coke, and when he didn't have them, he worried himself nervous, and it didn't take long before he was pants down, wiping himself down in any McDonald's bathroom with a stack of paper napkins nearly to his knee.

He opened the door, moved fast, rushing through his childhood home. His father made it too easy, kept everything too clean. The kitchen counters were spotless, just a coffee mug in the sink with a mashed wad of paper towels. Three vacuum stripes ran perfectly up and down the front hallway rug, and the screen of the TV in the small living room at the front of the house didn't have one fleck of dust. He took the stairs two at a time, pushed open the bathroom door, and held his head down as he opened the medicine cabinet, still afraid to run back into his twin.

But the shit caught up.

As he grabbed the codeine cough syrup from the top shelf, opened it, and swigged, the mirrored cabinet door swung closed. The man's mouth dropped open in terror. His bloodshot eyes streamed wet with tears. A scream tightened his dyed-red tongue, and the last of his teeth shivered in his bleeding gums. Deep cracks ran down his swollen face like he was born into a cage and grew with steel splitting his skin. He slapped at the mirror, sent the crying man away, and guzzled the promethazine as he went into his parents' bedroom and pulled open his father's nightstand drawer. A box of bullets and a bank sleeve of cash sat on top of a black leather Bible wrapped in his grandmother's pearl rosary.

When he picked up the cash, the crashing whirr of the garage door opening rattled through the house.

He put the top back on the cough syrup, shoved it into his pocket along with the money. He walked slowly down the front staircase, hand grazing the shiny oak banister admiring and remembering every dent in the wood. He'd nearly killed himself a thousand times on these stairs. Jumping from the top step, riding the banister backward, face-first, sideways like Mary Poppins, and every time, his father never batted an eye. While his mother screamed, slapped at his face, his father smiled, patted his head. As he stood by the front door waiting for the back door to the garage to open, the first kick of codeine dropped through his body. His face relaxed. His shoulders dropped heavy. His head dipped to his chest. He wanted to hug his old man, tell him he was sorry and thank him—thank him for caring, for making him who he was.

The back door opened. The front door shut.

"Georgie? . . . You here? . . . You here, son?"

The sky was black how he liked it. The street shivered like a river. His crumbling body carried him back through Evanston. Legs melting on every step, gut—like a baby's—filling taut with warm water. He chewed another clove of garlic, propped his head on the train window back into the city. His friend traveled with him, stared at him in the reflection. He asked for more remedy, and he obliged, holding the promethazine with just two fingers and taking dainty sips.

The city was cold, but he never knew.

He got off at Diversey, jammed up Lincoln, shoved brick walls all the way to Delilah's black front door. One-dollar beer steamed into the night as kids, gutter punks, and three-girl tribes in lipstick and Bettie Page cuts came in and out the front doors. He slid inside, let the loud music and cigarette smoke slap him a hair sober and christen his pale pocked jowls till they almost warmed to his natural shade of weakened blood. He shouldered up to the bar, pulled the bar stool out, put cash down, unzipped his jacket, unbuckled his belt, and let his jaw go slack when the love of his life walked into the bar.

As soon as he saw her, he wanted to rush her, ask her if she remembered the night they first met seven years ago when they both worked at that convenience store on the South Side. Did she remember how silly he looked in that guard's uniform that was two sizes too big? Did she remember it was his thirty-eighth birthday and they went for Chinese food down on Pershing Road? Did she remember he showed her his gun—his grandfather's service pistol that he'd stolen from his father only two nights before? Did she remember him grabbing the back of her head and laying on their first kiss?

Because he did.

Georgie remembered all of it. He cherished that first kiss and every single fuck that came after it. He thought about it more than he should. He remembered every high, every comedown, every three-day bender that blurred into hot dreams that all ended in his father's garage or some hourly rented motel. He remembered the good times when he used to give her advice, tell her how to deal with her sister, and how she made him feel strong. And he never forgot the bad times—their fights over money, how she wouldn't fuck who he wanted her to fuck. And no matter how much he drank, smoked, swallowed, or chased, he'd never found a way to blind his eyes to the worst day of his life—the day she disappeared—he woke up naked covered in her blood and found her gone.

Georgie pulled the bulk of his hand through the last of his slick dirty hair and stared at her because he knew she hated being stared at. She didn't notice. The bar filled with more bodies, got louder with louder music. She was gabbing, laughing with her dyke sister. Georgie ordered another beer, another shot, and winked at his old fat companion in the mirror behind the bar. For once, the man was happy. He pulled back his red-stained lips and returned a smile.

Chance counted the change in his hand as he ran up the stairs to catch the Brown Line train north. He was short on fare. Somewhere he'd lost a dollar bill. As he hit the top of the first flight of stairs, he ran his hands through his jacket pockets one last time before he vaulted himself over the turnstile and sprinted up the next flight of stairs to the platform. A late-evening crowd of straggling day shifters making their way home and folks on the night shift just starting their commute waited for the next train. Chance checked behind him to see if any CTA workers were on the chase and pushed himself through the crowd to the other edge of the platform just to be safe.

He wished he hadn't eaten.

He didn't know what he was thinking breaking his last five-dollar bill. But he'd been downtown looking for work, and it seemed like every other block another pizza spot was pulling a fresh pie. The cashier had given him a break—cut him an extra large slice—when he noticed Chance desperately counting and recounting his change on the counter next to the napkins and peppers. Chance had thanked the guy over and over. The slice was the best thing he'd eaten in weeks, and as he replayed taking the first deep bite into the mattress of cheese and sauce, he remembered wiping his hands on his jeans and figured that's when he'd lost that dollar bill. He shook his head as the train rounded the corner on its way out from the Loop. He should've just ordered a hot dog and run, snatched it out of the guy's hands like he'd done a million times—like a thieving gust of wind.

The train doors opened, and he shuffled inside with another six people and found a spot in the center of the car next to an older man in a collapsed fedora who smelled like fresh beer. The train knocked forward. People's heads dropped out of habit; their necks folded down into books, magazines, or the small candle of their phones like they were all expecting the lights to go dark. Chance smiled; he'd been in Chicago for six months and still couldn't get over city life. Everyone seemed to work like dogs, but no one seemed to smile. Back home if he was broke, he could still call a friend for a ride. Back home if he was broke, he'd still be able to hound down a good time. Back home, he wouldn't be rubbing nickels together trying to shave off a third.

The train picked up speed as it got out of downtown. Outside, brownstones spread wide in every direction. A quilt of streetlights and telephone wires rolled out as far as his eyes could see. Far off, he could make out a single tall, large building—a parking lot—lit up on every floor. If he squinted, it looked like a bread factory he'd seen as a kid in Missouri when he and his father drove across the state in a single night. They'd visited with family all day in Joplin, and on the way home the land panned out from the car's head-lamps in a rolling black sheet just like the city did now. Then two hours south of Caruthersville, the smell of honey and sweet baking filled the dark car. Chance, just ten years old, rolled down his window, stuck his head into the wind. He blinked his eyes over and over against the rushing night air. The factory rose from the farmland. Steam piped from its vents, dissolved into the stretching sky. As they passed, he could just make out the people working inside. They all wore white and milled around like a choir of deep country saints.

He got off at Diversey and ran down the stairs. The whole memory—that whole life—seemed like another country now. A foreign agrarian republic separated from the city by a twelve-hour passage on a packed Greyhound bus. People spoke a different language here, wore different clothes. They drank different, ate different, sang songs that at once struck him as familiar but when he closed his eyes and opened his mouth to join, the chorus inevitably changed. He'd run away from Missouri with the hopes of starting a new life. He'd abandoned everything—his home, his family—just for the chance to be faceless again, a person with no history. And in the end, he'd gotten what he wanted. In Chicago, he was nobody. The people on the street ignored him, looked right through him. No one would give him a job, and his word—even a passing promise—meant nothing. He'd done things he'd never had to do—begged, eaten trash, slept outside.

He was homeless.

He wished he'd never come to the city. He wished he'd never had to leave his home. Instead of pulling open this heavy black door to another sticky-floored bar he'd never been to, he could be opening the door to a sparsely furnished apartment. Yes, his back would be killing him, and his hands would be cut and aching from thirty days of work on a hopper barge. But his wallet would be full, and his stomach wouldn't already be banging for more food. And more than anything, he wouldn't be nervous when he met people like he was now as he approached Amanda and her sister, Stefy, at a table near the front door. He would be sure of himself, who he was. His mind wouldn't reel in a mash of lies and excuses as he conjured up believable answers to the constant questions of where he lived, where he came from, and why he was there. He could stand up straight like he used to. Talk loud like he used to. Look people in the eye because he had a closet—not a duffle bag—a bed—not a cot—and a single address—not a shelter—to call home.

"You're late," said Amanda.

"Had an interview at a bar downtown," said Chance as he sat down.

"How'd it go?"

"Good. So where do I get one of these dollar beers?"

"Try that long tall table where everyone is waiting in line," said Stefy, laughing.

"Good to see you too, Stefy," said Chance.

Under the table, Amanda squeezed Chance's hand and smiled. She looked beautiful, happy. Her long brown hair fell around her face, and in the low light of the bar, her entire face glowed. She was the only thing that he'd miss, that he could never find anywhere else in the world. When he was around her, he felt no judgment. They fit together. She laughed when he laughed and wasn't put off when he was quiet. He loved seeing her smile, and even more than that, loved feeling it.

"So why'd you leave Missouri, Chance Pritchard?" she asked him.

"You're not even gonna let me get a beer first?" he said.

"I'll make you a deal: I'm gonna go to the bathroom, and on the way back, I'll buy you a beer, *if you make me a promise* . . . "

"I don't like where this is going."

"It gets you a free beer."

"Alright," said Chance, feeling the small pile of change in his pocket.

Amanda leaned forward, coaxed Chance in with her finger. He leaned his ear toward her lips. Warm whiskey whispered with her breath.

"Promise me," she said into his ear, "you'll make me breakfast in bed."

"Get off me!"

Amanda slammed her fists against Georgie's chest. The shit didn't feel a thing. He pressed on her with all his weight and closed his hand around the bottom of her throat.

"You still think about me? Tell the truth."

He spit the words deep into her ear. She smelled cherry candy—codeine cough remedy—her ex-lover's favorite drink. She didn't recognize him; he didn't look the same. He had followed Amanda to the bar's bathroom and slid the bolt with his daddy's buck blade. He pinned her against the wall, covered her mouth. Her face was wet. She didn't know if it was sweat or tears. Her last drink came up her throat—bile spiked with Jim Beam. People knocked on the bathroom door—the top, the bottom. They slapped the sheet metal with open hands, pounded it with their fists.

"I'm embarrassed. I think about us more than I should."

He ripped open her shirt, spat on her chest. Her eyes went to the ceiling. Fluorescent light glared off her smudged glasses. The bathroom vent was choked with dust; cobwebs overtook the corners. Amanda's fingernails gnashed into her palms. Warm piss spilled down her legs.

"Look at me, Amanda. Please, baby. I pinned everything on you."

A hurricane was outside. The black walls boiled against her skin. Her pants dropped. Amanda screamed with all she had. Georgie's hand trapped her first prayer, but her second, third, and fourth cries broke her drunk just enough. She recognized tears drying on her face as Georgie slammed into her. Her fingers gouged deep into his eyes as he came.

"Ahhh! You, bitch!—"

Georgie fell back onto the open toilet. Amanda stomped his face and hands. She slammed the bolt open on the door and pushed past the swarming punks outside. Cigarette smoke filled her face. Goosebumps broke across her naked breasts. Her sister, Stefy, sat at the table across the bar. She was holding a tequila shot. Chance was where Amanda had left him—staring at the ground, running his hand back and forth across his freshly buzzed hair. Amanda stumbled towards them. She closed her shirt and tried to smile. At first, Stefy smiled back, but then she saw it all, and the color dropped from her face. Words rushed out of Amanda's mouth. Chills shook her body. She cried, pointed to the bathroom. Stefy shot up, covered Amanda with her jacket.

"Is he still back there?"

Amanda didn't answer and buried her face deeper into Stefy's arms. Chance pulled on her shoulder. His lips shook; his normally soft eyes turned to starving rage.

"Amanda—*is he still back there?*" he asked again.

"That's where I left him."

"What are you going to do, Chance?! Leave it alone," said Stefy.

Chance's boots hit the bar floor like hammers. Punks and

trash ran to the back of Delilah's bar as Amanda and Stefy walked out the front door. Voices hollered Chance on, and for a second, there was a man's scream above it all—a series of pleas. Then everything got quiet as Georgie's throat collapsed; his lungs filled with blood.

Three days later . . .

The sky warmed to gray then mustard pink.

Soon, the television in the living room would click on like it always did. The volume would be loud at first, but then her grandfather, Pap, would turn it down—a gentle reminder that he needed his medication and coffee. She hadn't slept in three nights. Her neck still hurt from Georgie's hands. Another night had passed and another two-dollar pint of Smirnoff and a half-pack of Parliament Lights lay empty on her windowsill. Amanda took a deep breath of the freezing morning air and watched the first shadow of the day—a distorted black web from the hanging electrical lines—hit the cratered cement of the alley and then disappear when a cloud stopped fire from the rising sun.

Amanda shut the window, picked up her glasses from her bedside table. Georgie had bent the frames. Now they sat crooked on her face. She wanted to take them in but didn't know if stores would charge her. Stefy said they wouldn't. Stefy said she'd pay if they did. She slowly opened her door and tiptoed past Pap's bedroom. The wood floor creaked; sharp grains of dust stuck to her bare feet. She held her breath, hoping that would quiet her steps, but when she turned the bathroom door's handle, Pap began to cough and then hack, unable to clear his chest.

"Pap, you up?" asked Amanda down the dark hallway.

" . . . Fine, Mandy. 'Morning—I'm fine."

His bed whined as he lay back down. Amanda shut the bathroom door, turned on the sink faucets, and waited for the water to warm. She ran her hand along her jaw in the mirror. She'd lost weight. Her bones glowed under the bathroom light. There were shadows where there hadn't been before, and her usually small dark blue eyes were larger than they'd ever been. Her brown hair fell just past her shoulders; she couldn't remember the last time it was cut. She tied it back and took off her glasses. The mirror clouded with steam. She rolled the bar soap in her hands, lathered her cheeks and the small bridge of her nose. As she dropped her head into the sink, her lower back pinched; her bruised thighs burned. Chatter of machine-gun fire erupted from the living room, rattling their old television's speaker. Pap turned up the volume. A reporter's muddled voice clipped in and out between the shots.

"What a mess, Mandy," Pap yelled. "Two more car bombs in the green zone overnight. You keeping score of this crap?"

"I'm coming. I'm just cleaning up a bit . . . Can you turn it down a little, Pap?"

"What's that? Is a window open? Oh, here we go, they're saying it's only going to take three more years—what a load. No one's coming home."

Amanda smiled, closed the bathroom window halfway. Her grandfather was still sharp, probably sharper than she'd ever be. It had been a week since his last chemo treatment, and the color had returned to his face. Behind his glasses, his eyes were bright again, and the night before, she found two crushed empty Old Styles in the kitchen sink. He was back to his favorite pastime. All good signs.

"This is something—just like '73. Nixon said the same load of shit when we got out of Vietnam, 'peace and honor' and the rest of it. Your dad would remember."

"Who you talking to, Pap?"

"Whoever's listening."

Amanda dried her hands on the bottom of her faded Bad Brains T-shirt and straightened her glasses as best she could. She went to the kitchen, started a kettle of water, and counted out two oxycodones from Pap's prescriptions on the counter. She put the pills on a plate, crushed them with the back of a spoon. As she tapped the white crumbs into her mug, the front door lock clicked open.

"Pap, Stefy's at the door," she called out. "Can you get the chain?"

"I'm on it."

While Pap struggled with the door lock, Amanda quickly filled her mug with water and choked down two bitter swallows.

"One sec . . . There we go . . . Hey, hey, hey, look at all this—"

Pap's voice brightened as he opened the door. She heard him kiss Stefy on the cheek. When Amanda went to the living room, Pap was coming down the front hall with a full grocery bag at his chest. Stefy followed him carrying two more.

"Amanda, will you help him please?" asked Stefy, struggling with the bags.

"I got it," said Pap.

Stefy was wearing their grandmother's orange plaid fur-collared jacket, and her hair was falling out in curls from under an army cap. She set the bags on the floor and took off her black Jackie-O's. She hadn't slept either; dark purple bags swelled under her eyes. She looked paler than usual, and the skin under her nose was rubbed raw from either the cold or the night before. Amanda picked up the bags, set them on the kitchen table.

"There's milk and eggs in there," said Stefy. "You should get those in the fridge. What's that smell?"

"Stefy, sit down," said Pap. "Mandy and I will take care of the shopping."

Amanda opened the fridge and unloaded the groceries onto the empty shelves.

"Stefy, do you want anything to drink?" she asked into the living room.

"Water—no ice."

"Good, because that's all we got. Pap, coffee's not ready, sorry—"

"I'm fine, Mandy. Get in here and quit with all the kitchen crap."

Amanda filled a coffee mug with water and carried it out to her sister.

"Don't you have a glass?" asked Stefy.

"They're dirty."

Amanda sat next to Stefy on the couch. Pap turned his recliner towards them and smiled. In front of them, the TV still blared dizzying green night footage of soldiers storming razed buildings and dirt-floor homes.

"What's that smell?" Stefy asked again.

"I thought you had to work today," said Amanda.

"I have to open the shop in an hour—Pap, did your check come?"

"No, I called the VA yesterday," said Pap. "I'm going to call them again and give 'em an earful."

"Don't forget 'cause it was slow this past week so I only have money for bills right now."

Stefy pulled an envelope from her pocket, slid it to Pap across the coffee table.

"Stefy, you're an angel," said Pap. "Thank you."

"Have you been taking your meds?" asked Stefy.

"Of course he has," answered Amanda.

"I wasn't asking you—Pap, you're taking the pain medication, right?"

A chill of guilt shot down Amanda's back. She inched away from her sister as if Stefy somehow knew what she'd just done. An advertisement for a tax law firm boomed into the living room.

"Can we turn that down?" asked Stefy.

Pap held up the TV remote and jabbed it at the screen; the news anchor's game-show voice quieted to a murmur. Suddenly, sweat broke at his brow; he shifted uncomfortably in his seat. Then, his eyes dropped to his lap. Amanda went to him, helped him up from his recliner.

"Do you need help?" she asked quietly.

"No, no, no. Stay with your sister."

Pap shuffled down the hallway. Amanda's face burned, and without warning, her eyes filled with tears. She quickly wiped them away before her sister noticed.

"Amanda . . . Are you okay?"

"I'm fine."

"If you need to see a doctor, we can work it out. I can ask Lee for an advance or a loan—"

"I said I'm fine," repeated Amanda.

"Well, you can go—that's all I'm saying . . . Sorry for trying to help."

Stefy pulled a crushed pack of Parliaments from her jacket pocket and fished a half-smoked butt from the bottom of the pack. She straightened it between her two fingers before lighting it with a paper match. She rolled the cigarette on the lip of the mug, tapping off the hard dead ash.

"Have you talked to Chance?" asked Amanda.

"No—I don't know where he is."

In the back of the apartment, something slapped onto the tiles of the bathroom floor. Stefy quickly got up, ducked her head down the hallway.

"You alright, Pap?" she called out.

The door cracked open, letting out Pap's cursing voice and the stench of fresh shit.

"Goddamnit—Mandy, can you get me some paper towels?"

"I'll get you some," said Stefy. "You okay?"

"I just need some towels, damnit! And I asked Amanda, not you."

"I'll be right there," said Amanda.

The door slammed shut. Amanda went to the kitchen and grabbed a stack of napkins off the counter.

"He wanted paper towels," said Stefy.

"Well, this is what we got, so it'll have to do."

Amanda tried to walk past her, but Stefy grabbed her arm.

"Just go to work. I'll come by later," said Amanda.

"I just wanted to see you guys," said Stefy. "I'm sorry."

"I know—*he knows.* Just go, you'll be late."

Stefy picked up her purse from the couch, tucked her hair under her hat, and started towards the front door. Amanda rushed down the hallway to the bathroom but stopped, trying to catch her sister before she left.

"Wait, Stefy. Thanks for the—"

The front door slammed shut, sending a gust of stale cigarette smoke into Amanda's face. She turned, knocked lightly on the bathroom door. Pap breathed deep heavy breaths inside.

"Watch your feet, Mandy . . ."

Dirty water spilled into the hallway. Scraps of soiled toilet paper collected in the slats of the hardwood. Amanda tried to step aside, but she was too late. Filth kissed the tips of her socks on its way to the living room. Her stomach retched, but she held all her sick down.

eorgie's ventilator haunted the room. Norman sat at his son's bedside conceding each of the machine's clicks and beeps with an ever-tightening grip on the linen handkerchief in his hand. The hospital had called Norman just past 2 AM. He didn't know why he was up. He'd been watching a new magic show on TV, sipping watered-down Tullamore, and ironing his cash for tomorrow's money clip. The crook on TV called himself a magician, but Norman didn't see it. The bastard walked around Harlem throwing perfectly good playing cards at passing cars and handing out winning scratch-off tickets like he was the second coming. The blacks were suckers for the cash—always—but the "magician" should've been ashamed of himself, raising people's spirits with gypsy parlor tricks.

I'd have arrested him right there. I'd have turned him out in the middle of the street, clubbed the fink till he apologized and told the truth. There ain't nothing for nobodies. Anybody can tell you that. Oh, I'd a had him.

The hospital said he needed to get over there right away. They couldn't drain the fluid from Georgie's lungs. Norman put on his brown suit with a freshly starched shirt from the cleaners. He tied his tie—the same one he wore when he retired from the force—in the front hallway mirror and slid his .38 revolver into the leather holster on his waist. While he polished the amber lenses of his gold-rimmed glasses, he said a prayer to St. Jude.

Bless my Georgie, dear apostle and martyr for Christ. My wayward son is at a desperate stage. Please forgive him for his barbarous ways and allow him one more chance to renounce all his sins. Oh, servant of Jesus, give Georgie strength and come to his assistance in his time of need. Pray for me who feels so hopeless and hasten to my son's aid. I will always honor you as my special patron and do all in my power to encourage devotion to you. Amen.

From Evanston, Norman drove south on Chicago Avenue until it turned into Clark. He crossed over to Lake Shore and gunned his Ford Explorer down the parkway to St. Joseph's Hospital. Outside his speeding windshield, his city rose from Lake Michigan like a steel-shouldered Samson. The high-rises embraced the lake, and all their lights glared to the midnight sky like a hundred thousand merciful eyes. By the time he got to Georgie's room, they had sedated his son and put him back on a ventilator. Norman listened to the tired doctor on duty and nodded his head when she said his son was "touch and go." He knew what that meant and waited for the doctor to leave before he pulled his linen handkerchief from his pocket and dragged a chair closer to his son's bed.

The mess was fitting for the little shit.

Georgie had finally screwed with someone who didn't give a damn. Norman had told his son a hundred times, "Keep it up. One day, you're going to fuck with the wrong man, and he's going to kick you till your kidneys bleed or worse." But Georgie didn't heed, and Norman would be lying if he said he never wished a righteous, lethal beating on his own son—for someone to do what he couldn't. But Georgie just kept on—fucking around with all that bullshit, shooting up, snorting anything he could get his dirty fucking hands on, and look what happened: *Was he happy now?* It happened just like Norman said it would, just like he'd seen during his thirty-some-odd years in homicide. You live like scum, you die like scum. The fucking Cubs tickets were a waste. Now what? Was he supposed to go to all those games alone? They were going to ride the Purple Line holding hands, cutting up just like when Georgie was young. Norman had it all planned out. In one special day—the train ride and a sunny game at Wrigley—he was going to get through to his forty-five-year-old son.

You gotta quit the shit. You've still got good years. I talked to a friend. He'll give you a job if you just clean up. Do it for me, if you won't do it for yourself. Do it for your mother. God rest her bitching soul.

Norman squeezed his handkerchief, held it at his eyes until the weathered linen became damp. His knuckles cracked, popped. Cold dead air filled every gap in the room.

manda folded the earflaps down on her black ushanka hat and buttoned her old denim jacket to her throat as she waited for the 56 bus under the blue awning of the Logan Square stop. Three blocks away, the bus lurched down the street—an ailing whale in the rush of shiny Toyotas and rusted-out Cavaliers. In front of Amanda, two elderly women dressed identically in plastic rain bonnets and gray wool coats moved to the edge of the curb. They raised their hands together, flagging down the bus even though it was still more than a block away. A teenage Mexican girl talking on her phone laughed at the two women. She wore tight, ankle-short jeans, a purple tank top ripped low into her chest, and bright pink plastic sandals that looked like glass in the brief patch of sun. The bus squealed to a stop and opened its doors. Amanda got in line behind one of the older women while the knot of people exiting the bus broke onto the sidewalk in every direction. Some held their jackets closed as they trotted down to the subway; others walked straight to the light at Milwaukee and Kedzie.

Amanda inched forward in line bumping the old woman in front of her. Her eyes followed a young woman who had just left the bus. She reminded Amanda of her mother. The way her short brown hair swept perfect to her chin—somehow shining despite the overcast sky. Her eyes, skin, and lips were powdered flawless. If she was cold, she didn't let on. She didn't hear the horns or smell the lingering exhaust. Her feet fell in a privileged march as she crossed the intersection. She was beautiful—an exception to everything around her.

"How much you got on your card, girl?"

The voice came from behind her. Amanda turned around to the girl in the plastic shoes. The wind had picked up, and the girl was rubbing her bare shoulders trying to stay warm.

"What's that?" asked Amanda.

"I said, 'How much you got on your card?' Can you cover my ride?"

Amanda dug out two single dollars from the front pocket of her jeans and held them up.

"I'm paying cash. Sorry—"

"Can you give me a spot on this one?" the girl pressed. "I'll get you back. It's straight up cold out here."

"I can't . . . You should've brought a jacket. What were you thinking?"

"Look, you don't gotta be a bitch about it. Just say no. Psssh."

The driver leaned towards the open door, already halfway to pissed.

"Miss, you in or out?" he asked

Amanda stepped onto the bus. Outside, the girl stared her down through the closing doors.

"That's right, look the other way, white girl. You ain't better," she shouted. "I see your drunk broke ass all the time."

"Looks like you made a friend," said the driver, shaking his head.

As she pushed and sidestepped her way through the packed bus, Amanda wished she'd taken the train. It was right there. Stupidly, she'd not accounted for rush hour when she decided that taking the bus would be a great way to put off seeing Stefy a little longer. She wasn't ready. She didn't want to say it, but she wasn't comfortable being around anyone except Pap. When she got to the back, she locked eyes with a mother in a denim jacket just like hers with a toddler son. The woman was black, wasn't much older than Amanda; she smiled, put her son on her lap, and tapped on the empty seat.

"Thanks," said Amanda, sitting down. "I appreciate it."

The woman smiled back, but didn't answer. Her son eyed Amanda for three stops before a string of speeding police cars going the other way stole his attention. They rode the rest of the way down Homan Avenue looking out the window, staring at the faces coming on and off, and avoiding grazing and touching each other until the monotony of the bouncing, jerking starts and stops overtook them. Their bodies relaxed. The little boy's sneaker dug into Amanda's side, and the woman's elbow rested on Amanda's thigh. Amanda didn't shift in her seat or try anything else to buck them off. She closed her eyes, let her head fall back on the window behind them, and when her shoulder relaxed against the woman's warm body, she felt safe. Half-awake, her body jarring with the road and the snap of lowered voices over the grating whine of the engine beating into a lush of noise, Amanda wished the stranger was her sister. That Stefy was warm, kind, silent.

Every time she'd seen her sister in the past three days, Stefy had asked the same question—*Are you okay?*—at least once, sometimes twice. Amanda wanted to shake her, slap her, scream, *What do you think?! Have I ever been okay?*

Stefy wanted answers that Amanda didn't have. Part of her felt like the rape had been a relief—the other shoe that she'd been waiting to drop for the past four years. When she broke up with Georgie, she'd done everything Stefy had told her. She got a restraining order, grew out her hair, and disappeared. But the whole time it didn't feel right—it was just too easy. Stefy told her to get on with her life, and she'd honestly tried fighting the feeling that Georgie was around every corner, in every empty room, or behind the convenience store where she shopped or in the bathroom at her new favorite bar. And he had been. He was. The rape was the worst kind of validation, physical evidence of all that she'd known.

Amanda pulled the stop cord as the bus neared Armitage, got off, and started making her way over to Damen. The afternoon sky became dark, overcast, threatening rain. She walked as fast as she could. Even though her legs still hurt from being throttled against the wall, and the rough collar of her jacket chafed back and forth against her scratched neck, she willed her feet to pound fast against the cement and demanded her ankles to snap her forward until her whole body shook with movement just short of a run.

Are you okay?

Tears crested her eyes as she turned onto Damen and saw Ghost Town's fluorescent TATTOO sign blinking at the middle of the block. She was cold. She was hurt. She was hungry. She was broke. She was ashamed. She was scared. She was tired. She felt like a bad joke. How did she not recognize Georgie? How could she have missed him? Yes, he was fatter, weaker, but his face was the same. His skin was still creased deep and black. His nose was still an axe. His wired dilated eyes still darted around in convulsing storms. She felt like an idiot, that's what she couldn't say. She felt guilty, stupid. Like a baby shown a card trick or a blind person given a plate of trash, she couldn't see what was right in front of her.

"Didn't think you'd show."

Stefy didn't raise her head. She kept her eyes focused on the lace heart she was inking on the bony chest in front of her.

"I made Pap his lunch," said Amanda. "But he fell asleep before I gave it to him."

Stefy held the boy's pale skin taut while she scrubbed the needle in small circles across his skin. The tattoo pistol buzzed on and off in quick bursts as her right foot worked the power pedal up and down. With every buzz, the boy clenched his jaw tight, fixed his eyes on the dancing black and silver skeletons on the shop's ceilings and walls. Stefy wiped the fresh blood off her work with a wad of paper towels and smeared Vaseline onto the center of the boy's chest.

"Okay, buddy, go check it out," she said.

"We're done, already?" asked the kid. "That was so fast."

"Go take a look," said Stefy, pointing to a full-length mirror at the back of the shop.

The boy got up from the table, flipped back his long greasy hair. His flushed red face winced with every step.

"I love this part," Stefy whispered to Amanda. "The look on their faces."

"Is he even old enough to be in here?" asked Amanda.

"We only have one policy: Pay in cash."

When the boy looked in the mirror, a broad dumb smile broke across his face.

"This is incredible . . . This is just how I saw it, better even—"

"Couldn't have done it without you, kid," said Stefy as she snapped off a pair of black rubber gloves.

The boy pivoted back and forth in the mirror, admiring the delicate swelling valentine from every angle.

"It looks like a doily," said Amanda.

"Quit killing his buzz. It's what he wanted," said Stefy. "Hey, Rambo, get over here. I need to bandage you up."

The boy came back, held his arms up while Stefy wrapped his chest in plastic wrap and sealed it with surgical tape.

"Keep it clean. Don't get it wet, and no showboating for the tramps," she said.

"How much do I—"

"Three-fifty without tip," said Stefy. "And I expect one—*a good one* or I'll tell all your friends you cried."

The boy carefully slid his shirt back, pulled out his wallet, and flipped out the money. Stefy counted it again, smiled.

"That's how you treat a lady. Now, go get in some trouble."

The boy walked out the front door light on his feet, the same struck smile still holding his face. Stefy opened a White Owl cigar box on her work tray and dropped the stack of cash inside.

"In the register, Beaumont!"

Lee's booming voice carried over the shop. He walked out from the back office in a blue Dickies work suit unzipped to the middle of his barrel chest. His dyed-black hair was tied back in a ponytail, and his gray beard grew wild on his face. He tried his best to appear angry, but when he saw Amanda, he smiled.

"Your sister is set on getting my shop robbed," Lee said to Amanda. "How you doing, baby girl?"

Lee wrapped Amanda in his huge tattooed arms, kissed her on the cheek.

"Been better," said Amanda.

"No shame in tears," said Lee.

Lee pulled open his work suit, lifted out his left arm. A giant Celtic battle axe ran the length of his hairy body from his armpit to his waist. He took Amanda's hand, ran it back and forth across the bruised knotted cheeks of the axe.

"That's what happens when you get cuffed to an iron radiator for three hours in lockup," he said.

"You never showed me that," said Stefy.

"I'm not a damn scratch 'n' sniff," said Lee. "My point is: I know hurt, Amanda. I know what it feels like to be helpless—"

Lee stopped himself, wiped his reddening face with a bandanna from his back pocket.

"I'm fine, Lee—*really*. Don't worry," said Amanda.

Stefy walked to the brass register at the center of the shop; it popped opened with a ring. She dropped the money in the drawer, spun around, and curtsied towards Lee.

"Happy now, boss?" she asked.

"Oh, I like it when you call me that. 'Bout time I get some respect around here."

"Hey, Lee," Amanda said, "have you seen Chance?"

"I'm about to go pick him up right now," said Lee, zipping up his work suit and pulling out his keys.

"How is he?" asked Amanda.

"Alive."

In one short hour, the color vanished from Georgie's face like stained fog off the lake. His bloated, scratched skin turned gray. His bulging eyes went blank, searching. And whether or not it was real, Norman smelled the same rotten stench that used to seize his face when he came upon week-old cadavers in tenements across the city. As he stared at the lifeless body, Norman twisted his gold wedding band around his finger as if rubbing his old skin raw would be an adequate sacrifice to bring back the dead.

"Take as much time as you need, Mr. Quinn," said the waiting nurse.

"Nah, I don't need much," said Norman. "Just this."

Norman loosened his tie, unbuttoned his shirt, and removed his gold St. Christopher necklace from around his neck. He lifted Georgie's head and clasped it around his son.

"That's all."

The young nurse pulled the sheet over Georgie's head and pulled the IV from his arm. Two quiet knocks came at the door. The nurse looked at Norman, checking to see if it was okay.

"Go ahead. Open it," said Norman. "You people gotta work."

Before she could get to it, the door creaked open and a man's quiet voice called inside.

"Norman, you in here?"

"Yeah," replied Norman. "Come on in, Paul."

Norman's old partner, Paul Colsky, stepped into the hospital room. He still moved like an elephant on his last legs—head down, throwing his weight side to side after every step. He took off his hat and unzipped his blue Bears parka. Instantly, the bite of tzatziki sauce filled the room. Paul wiped his mouth with a crumpled napkin from his pocket and then swatted at the top of his head trying in vain to tame his last few dancing gray hairs into a comb-over.

"Traffic was a son of a bitch," said Paul. "Clark's backed up all the way past Wrigley."

"You should've taken Lake Shore, that's what I did," said Norman.

"Yeah, well . . . Sheila's in the hallway. We're sorry, Norman. It's a Goddamn tragedy."

"Thank you, Paul. Could we have a second?" Norman asked the nurse.

"Of course. Take your time, Mr. Quinn."

Norman walked the nurse to the door and closed it behind her. Paul pulled the sheet back from Georgie's face and stared at his body.

"What's the matter, Paul? You look like you've never seen a stiff."

"Ah, it's not that. It's just that it's Georgie, you know—I watched him grow up."

"Well, he's dead like a big grown-up now, ain't he?" Norman scoffed.

"C'mon, Norman. Quit with that. He's your son, for Christ's sake."

"Exactly. He's my son. My rotten, selfish son who never listened to his father, and now he's dead. Thank God his mother's not alive to see this."

"It would've killed Eileen," agreed Paul.

"His past twenty years would've killed her. *This guy*—"

Norman's voice cracked; he kicked at the bed. Georgie's body quivered.

"Do you know how many times I saved his ass, Paul?"

"I even called in favors."

"You never told me that."

"He got picked up a couple of times when he was a kid. I guess he was scared to call you."

"He was right to be scared. I kicked the shit out of him every time. I can't believe you never said anything."

"This was years ago, Norman. Georgie must've been sixteen—seventeen."

"Oh, that was some of his best work . . . Little shit."

At once, grief overtook Norman. Tears fell down his face. He pushed them off, rubbing his handkerchief quickly over his eyes.

"Ah, Norman, I'm sorry," said Paul. "You want me to get Sheila?"

"No, no, don't trouble her—did you talk to Terry?"

"Why don't we go get some coffee, Norman?"

"What did he say?"

"How long have you been here? Let's go down to the cafeteria and talk about it."

"What the fuck did he say, Paul?"

"Norman, they've got a full bar of witnesses saying Georgie was raping the girl before he got beat down."

"So?"

"So they're not touching it—cop's son or not. You know that."

"This is murder, Paul, manslaughter at the least."

"They don't see it that way, Norman."

Norman stepped to the window, shook his head back and forth as he stared at a roll of heavy black clouds flattening over the city from the lake. Strips of lightning jumped back and forth over the North Side, and far out—over the pitch water—Norman could make out a sheer wall of rain.

"Fucking Terry, kraut son of a bitch—guess he's too good for us now."

"I don't know, Norman—"

"Of course he is. Limp dick's a big commander now. Doesn't have time to help the people who got him there—"

"It's bullshit, I know."

"He's my son, Paul!"

The door creaked open, checking Norman's mounting rage. Paul's wife, Sheila, peeked her head inside. Thirty years ago—when they first met—Norman had named her "country mouse," and she still struck him as out of place, a scared rodent, a stout mama squirrel now in her old age. Her brown hair spilled out from under her pink wool cloche, and her nervous dull eyes darted back and forth.

"Everything okay?" she asked.

"Sheila . . . Thank you for coming," said Norman, collecting himself. "Everything's fine."

"Honey, can you get us a couple of coffees?" asked Paul.

"Where's the cafeteria?"

"Third floor," said Norman.

"You want any cream? Sugar?" asked Sheila.

"Black, sugar," the two men said together like they'd said a thousand times before, and then they both waited for the door to click closed.

"He's my son, Paul."

"I'm gonna talk to him again today."

"My only son."

"I know."

Chris' Bar sat on the corner of North Avenue and Ashland on the outskirts of Wicker Park. The building used to be an auto garage, and the only thing the new owner had changed was the installation of a long, scuffed oak bar that ran the length of one of the painted cement walls. Under low-hanging fluorescents, oil stains faded on the concrete floors, and a donated threadbare pool table sat on top of the old auto shop's sole lift. Chance tried his best to appear sober when Lee and the girls walked in. He wiped his mouth with a cocktail napkin, straightened himself up on his bar stool, and ran his bandaged right hand over his buzzed hair. He hadn't expected to see a soul.

"Lee, what'd you bring all these people for?" he slurred.

"Christ, Chance, it's not even dark yet," said Stefy.

Chance put a hand on the bar, steadied himself up. His bloodshot eyes clipped back and forth from Amanda to Lee. A young Mexican barkeep who couldn't have been older than sixteen pushed a shot of clear liquor in front of him. Lee grabbed it before Chance could, drank it down.

"How long has he been here?" Lee asked the barkeep.

"Ahhh, you know, an hour, two," said the kid in clipped English. "He waits for you. He helps. He's alright—"

"See, I'm alright," said Chance.

Lee set two hundred-dollar bills on the bar and pointed to a bottle of Beam on the back wall.

"That bottle of bourbon, three glasses with ice, and keep the beers coming. *¿Comprende, mi amigo?*"

"*Sí, sí.*"

"And no more for him, yes?" Lee said, patting Chance on the back.

"Lee, why'd you bring them? I told you—"

Lee grabbed the back of Chance's arm, leaned in close, and whispered something into his ear. Chance closed his eyes and shook his head.

"I'm serious, Chance. I'm not fucking around," said Lee.

Amanda took the bar stool next to Chance and held out her hands, trying to steady him. Every few seconds, he licked his lips while his wobbling body pitched back and forth.

"I didn't know how to get a hold of you," said Amanda. "I wanted to see if you were alright."

"Lee says I gotta sober up or he's not giving me a ride."

"Stefy can give you a ride. We can drop you off. What side of town are you on?"

Chance pursed his lips, squeezed his eyes tight. The barkeep struggled to pick up the full tray of glasses and bottles off the bar and balance them as he walked to Stefy and Lee.

"Can you get him a glass of water?" Amanda asked the barkeep.

"*Sí, sí,* I come back—"

Chance dropped forward; vomit spilled from his mouth. Amanda held his bandaged arm trying to hold him up. Lee ran across the bar, lifted him back onto the bar stool, and shoved a fold of cash into Amanda's hand.

"Get him the fuck out of here," he said. "He's done."

Amanda took Chance by the arm and walked him out the front door. Outside was cold, just turning into evening. Rush-hour traffic surged up and down North Avenue in the freezing air until it was just one long wind of honking, flashing lights. They held hands, but Amanda didn't know why. Her stomach turned when she thought of the sight, when she imagined being one of those stampeding cars. Her body stretched, hardened into oxidized metal. Her limbs rolled and pressed into tires filled with decade-old air. Would she honk, piss gas when she saw herself— a skinny, sour-faced woman holding hands with a stumbling, baby-faced drunk? She'd run them down is what she would do. Laugh, do them a favor. Chance let go of her, blew his nose into a cocktail napkin.

"You okay?" she asked.

"Yeah . . . better."

She remembered the first night they'd kissed. Stefy had picked her up from the apartment late at night—past two. Stefy was drunk, and they immediately got into a fight, yelled at each other in a whisper because Amanda didn't want to leave Pap in the apartment alone. He'd been through a rough course of chemo and wasn't bouncing back as quickly as before. But Stefy wouldn't let it go, she pulled the sheet off Amanda, forced her to put on jeans, and then they tiptoed out the apartment and down the front steps. Lee and Chance were waiting in Lee's Lincoln. Late at night under the yellow streetlamps, the giant car looked like an old rumbling warship from one of those history shows Pap liked to watch. She got in the backseat with Chance, and Lee drove them through the city all night. They passed a bottle of vodka around the car and listened to music so loud that her ears rang the whole next day. She remembered feeling the car sway back and forth, the city turning into a scream of drums and lights, Lee and Stefy laughing in the front seat, and her head falling into Chance's lap because she was tired of trying to shout over the music. He ran his hand through her hair over and over until her eyes closed, and then she felt his breath near her face and his lips on hers. He spoke into her ear, told her she made him so happy. Amanda didn't say anything back because he was drunk just like now. He stank of liquor just like now. He was still a stranger just like now.

"Why'd you move to Chicago? You never told me—you were about to before I went to the bathroom the other night."

"I don't remember," said Chance.

"You don't remember why you moved here or you don't remember the other night?"

A block ahead, a westbound bus stopped and opened its doors. After a mob of people stepped off, the bus swelled up—visibly lighter—and roared past them.

"Was that my bus?" asked Chance.

"I'd say yes, but I don't know where you live—*where are you going, Chance?*"

Chance pulled a wad of cash from the front pocket of his jeans, uncrumpled the bills, and counted them out one by one.

"I don't got shit, Amanda."

"Neither do I."

"No, you don't understand—I stay at a shelter downtown."

Chance pulled up the sleeve of his jacket, winced as he opened and closed his busted hand. He pinched each of his fingertips over and over, curled them to his palm one by one.

"Back home, I grew up with this older kid, Lonnie Crete—ugly redheaded motherfucker. He'd game anyone for anything. He robbed me twice, and I knew him since we were kids—got me drunk and cleaned out my wallet both times. I was nineteen, and Lonnie must have been like twenty-four or twenty-five at the time. We'd broken into the high-school lab the night before and ganked this magnum of ether. We soaked up some old dress socks and sealed them up in a Ziploc bag. We were just cruising Lonnie's old LeBaron, huffing those socks back and forth till they were dry. His mom worked as a card dealer at this riverboat casino. It was this old fucking hopper barge they redid from top to bottom."

Chance bounced at his knees, talked faster as if rushing his words would keep him warm.

"We're sitting in Lonnie's car in that casino parking lot getting up on that ether, and Lonnie points out the window and whispers like a retard, 'There . . . goes . . . my . . . mom.' And he starts the car, and the whole time I'm thinking he's just making sure she gets home safe. And then she stops at the store, and Lonnie isn't saying anything—*nothing*. His mom comes out carrying a bag with a can of Pringles sticking out the top—I remember that 'cause I said to him, 'I call dibs on those chips,' thinking we were gonna eat them when we all got home. But then, Lonnie gets out of the car—it was freezing out, and he didn't have a jacket, just this stupid Steve Austin shirt on—and he just walks up on his mom while she's unlocking her door and shoots her in the face. He killed her right there. I watched him pick up her purse, the paper bag, and carry it all back to the car. That motherfucker got in, threw the chips at me. He didn't say a word."

Chance kicked at the sidewalk, looked at the darkening sky, the street, the cratered sidewalk, sucked up and swallowed his snot over and over—anything to avoid Amanda's frozen eyes.

"I wasn't gonna say a thing, Amanda. I went down to the dock the next day and got a job as a deckhand on an Ingram boat. I was making a buck-twenty a day. I just tried to forget everything. Then like a month later, Lonnie gets arrested for murder. I did twelve years in Jefferson City Penitentiary in Missouri—"

"So?"

The word came out of her mouth before Amanda heard what Chance had said. She smiled, but her face was uncomfortable, inadequate. His voice shook, threatening to crack, and his eyes went wide, electric with anger and tears.

"I was an accessory to murder, Amanda. For twelve years, I thought about how I failed that woman. I promised myself if I was ever put in a situation like that again, I wouldn't sit by and do nothing. There's nothing left for me back home. Everyone knows what I did. They all think I'm a coward."

Amanda pulled out one of Pap's oxycodones from her pocket, held it out.

"This will help with your hand," she said.

Chance swallowed the pill dry. After a few blocks, she found her hand back in his. When they passed under the Dan Ryan,

Amanda covered her ears. Above their heads, tires snapped against the concrete in a stampede of whips. She wanted to tell Chance about her father—how he fought in a war and drank bottles trying to right his disgraced spine. She wanted to recite what her father used to say—how he sounded like a sea-addled radio when he rambled about the oil fires and the names of his devoted guns. She wanted to recount the last moments of her mother's life—how hard she had fought and what Amanda had learned. She wanted to tell him all her short memories of growing up in Maryland like he'd told her about Missouri—how the white ash trees tore at the summer skies, and the winter beach smelled like fish guts, brandy, and the leaking gas line of her father's Chrysler. She wanted to say there was a time when she and Stefy ran away. They rode a train to California looking for a better life just like him.

"Should we turn back?" asked Chance.

Amanda dried her eyes as they looked on the north end of the Chicago River. She took Chance's cold face in her hands, kissed him on the lips.

"Too late," she said.

Norman got there before they opened, just before dawn. He pulled his Explorer to the front gates of Calvary Cemetery, pushed his bumper against the black steel, and sipped at his mug of coffee while he watched the sun rise over Evanston in his rearview mirror. The morning clouds slogged over the city and twisted straight over the lake like a line of wet rags in the sky. They hung in the air in strings of ash gray and fire-smoke white. For two hours, Norman watched the sky in silence while he worked his rosary on top of his thigh. At 8 AM on the dot, a groundskeeper opened the gates and waved him in, and at eight twenty-seven—three minutes early—his old partner, Paul, parked behind him at Georgie's gravesite as misting rain started in off the lake.

Say what you want, but Paul Colsky was a good man. Norman knew his old partner didn't want to be at Georgie's funeral this Sunday morning. Paul could've been at home watching the game. The Bears had been showing up this season, and there was nothing that Paul enjoyed more than sitting on his fat walrus ass mauling down Italian beefs and crap beer. Norman had done it with him a thousand times. And there was his car—that shit black Nissan that Norman had told him not to buy. The engine was burning oil; thick white smoke billowed out the exhaust like an old freight train. Paul could've taken the car into the shop today, gotten it washed at least, but he was here instead—in his cheap black suit that stretched over his gut like a worn-out bedsheet. He even dragged Sheila, his tub of a wife, and they both stood in the rain next to Georgie's grave. Besides Father Healy, who was just pulling in, they were the only people that showed.

"Sorry about the short notice, Father," said Norman, getting out of his truck. "They gave me a deal because of the weather."

Father Healy held an umbrella in one hand, and in his other a cracked leather-bound Bible with gold and red letters flaking off the cover. His thin white hair was already soaked through, revealing dark liver spots staining his scalp.

"I understand. I just feel bad that I don't have anything special prepared."

"You don't worry about that, Father. Your regular will do," said Norman.

"Whatever you'd like. Should we get started?"

"Yes, of course," said Norman. "People got things to do. If more come, they come, you know?"

Rain dripped from the bill of Norman's black fedora onto his chin as they walked to the gravesite. As they approached, Paul wiped his face with his hand and put his arm around Sheila, who was bundled up in a quilted mauve winter coat that fell past her knees.

"I'm sorry about the weather," said Norman, straining a smile. "I talked to the man upstairs last night, but I guess he's busy with the world's troubles. Don't worry. This won't take long."

"Norman, don't be silly," said Sheila. "Get under the umbrella."

Norman stood with his friends as Father Healy put his Bible under the arm of his wet black trench coat and pulled out a crystal flask of holy water from his breast pocket.

"Let us pray," he began. "Grant this mercy, O Lord. We beseech thee to thy servant departed, that he may not receive in punishment the requital of his deeds who in desire did keep thy will."

With a practiced flick of the wrist, Father Healy shook the flask forward, casting holy water over Georgie's dripping coffin.

"And as the true faith here united him to the company of the faithful, so may thy mercy unite him above to the choirs of angels. Through Jesus Christ, our Lord, amen."

Father Healy capped the flask, put it back into his jacket. Norman stood frozen staring at his own warped reflection in the swirls of the coffin's lacquered wood. He took off his fedora, stepped out from under Paul and Sheila's umbrella. He ran his hand down the side of Georgie's coffin, tapped it twice with his fingertips.

"Thank you, Father, for that beautiful prayer. And thank you, Paul and Sheila, for coming out. You don't how much it means to me and how much it would've meant to Georgie."

Norman's throat tightened. His cheeks filled with hot shaking tears.

"Georgie loved you like family, Paul, and I thank you for loving him right back. He could be a handful sometimes. But like Father says, God never gives us more than we can handle. And underneath it all—even at his worst—Georgie was a good kid."

Norman took off his glasses, rubbed at his eyes trying in vain to shake off his heartache. The rain increased, soaking through his overcoat, sending a chill down his shoulders and the small of his back. From his jacket pocket, Norman pulled out his pocket-sized Bible and flipped the red ribbon to the back. Fat raindrops fell onto the tiny pages in front of him.

"My soul is deprived of peace," he read in a loud low voice. "I have forgotten what happiness is. I tell myself my future is lost, all that I hoped for from the Lord. The thought of my homeless poverty is wormwood and gall, remembering it over and over leaves my soul downcast within me."

The rain increased with Norman's words. Father Healy took a step towards him, holding out his umbrella, but Norman waved him away.

"It's alright, Father," he said. "My prayers need to go straight into the sky today."

Norman ran his finger down the wet page, searching for the spot where he had stopped. When he found it, he placed the tip of his index finger over the words and looked up to check again on his friends. He smiled another hurt smile, trying to calm his shaking chest, but then sorrow flooded him. His face turned a deep dark red, and his whole body seemed to sob then break. His hand shot out, caught him on the side of Georgie's coffin.

"I can't—I can't do it—"

Paul stepped forward, took Norman in his arms, and squeezed his old partner tight.

"They stomped him like a dog, Paul," Norman choked out. "They collapsed his fucking chest like a fucking dog. I wish them hell. I've been praying, but I wish them hell. Every last one. They all just sat and watched . . . Oh God, this cursed shit—"

"I know, I know," said Paul, patting him on the back. "C'mon, show me where you are. We'll finish it together."

Norman lifted his wet face from Paul's shoulder and pointed to the center of the page. Paul took the Bible, squinted his eyes, held it close to his face attempting to make sense of the small drenched words.

"But I will . . . call this to mind as my reason . . . as my reason to hope. The favors of the Lord are not exhausted. His, His . . . His mercies are not spent. They are renewed—each morning . . . so great is his faithfulness . . . My portion is, ah, the Lord . . . says my soul. Therefore will I . . . I can't—what is that there?"

"Hope," Norman blurted out. "Fucking hope, Paul."

"Right—oh, right. Therefore will I *hope* in him. Good is the Lord to one . . . who waits for him, to the—to the soul that serves him. It is good to hope in . . . in silence for the saving help . . . of the Lord."

Paul closed the Bible, let out a long, strained breath. Sheila went to the two men, kissed Paul, took Norman in her arms.

"That was beautiful, you two," she said. "Georgie's safe now."

"I hate to leave you," interrupted Father Healy. "I've got two services today and—"

"No, it's alright, Father," said Norman. "Thank you for making the time."

Father Healy rubbed Norman's shoulder up and down one last time and then turned and headed towards his car.

"Honey, can you give us a minute?" asked Paul, handing Sheila his keys.

"Maybe we can all go out to breakfast?" said Sheila.

"Yeah, maybe," said Paul.

Paul watched Sheila walk away, waited until she was out of earshot. Again, Norman ran his hand down Georgie's coffin, snapped the water out to the ground. He pulled a handkerchief from the pocket of his slacks and dried his hands. He raised the damp cloth to his face, wiped carefully beneath his still red clouded eyes.

"You okay?" asked Paul.

"I don't know."

"I got the kid's name for you."

Stone angels, marble children, and towering green patinated Holy Marys scattered across the cemetery. Some hid between trees; others gazed out—faced the spitting wind of Lake Michigan. Norman kicked at the pile of soaking dirt next to Georgie's freshly dug grave. A brick of mud landed with a splash.

"No address?" he asked.

"Just a church shelter downtown."

"For bums?"

"That's what he wrote down at the hospital—guess he busted up his hand pretty bad. Looks like it was old Father Whelan's parish by the address."

Paul pulled a scrap of paper from his jacket pocket and held it out.

"Norman, promise me you won't do anything."

"I just wanna hear his side, Paul."

Norman took the paper, folded it, put it straight into his pocket.

"Aren't you going to read it?"

"Enough reading for today."

Norman tilted his hat over his brow and walked towards the lake. Wet bursting wind swirled down his body and stretched the branches of all the short bushes and plastered the tall grass to the ground. He watched his every step, avoided the growing black puddles and tiny marshes eddying around the headstones that were closest to the water. When he reached the end of the cemetery, he stood at the fence and pressed his face against the cold steel fence posts. On the other side, huge white stones—the size of cars—separated him from the lake. If he wanted, he could break them. Norman was sure his pain could crush them to bits.

Amanda clutched her purse as she stepped off the Green Line L at the Garfield stop. Four black boys—none of them older than fifteen—had eyed her since she got on the train downtown. They all wore backpacks, and oversized blue jeans sagged at their waist. Their eyes were puffy and high, and three of them fought over a giant yellow bag of Funyons. The last one didn't bother. He kept one eye on the message he was typing on his cell phone and the other on Amanda until his friends noticed. After that, they all smiled and clocked her up and down. She pretended she didn't care, but when she got off and the train doors closed behind her, she exhaled and realized she'd been digging her nails into her palms for the past half-hour.

The city was still green this far south. Heavy clouds had been choking the North Side all week, but in Hyde Park, a late summer sun was sticking around. The empty lots that dotted the boulevard and side streets looked deliberate and alive. They would take on another life in the snow—bare reminders to the locals no one would pay a dollar for their land as long as they resided there. Stefy lived in a one-bedroom in an old brick high-rise that overlooked the lake. Amanda had stayed there for close to two years when she first moved to Chicago, and as she opened the door and stood nearly inside the kitchen, she remembered why she longed to move out. The apartment was tiny, too small for both of them.

"He's what?"

It was four in the afternoon; Stefy had just woken up. All she had on was a pair of men's white boxers and a bleached-out black tank top. With her streaked makeup, she looked like a puppet—a life-size Muppet with exploding red hair. Her eyes were barely open—morning bloodshot—but they still glared at Amanda with baffled scorn.

"Chance is going to stay with us until everything blows over," said Amanda.

Stefy got off the couch and immediately started stalking around the living room, lifting magazines, throwing envelopes off the short coffee table.

"Start over—*have you lost your fucking mind?*" asked Stefy.

"He doesn't have anywhere to go," said Amanda.

"Not your problem."

Stefy shoved a stack of unopened bills onto the ground, sifted them with her bare foot.

"What are you doing?" asked Amanda.

"Looking for my fucking lighter."

Amanda pulled a book of matches from her jacket, threw them to Stefy on the couch. Stefy lit her Parliament and flicked the tip into an empty White Castle cup.

"It's temporary until he can get a job," said Amanda.

"How's Pap doing?"

"He's fine. He loves it—they get along."

"No, how's he *doing*?" asked Stefy, taking a long drag.

"He seems alright. He's been eating."

Stefy rubbed her eyes, ran a hand through her hair. She stared at the overflowing bags of half-eaten gyros, empty Chicago's Pizza boxes, and a quarter-full handle of Beam.

"Amanda, you know it's not temporary," she said.

"He's going to get his own place."

"When? He's been in the city for four months."

"It's barely three."

Stefy took a long drag and dropped the rest of the cigarette into the cup.

"Did he tell you he was locked up?" she asked.

Amanda bit her lip, gripped her purse in her lap, and at once felt like an idiot for thinking that this wasn't going to come up.

"Lee told me," said Stefy. "Did Chance say anything to you?"

"Yeah, he did. So?"

Stefy stood up, walked to the one huge window in the living room. After a block of buildings and a brief patch of wooded green park, Lake Michigan's black water broke long and wide to the horizon.

"You don't see it, do you?" she asked Amanda.

"What?"

"First Georgie. Now Chance. You screwing him, aren't you? You screwed him and now you think he's an angel just like Georgie. Can't you just fuck and be done with it? Christ, it's not like we don't have enough problems as it is."

"Chance is nothing like Georgie."

"You're right. Chance didn't beat you for three years and then fucking stalk you to a bar and attack you. He didn't leave you for dead in his fucking garage so I could find you and drag you in the backseat of my car while you were bleeding out and talking crazy. Do you even remember going to the hospital, Amanda?"

Amanda didn't move. She stared at Stefy's tattered tank top, her protruding ribs, her pale freckled skin that she remembered pinching, slapping, and clutching as a child. She had long memories where Stefy was her entire world. Whenever she wanted to, she could close her eyes and feel her sister's arms around her, cradling her when she was a baby, comforting her when she was a teenager or dragging her—just four years ago—from Georgie's garage. She could rub her fingers together and feel the tips of Stefy's fingers pressing back because of how often she'd held her sister's hands. No matter what—for better or for worse—Stefy would always love her, care for her, treat her like a child.

"What do you want me to say, Amanda? You want my fucking blessing? No—sorry, I'm not our mother."

Amanda buttoned her jacket, picked up her purse, and headed for the door. Stefy lit her last cigarette, dropped the empty pack next to two more on the ground.

"You know Georgie's dad was a cop, right?" Stefy said after her. "He put Lee away. You're kidding yourself if you think this is just going to disappear . . . Amanda?"

"I wanted to talk to you. I need my sister, but I'm sitting here listening to your hung-over strung-out bullshit."

"Amanda, look at me."

"Fuck off."

"Look at me, Amanda."

Amanda stopped, turned around. Stefy hadn't moved from the window. Her skinny arms wrapped around her even skinnier waist, and without her makeup, her sister looked old, tired.

"Please, don't do this," she said.

"We need groceries," said Amanda.

"Get a job."

The cold stuck. Everything was gray. An overcast sky brought a freezing Monday morning to the city. Norman didn't mind winter. It was part of life. What he couldn't live with was cold coffee, and as he parked his Explorer on Chicago Avenue, he forced down one last bitter sip before he opened his door and emptied the large Styrofoam cup onto the sidewalk.

"Hey, don't be doing that—"

Norman ignored the voice coming from behind him and shook the last drops from the cup and got out.

"Why you gotta do that, man? Father Dunne hates when people litter out here."

The man's purple suit was two sizes too big, most likely a donation, a piece of charity like his job. He stood at the front door of Cathedral Shelter holding a clipboard in his leather-gloved hands. He was black—probably in his late forties—but his dry gray skin and worn eyes made him look ten years older.

"Relax," said Norman. "It'll wash away. We're supposed to be getting more rain."

"Well, Father Dunne ain't gonna hear that. Now, I gotta get the hose and spray it down."

"I'm sorry," said Norman.

"Sorry ain't gonna hold that freezing hose out here."

"I'll tell the father I did it."

The man's head cocked to the side; his chest drew up and back. Norman recognized the gestures. He'd just been made.

"You a cop, ain't you?" asked the man.

"Retired," said Norman.

"Yeah, I know that look—the way y'all be clockin' the brothers. It's in your blood, am I right?"

"Or you got a guilty conscience," said Norman, smiling.

"Man, I did my time. I been clean for six years. The only thing I'm guilty of is loving the Lord."

"That makes two of us," said Norman.

The man pulled off one of his gloves, held out his hand to Norman.

"Well, in that case, I'm Edmund. Nice to meet you. Everyone around here calls me Eddie."

"Good to meet you, Eddie," said Norman, shaking his hand. "I'm Norman. Everybody calls me Norman."

"Ha! You gotta roll with what you got. What brings you down our way?"

"I'm looking for Father Dunne."

"Do you have an appointment?"

Eddie held up the clipboard, knocked it twice with his fist.

"You gotta have an appointment—them the rules," he said.

"I don't, Eddie, but I'm willing to bet a man in your position could help me out."

"You'd be betting right, Norman. But you know, stickup kids

be trying to hustle their way inside the shelter all the time, robbing folks in their sleep. These people already have nothing, and them shits trying to take nothing from nothing. So I'll ask you what I ask them—and don't lie because I know when a motherfucker's lying—are you here doing God's work or the devil's?"

"Eddie, I'm retired police—"

"That's not what I asked you, Norman."

Norman smiled. Eddie smiled back.

"It's a simple question," said Eddie.

"God's work, Eddie. I'm here because my son—"

"That's all you gotta say."

Eddie shoved the clipboard under his arm, turned around, and buzzed the building's intercom. A woman's voice cracked through the small speaker.

"Cathedral Shelter, how may I help you?"

"Hey, Mary, this is Eddie out front. I've got a friend of mine—a cop out here—"

"Retired," said Norman, correcting him.

"I'm gonna send him up to you, alright? He needs to talk to Father Dunne."

"Okay, send him to the office. I'll be waiting."

The door lock rattled; Eddie pulled open the door and held it while Norman slid out a crisp ten-dollar bill from his money clip.

"This ain't no casino, Norman. Give it to the shelter."

"You sure?"

"Come on, man. I ain't no valet. Just do me a favor: Tell Father Dunne you're the one who spilled all over her street."

"*Her?*" asked Norman.

"How long you been retired? Office is at the end of the hallway."

Norman patted Eddie on the shoulder and stepped inside. As the door creaked closed, the warm smell of garlic and detergent replaced the cold city air. He had expected a zoo—bodies on top of bodies—men stinking just like county jail. But instead, the shelter reminded him of Georgie's old school, Sullivan High, up on Bosworth. He walked slowly down the fluorescent-lit hallway. Behind the small windows on every lacquered pine door, men and women peeked up from their classes and groups to see whose shoes were clacking down the hall. When he stepped inside the office, he thought it was empty until a woman's voice came from behind a computer monitor on top of a desk stacked high with a rainbow of file folders.

"You're here to see Father Dunne?"

"Mary?"

"That's me—"

Mary peeked her head out from behind the monitor. She was white, in her forties, her brown hair was pulled back and she was wearing a green turtleneck that sagged around her neck. Norman pulled out the scrap of paper that Paul had given him, held it out low, and squinted at the words.

"I was hoping to, if she has the time. I'm looking for someone who's staying here—Chance Pritchard."

"And your name?"

"Norman Quinn."

"And you're a police officer?"

"Retired. But yes, I was—homicide detective."

Mary picked up a huge RadioShack walkie-talkie off one of

the stacks of file folders on her desk and held it with both hands as she pressed the orange button and spoke.

"Father Dunne, are you on property?"

The walkie spat back two patches of buzzing static before a woman's light voice spoke back.

"I'm in the gym with the outreach team, Mary. What's up?"

"I've got an Officer Quinn here to speak with you about one of our clients—Chance Pritchard."

The radio popped, hissed, and went quiet. After a long moment—long enough for Norman to start looking for a seat—Father Dunne came back on.

"Okay, tell him I'll be right up."

"She'll be a few moments," Mary said to Norman. "Do you want a glass of water? Coffee?"

"That's fine. I'll wait," replied Norman.

On the other side of the room, two large bulletin boards hung on the brick wall outside the father's office. The boards were covered with thank-you letters photocopied on pink paper and snapshots of smiling people of all colors. In the pictures, all the people stood in front of apartment buildings holding up thick sheaves of paper to the camera.

"Those are some of our success stories."

Norman turned; Father Dunne's short blonde hair was wet and pasted to her head. Her face was flushed, shiny with sweat. She wore a set of plain gray sweats, and an orange towel hung around her neck. She was as tall as Norman, but had the lean square shoulders of an athlete and the piercing eyes to match.

"Those leases in their hands?" asked Norman, smiling.

"Some are month-to-month, but most are six," said the father. "We try to get the landlords to commit to at least three months so our people have a decent chance to get settled. But not everyone is sympathetic to our work."

"They got bills to pay too," said Norman.

"They also have empty units that aren't making them a dime." She wiped her hand on the towel, held it out.

"Sara Dunne."

"Norman Quinn. Should I call you Father? I mean—"

"That's what most people call me."

"I promised Eddie I'd let you know I spilled some coffee in front of your building."

"Don't worry about it. I'll show you where the hose is on your way out."

Norman waited for her to say she was kidding, but instead, she pushed opened her office door and kicked down the door stop. Inside, she moved quickly—turning on the lights, clearing a chair filled with books in front of her desk. She rubbed her head with the towel, tried to fix her hair in a tall mirror leaning on a bookshelf.

"You caught me during our weekly basketball game. It's good for the staff—gets our mind off the work."

"I have a punching bag in my basement at home," said Norman.

"I've found you have to stay active with this kind of work—"

"Oh, *I know*, believe me. There were some times. Oh boy, Father, without that punching bag, it would have been some-body's face."

He'd said something wrong. The father stared at him with

another look he recognized—the start of disgust. Norman could tell she wanted to reply, scold him, but instead she just sat down behind a gray steel desk that looked identical to his when he was on the force. The top was covered with stacks of file folders just like his. She even had one of those brass library lamps with a green glass shade pushed to the right. The only difference was the pair of threadbare leather-bound Bibles in arm's reach; Norman only had just the one.

"So what do you want with Chance?" she asked.

"I was hoping I could talk to the kid."

"About?"

"With all due respect, Father, that would be between me and Mr. Pritchard."

"Is he in trouble?" asked Father Dunne.

"I wouldn't call it that," said Norman.

"Well, with all due respect to you, we don't give out client information to anyone but immediate family."

"Even the police?"

"*But you're retired*, aren't you, Mr. Quinn?"

"Six years this December, thirty-six years on."

"Then you—more than most—would understand how important client confidentiality is."

"Father—a simple conversation is all I'm asking."

Father Dunne closed the folder in front of her, straightened two pens into a line, and then leaned forward on her desk.

"I'll level with you, Norman, and hopefully spare us both any more bullshit as I assume you've got better things to do much like myself. I can't and won't provide any information regarding any of our clients unless you've got a valid warrant or subpoena for our records. A lot of our clients are just getting back onto their feet, starting to make amends for their former lives. I can assure you—if they're here, they're trying, and that's good enough for us."

"Father, I thought you were in the business of helping people," said Norman, clenching his fists on his lap.

"We help those who want to better themselves, but for whatever reason can't. We provide the resources, emotional and otherwise. So unless you're sleeping under the Dan Ryan or don't know where your next meal is coming from, I really don't have anything for you."

The father rolled up her sleeve, checked her watch.

"Speaking of which, it's spaghetti night. You're welcome to stay. We've always got enough. Otherwise, I'll have Mary show you where the maintenance room is."

"*The what?*" asked Norman.

"For the hose, Norman—to wash out our drive."

E ddie stood at his post at the front door of Cathedral Shelter smoking a Newport and laughing while Norman filled a five-gallon bucket from a hose at the side of the building.

"Don't get your slacks all wet, Norman," he said. "You'll freeze right up."

"No shit—and I just got this suit back from the cleaners."

With both hands, Norman picked up the bucket by its handle and struggled to make the four steps to his Explorer without spilling. When he reached the puddle of his coffee on the sidewalk, he took a step back and awkwardly poured the water out.

"There you go," said Eddie. "Don't worry about that suit. I work at a cleaners up on North. I can get it cleaned for you."

Norman upended the bucket and shook out the last drops of water. He carried it back to Eddie, set it at his feet.

"Which cleaners?" asked Norman.

"Best Value up on Wells. I do two days there and three here. That's how I stay looking fresh."

"That's a good deal for you," said Norman. "A solid living."

"Works for me. Keeps my lips dry and my nose clean," said Eddie, laughing.

Norman checked up and down the street. The shelter shared the block with a warehouse and a towering self-storage facility. There was traffic—just a few cars—at the intersection at the south end of the block, but otherwise the street was quiet.

"You must've said *something*, Norman. Father's usually much more kind to our guests."

"Guess it's in my blood like you said, Eddie. You got a spare smoke?"

Eddie took off his gloves, reached inside the breast pocket of his jacket. Norman peered through the shelter's front door; the front hallway was empty.

"How come you're not getting dinner with everyone else?" asked Norman.

"Ah, you know, I'm not really a Chef Boyardee kinda man."

"Me neither—"

Norman grabbed Eddie by the collar, shoved him back against the brick wall. In one motion—his oldest reflex—Norman pulled his revolver and jammed it deep under Eddie's lower ribs.

"What are you doing—"

"This can go a whole lotta ways, Eddie," said Norman, wetting his lips. "You can give me the information I need, and I'll leave you and all your fucking degenerate friends alone or we can take a ride in my truck, and after I beat your sorry ass for a couple of hours, I'll call some of my old friends at the precinct, and I bet they got room for your nigger ass in county. Whaddya' think?"

"I didn't do shit—"

Again—in a flash, *simple as putting on a jacket*—Norman smashed the butt of his pistol on Eddie's face, snapping his head against the brick wall. Blood started from his nose.

"It's a simple question, Eddie."

A smile spread across Norman's face as he dug the barrel under Eddie's jaw and leaned on it with all his weight. Eddie clenched his teeth. Sweat broke across his brow despite the biting air condensing his quick heaving breaths.

"What do you want to know?" he asked.

"Chance Pritchard—what do you know about him?"

"Who?"

"*Chance Pritchard.* Don't fuck with me, Eddie."

"I'm not, I'm not—"

Norman's forearms burned. It'd been so long. His heart sped, excited. He kept the pistol at Eddie's throat and jammed him again against the brick wall as he enjoyed the rush, the pain.

"What do you know?!"

"White boy. Shaved head. Keeps to himself. Few day ago, he came around with a busted-up arm. I asked him about it, but he didn't say shit. He's got a buddy that drops him off—big white motherfucker with tattoos, looks like he's been inside."

"What's his name?"

"I don't know—"

"Bullshit."

Norman whipped Eddie across the face with the pistol. Blood sprayed from his right eyebrow onto Norman's shirt.

"You see everything, Eddie. Don't insult me. Don't insult yourself."

"Why are you doing this?"

Eddie's voice shook; tears fell down his cheeks.

"What's the friend's name?!" Norman demanded.

"Lee . . . I think. He's older, probably as old as you. He's got one of them biker beards."

"When's the last time you saw them?"

"Ah, man, come on, Norman . . . I don't know. I told you four—five days ago—sometime. Do you know how many motherfuckers be coming in and out of here?"

Norman relaxed the pistol. Eddie's face was already swelling. Blood covered his cheek and lips.

"Look at this shit—why you gotta come at me like that, Norman? My face, my fucking suit, I thought we was friends."

"We ain't shit, Eddie," said Norman, holstering his gun. "And if you say anything about this—"

"I know. You'll string up my black ass. I heard it all before, mister. You ain't got one new word."

Norman glided to his truck. He didn't feel the ground. When he lifted the handle on his door, he felt his entire right arm pinch and start to ache. He started his car; the engine cracked and spit to life. He pulled the gearshift towards himself and down. The three knocks to drive snapped from his burning hand all the way into the middle of his cramping back. At the end of the block, he rolled down his window. Cold air filled the car. The scent of Eddie's blood swirled around him and mixed with the fresh gun oil from his revolver in his jacket. He smelled the drops of coffee that he'd left on the street, every garbage can that he sped by as he floored his truck, and if he breathed deep, he could smell the wet grass still soaking on Georgie's coffin across town. He smiled.

A manda sat on Pap's bed watching him struggle with the blinds in his dark bedroom.

"There, there—come on, stay up—damnit—"

"Pull it to the right," said Amanda. "The cord."

The blinds reeled up one last time and stuck to the top of the window; dim afternoon light filled the room. It was just bright enough to light up the layer of dust covering Pap's bedside lampshade and an old space heater that ran the length of the wall. Pap pulled a tissue from his cardigan pocket, blew his nose, and circled the room kicking the baseboard with the side of his leather slipper.

"There's a rat in these walls. Bastard waits until my eyes are heavy as diving bells before he starts up. The academics swear the animal kingdom cannot comprehend all our two-legged foibles, but I'm here to tell you—after eighty-two years—they're just the same as us. They love, they hate, and they enjoy a good ribbing as much as the next man—you hear that?"

Pap crouched down, brought his head nearly to the floor, and closed his eyes. Amanda held her breath and leaned in, but all she heard was the muted buzz of the warming space heater and, behind that, the building's pipes filling and emptying with water.

"I think it's just the plumbing," she said.

"You don't hear that?" Pap shouted in a whisper, jabbing his hand at the seam on the floor.

"Pap, there's nothing in there."

Pap shot up, stomped to the front of the apartment. Amanda heard him open the front closet and drag out his huge steel toolbox. The metal let out a long scrape against the hardwood floor. After a moment, he came back carrying his old fat plug-in drill and a small handsaw half the length of his arm. Before she could stop him, he dropped to his knees, plugged in the drill next to the space heater, and continued tapping back and forth along the base of the wall.

"Once they breed, it's over, Mandy. We'll have to move out," he said. "Bring me the borax from the kitchen."

"Pap, I don't think this is a good idea."

"Go get me the fucking borax, Mandy, or I'll tell your sister who's been stealing my pills."

Amanda stared at Pap, got up slowly from the bed. He'd never spoken to her like that before—*ever*. Sweat dripped at the back of his neck as he crawled back and forth on the ground. With both hands, he placed the thick bit against the wall and pulled the trigger of the drill. Amanda backed out of the room, went to the kitchen, and searched for the borax beneath the sink. The sound of the drill—a cracking drone—filled the entire apartment, and then the old machine hissed and screamed like it was eating tacks as Pap drilled hole after hole into the wall. Amanda pulled the box of borax from the back of the cupboard and carried it back to the room. A cloud of minced plaster filled the air. She took the box to Pap, tapped him on the shoulder.

"What—Goddamnit!"

Pap jumped; the drill bucked in his hand. He fell back from the wall, caught himself on the ground.

"You don't just sneak up on someone when they're working! Are you an idiot?"

Plaster dust covered his face and arms. He wiped at his forehead; blood smeared across his brow.

"Your hand," said Amanda.

Blood dripped from a short cut down the base of his palm and trailed across the floor to the handsaw behind him.

"Damnit," he said. "I'm making a mess."

"Let's go wash it out," said Amanda, taking his arm. "Come on."

She helped him up, walked him to the kitchen, and ran his hand under the faucet. Blood splattered inside the steel sink before it thinned to pink and drained away. Amanda wrapped his hand in a dishrag and sat him down at their small kitchen table while she pulled the first aid kit from the cupboard.

"What was the borax for?" she asked.

"The coward's sword: poison."

Amanda sat at the table, pulled his hand forward. She dabbed it dry with the dishtowel before she stretched a butterfly bandage across the small cut.

"Sound crazy, don't I?" asked Pap.

"Just angry," said Amanda. "I'll talk to Chance, have him get some traps."

Pap scanned the kitchen's yellowed walls up and down. A long deep crack—just right of the fridge in front of him—burrowed back and forth through the plaster like a blind child feeling for the floor. Pap set his hand on top of Amanda's, patted lightly like he was tapping a drum.

"Thank you, Mandy," he said quietly. "I'm sorry."

Amanda watched his hand jump up and down on hers. Dark purple veins braided back and forth under his skin before they broke into dots and tiny red pricks running up his arm.

"You know when your sister calls, we talk about you, always have. When I hear her voice, I'm struck. I hear your mother—I hear myself talking to your mother."

Pap got up and opened the cupboard underneath the sink and squatted down. At once, he looked old to Amanda—older than he ever had. His body curved, bent into a question mark after years of doing more than he should. He groaned as he reached to the back and pulled out an empty spray bottle of Windex, an empty box of S.O.S pads, and two of Amanda's T-shirts that she'd cut up into rags. He ducked his head into the dark space and then came back out holding up an old, unopened package of two large mousetraps.

"I remembered these as soon as you said it," he said, smiling.

"Why did my mom leave, Pap?"

Pap tore open the package and pulled out of one of the traps. He flicked at the copper bait switch over and over and then lifted the spring arm and let it snap back.

"You would've done the same thing, Mandy."

"Not if I had kids."

Pap held out his arm. Amanda got up from the table and pulled him to his feet. Immediately, he went back down the hallway to the front closet and pulled a small box from the top shelf. He carried it back to Amanda, put it on the kitchen table.

"You should have these."

The black velvet box was small and long—the kind that held necklaces or a precious set of pens. Amanda pulled it open; the small hinge creaked apart. Inside, two tarnished army medals— a Bronze Star and a Purple Heart—lay pinned to the cushioned cloth by their individual ribbons.

"Your father enlisted because of me. He'd never admit to it, but I know. When he was young, I'd tell him about my journeys in France and the rest of it. He wanted his own stories—something to tell his kids, make me proud, all that. When he came back from Iraq—the Desert Storm or Desert Shield, whatever the hell they ended up calling it—he didn't look the same, didn't talk the same. He'd get drunk and start going on about the war—the oil fires, his guns. He'd called himself the dead's shepherd. He'd say he was the cross, the sheriff, the gold. I can still hear him now. It was crazy talk, Mandy, coming from my own. He'd get so worked up, I thought he'd hurt your mother or worse."

As Pap spoke, Amanda set the box in her lap and traced the same crack in the wall over and over with her eyes—up to down, left to right—searching for a shadow of the failing, cleaving stud that had started it all.

"We gave your parents the house in Maryland because we thought it would help. Me and your grandmother thought it was just the stress of making ends meet that was getting to him. We should've never left is my point. Your mother called me when she decided to move to Baltimore. It wasn't an easy decision for her, Mandy. You have to know that. But she couldn't take it anymore. Wayne was . . . gone. And you girls were old enough—*no, you weren't old enough.* But you weren't babies anymore, you see? We decided—me and your mother—that it was what was best for everyone. Maybe we were wrong."

Tears filled Amanda's eyes. She tried to fight it off, but her chest still caved. Her face fell into her hands. Pap wrapped her in his arms, rocked her back and forth.

"Oh, baby, don't. You remind me so much of your dad sometimes. You carry all that hurt in your chest just like he did, and it just eats you two up the same."

"I just want to be normal. I just want a job and a life. I want to come home and live like a regular fucking person. I don't fight with Stefy. I don't worry about money, and I don't feel all this—*shit*—all the time. "

Pap held her at arm's length, looked deep into Amanda's eyes.

"Then do it, Mandy. I'll be fine. I know more than you think, and I know it hurts, but you can't let it eat you up. Not like your dad."

Amanda cried into Pap's chest. Her tears soaked into his old thick cardigan and softened the wires of wool into a warm damp pillow that smelled of the same aftershave and pomade he'd worn her whole life. His heartbeat tapped inside her ear, steady and quiet beneath his short breaths.

"All that past hell—that's the rub for all of us."

The midnight Blue Line train shook Ghost Town's walls as it tore overhead, drowning out the screams of the naked girl bent over Lee's desk. Her tattoo—a tall masked gypsy girl with the golden brown wings of a young eagle—was still fresh, swollen and pink across her freckled white back. As he held her hips, Lee watched his huge belly hulk over the young girl in one of the five security camera monitors on the shelf above his desk. Three of the monitors covered the front of the shop. One focused on the tinted front door, another on the antique brass register at the center of the shop, and the last just over Lee's workstation focused close and tight on his barber chair. Stefy had asked him a thousand times why there wasn't a camera on her chair, and every time Lee had given her a version of the same answer—"When you do something worth looking at."

The last two monitors covered the back of the shop. One aimed at the back door near the steps to the basement, and the other—the one Lee was watching as he grabbed the girl's long black hair like a horse's rein and yanked back, fucking her harder as he finished—was on the ceiling behind him pointed at his long, always clean desk. He let go of the girl's hair; she collapsed onto the register drawer still full of cash.

"Did you come?" he asked.

"Close, but it's okay," said the girl, standing up.

"Just gimme a second, my heart feels like it's gonna explode."

Lee sat at his desk, shoved the register drawer from in front of him. Fives, tens, and twenties fell into a pile on top of an old issue of *Tattoo*. While the girl stood naked admiring her new tattoo in the long mirror behind him, Lee reached into his jeans pocket and pulled out his small bottle of nitroglycerine tablets.

"My art looks good on you, if I do say so," he said, tapping out his last five pills. "Makes your ass float."

"Can we go another round?"

"Inking or fucking?" Lee asked, smiling.

"You don't get one without the other," said the girl, slipping back into her dress. "I'm gonna go have a smoke."

The girl put on Lee's huge black Carhartt and walked down the dark back hallway of the shop. The steel door punched open, letting in a gust of freezing air.

"Don't go too far," Lee called out.

"Bad advice."

Norman stepped from the shadows of the back hallway. Lee jumped, pulling up his jeans. Cash and pills scattered to the ground. He yanked at his desk drawer, trying to get it open.

"Don't bother. I got it right here," said Norman.

Norman held up Lee's chrome .45 pistol in the low light. Despite the late hour, his thick, silver hair was combed neatly to the side and back. His face was freshly shaved, and his black suit and gray overcoat were cleaned and pressed.

"Don't worry," said Norman. "I'll give it back. It's much too fancy for me. I like hammers and bullets, never really needed anything else."

"That's not how I remember it, Norman. If I recall, you've got a weakness for radiators and vice clamps."

"Ah, the good old days. We can't all be tough guys like you, Lee, slicing people up with straight blades."

Lee's heart slammed away in his chest. He groaned as he leaned forward in his chair and picked up the cash off the ground. He piled the money on his desk and sifted through it, looking for his pills. Just then, the back door grated back open; the clap of the girl's boots echoed down the dark hallway.

"Some asshole parked me in," the girl called out. "And it's starting to snow."

Lee wiped his reddening face, grabbed three twenties from the pile of cash in front of him, and quickly got up and stopped the girl in the back hallway before she could make it all the way to the office.

"Take a cab," he said, holding out the money. "You can come by tomorrow and pick up your car."

The girl stared at Lee. Even in the little bit of light, she could see his cheeks were a deep red—almost purple—and sweat streamed from his temple in fat drops.

"Are you okay?" she asked.

"Yeah," said Lee. "Just take a cab."

"I don't want my car to get towed."

"It won't. I'm gonna be here for a while."

"How long?" asked the girl.

Norman stepped from behind Lee, swinging his pistol in his hand.

"Do your parents know where you are, young lady?" he asked.

Lee grabbed the girl by the arm and pulled her back down the hallway to the back door.

"Who the fuck is that?" she asked.

"Come by tomorrow," said Lee, pushing open the door.

"Do you want me to call the cops?" the girl whispered.

"Yes!" shouted Norman. "Let's make it a real party."

Lee shoved the girl out and yanked the door shut. He held the bare brick wall, took deep breaths as he made his way back to the office. Norman waited for him on a stool with his overcoat unbuttoned, kicking at the ground like a lonely twelve-year-old ready to spin a yarn to anyone that would listen.

"You're gonna love this, Lee. So I'm shaking down this particular hapless fuck, and he starts blabbering on about a tall tattooed asshole goes by the name of Lee, and I'm thinking to myself, *I know a Lee, I know a Lee real well, but it can't be the same guy.* I mean, dash it all, what are the odds? So I go to that shithole bar where my boy is stomped—what is it? Darla's? Help me, what's the name, Lee?"

"Delilah's," said Lee, sitting back down at his desk.

"Yes, Delilah's. And you know what, Lee? The owner is a fucking saint. I knew his father coming up, Benji Miller—*Butcher to the Stars.* Best beef on the lake. This guy—God bless him— gives me a drink, and we talk. He tells me everything. He tells me about that little whore Georgie loved so much. He tells me about her tattooing sister, who she works for, and where they congregate like a bunch of fucking dumpster rats—his words, not mine, Lee—and now a part of me is thinking, *This has to be the same*

Lee, but I still don't want to believe it. Do you know how much I don't want to believe it, Lee? Guess. Guess for Christ's sake."

"How much, Norman?"

"I don't want to believe it so much, I drive around this fucking block five times rechecking the address. I pass your pretty Lincoln five times, Lee. The same car I picked you up in way back when. I must have burned through half a tank not believing what was right in front of my eyes."

Norman pulled a handkerchief from his lapel pocket, wiped spittle from the sides of his mouth, and threw it on Lee's desk.

"Wipe your face, Lee. You're sweating on your money. You've done a great job with the building, by the way. And the neighborhood—I didn't even recognize it. I remember when you couldn't walk three steps without tripping over a hippie nodding out in the streets. I used to carry a pair of scissors—do you remember that?—I'd chop those greaseballs' hair right off their head. I'd tell 'em, 'Go home and take a shower, you stinking faggot!' Remember that?"

A police siren wailed out somewhere near. Out of habit—their shared history—both the men froze waiting for the sound to fade back into the whirr, pop, and hiss of the building's radiator. Lee pushed the stacks of cash to the side, slid a shot glass to the center of his desk. He opened his desk drawer and pulled out a bottle of Beam. He poured a shot with his shaking hand, drank it, poured another.

"Georgie's dead, Lee."

Lee's blood slammed inside his head, and his arms tingled, felt cold and numb at his fingertips. He slowly pushed his hands through the cash in front of him and felt one of his pills roll under his palm. He pulled it to the side out of Norman's sight and ran his hand across his desk searching for another.

"Sorry for your loss," said Lee.

"Save your fucking pity."

"Oh, I don't pity you, Norman, or your fucking junkie kid."

Norman set Lee's pistol on the edge of the desk and pulled his own revolver from his holster and pulled back the hammer. Lee cocked his pistol, turned around, rested it on top of his leg.

"Where's Chance?" asked Norman.

"Go home, Norman. Bury your son."

"Already did."

Norman snatched the shot glass off Lee's desk, drank it, and dropped it back. It rolled in a long circle before it came to a stop in the pile of money. Whiskey wet the bills.

"You think I covered up that murder for free? Do you know the difference between first-degree murder and aggravated robbery, Lee? *A fucking lifetime.* All it takes is one call. There's no statute of limitations. I still got the bloody knife you killed Cupid Calloway with, and it's still got your fingerprints all over it. I bet you all that cash in front of you: They go digging around in this basement, you and your DNA will be all over it. There goes your shithole shop, your fancy fucking gun, and everything that's precious to you. You owe me—"

Lee slammed his fist down, and with all his trembling strength, pushed himself up to his feet and raised the pistol on Norman's gut.

"I don't owe you shit. For twenty years, I paid you in cash. We are square. You said so yourself. So don't come breaking into my life again ten years later telling me I owe you because your man-child got got. Hell, I probably paid for that crackerjack house in Evanston. That's right, I know where you live, Norman Quinn. I got your number a long time ago, old man."

"Chicago problems—Chicago solutions."

"You're Goddamned right," snapped Lee. "I'm surprised you remember that."

"I remember everything, Lee. I remember you got a weak heart in more ways than one."

Norman flicked one of his old CPD cards onto Lee's desk. The work phone had been crossed out and replaced with a handwritten number.

"Give me Chance Pritchard or I bring in the sisters, and we can see how much they like radiators and clamps."

Sweat dripped from Lee's chin. His temples stretched and pounded, threatening to explode. He drank straight from the bottle, choked down two huge swallows, spilling it over his cheeks.

"If I do this, we're done, Norman. Forever."

Norman holstered his revolver, buttoned his overcoat back up.

"I heard they're closing O'Hare tonight. Same with Midway," he said. "Gonna be hard to get out of town."

"What are you going to do with Chance?"

"I'm a peace officer, Lee. I seek justice."

Norman walked back down the dark hallway. When he opened the door, a cold gust cooled Lee's boiling neck. He waited for the door to bang shut, but all he heard was his pulse slamming, his heart thrashing. He shoved the lone pill in his mouth, chewed it, and scrubbed his hands in frantic circles searching for the other four.

"Every vehicle you see out there has a wondrous story," said Pap. "Germany, Japan, the Danes—all represented by combustion engines and a faculty of international rubbers and plastics—damn me, I love this town."

Steady morning rain dotted the windshield of Stefy's Toyota. She'd picked them up at nine; Pap's appointment was in another hour at the veteran's hospital across town. Chance held Amanda's hand in the backseat as they sat in packed traffic on the Dan Ryan. Amanda was hungry—starving—her stomach turned on itself, starting a stab of a headache behind her eyes.

"The city is booming," Pap said in the front seat. "The fury of the ants!"

He'd been like this since he woke up. He had no coffee, no breakfast, but was still full of a buzzing busy energy that Amanda hadn't seen in a long time. She'd woken up to him spraying WD-40 on every hinge in the apartment, and after that he'd walked down to the convenience store with Chance and tried to race him back. Amanda hoped it meant that he was finally turning a corner, that the last cycle of chemotherapy had finally made a difference. The possibility of that slowed the pounding in her head. She smiled as he jabbed his hand through Stefy's arms on the steering wheel and laid on the horn.

"Quit it, Pap. I'm driving—" said Stefy

"I'm serious, Chicago—my kind of fucking town!"

Pap didn't let off. He pushed over and over. The horn squealed while he waved at the other cars creeping by. Stefy grabbed his hand, threw it off.

"Pap, stop!" she yelled.

"That's right!" shouted Pap. "I'm serious. Serious as a—what is it, Chance?"

"Heart attack," Chance said from the backseat.

"That's right. Serious as a fucking heart attack."

"Has he been drinking?" asked Stefy, glaring at Amanda in the rearview mirror.

"Do frogs have wet assholes?" said Pap.

Chance dropped his head and put his fist to his mouth, trying to stifle his laughter.

"Nice," said Stefy. "Amanda, did you get him drunk?"

"Of course, I poured his beer in a bowl and left it on the kitchen floor—fuck you," sniped Amanda.

"Serious as a faggot with a soda bottle."

Chance broke, busted into laughter in the backseat.

"You like that one, Chance? I got some more: serious as this shit bag on my chest—"

"Shut up, Pap—I could kill you right now," Stefy said to Amanda.

"Stefy, I love you, darling, but I'd sock you in the kidneys if you tried," replied Pap.

"I'm not talking to you, Pap."

Suddenly, he coughed into his hand. He shook his head back and forth holding at his stomach. Vomit flew out of his mouth onto the dashboard.

"Ouch," Pap choked out.

He wretched again. Thin, blood-tinged puke poured from his mouth. He batted at his face trying to wipe his chin; his neck gave way, pitching his head back and forth like a rag doll.

"Can someone help him?!" shouted Stefy, swerving into the next lane.

Horns blared all around them. Amanda leaned forward, tried to steady Pap.

"Keep your eyes on the road, Stefy!" she yelled.

"What's wrong with him?"

"I—I don't know," said Amanda. "Pap? Pap?"

"I'm alright, Mandy. I'm fine," he croaked out.

Pap blinked over and over as the color dropped from his face. Beads of cold sweat broke across his forehead, and his breath shortened to gasps.

"I'm fine—Chance—tell her, I'm fine," he managed.

Amanda wiped Pap's face with one hand and held his head straight with the other. Her heart dropped inside her chest. Stefy slammed the wheel to the right and sent the Toyota across two lanes, barely making the exit to Lake Street.

"What are you doing?!" shouted Amanda.

"I have to take the streets or we're never gonna get there—"

Stefy floored the gas and honked over and over as she ran a red light. Cars swerved around them squealing to a stop in the middle of the intersection. Pap's eyes closed. His body went limp in his seat. Amanda pushed herself forward, wrapped her arms around his body, trying to hold it up. A block ahead, the hospital barreled towards them. Stefy downshifted; the Toyota's engine wailed and bucked as they barely made the entrance of the hospital.

"There, there, go straight," Amanda said, pointing to two ambulances parked in a driveway.

Stefy sped up and slammed on the breaks. The Toyota skidded to a stop, nearly hitting one of the ambulances. Pap lurched towards the windshield, but Amanda held him tight.

"Hurry up! Take him in!" said Stefy.

"You're not coming?" asked Amanda.

"I have to park the car, and I need to call Lee."

Chance jumped out; Amanda followed. He opened the passenger door, squatted down, and lifted Pap out. Amanda ran ahead of him through the sliding glass doors of Brown Medical Center's emergency ward. In just a few steps, both Pap and Chance were soaked with rain and bleeding red vomit.

"What do we do?" Chance asked between heavy breaths.

The long white waiting room was empty and quiet except for two older men—black and white—laughing by the bay of payphones near the front doors. They both wore faded green army field jackets and soaked tattered sneakers wrapped and patched with strips of failing duct tape. A short rolling oxygen tank stood next to the black man's leg; a set of clear tubes ran up to his nose.

He wheezed in scraping breaths and stared at Amanda, Chance, and Pap. The white man scratched at his beard and turned to see what his friend had noticed. When he turned, Amanda could see half his face was scabbed-up and raw.

"You need some help?" he asked.

Amanda fought back tears. Her voice was strange—faint—from another part of her body.

"No, we're fine—wait—where do we go?" she asked.

"You wanna go right up there, honey."

The white man pointed to a glass window on the far side of the room. His hand shook in the air. He pulled it back, embarrassed by the sight.

"You might have to knock or buzz. Sometimes, I just yell," he said. "Sometimes you wanna scream."

Norman closed his eyes and saw heaven as he knew it. Polished white marble beamed under yellow clouds. Angels moved in flaring silver swarms. Their powdered faces smiled while their pipe-organ voices cooed the choruses of his favorite hymns. Their razor-sharp wings lifted them from a hundred miles away in a semicircle sun. Georgie was nowhere to be seen, but Norman knew once he was deep in prayer his son would arrive in diamond chain mail to welcome him into paradise with a flock of giant doves trailing ribbons of God's blonde curling beard.

Norman kneeled in the pew, let the Eucharist melt on his tongue. He squeezed his hands together and lowered his forehead to his fists. The morning Mass had been beautiful, the best he'd heard in a long time. Father Healy had dedicated his homily to the holy family—Mary, Joseph, and the baby Jesus—and for Norman, the sermon couldn't have been any more timely. He related, found solace in the words. The way Father Healy explained the challenges that Mary and Joseph must have felt explaining to their friends and family that their child was divinely conceived were some of the same feelings Norman and his wife had felt when they had to explain to their families how Georgie came to be. By then, it had been no secret that they'd had problems getting pregnant, and when Eileen began to show, the skeptical stares were as abundant as the weeping congratulations. It was different back then. Bringing doctors into the bedroom meant you were weak. Even Norman's own father, the kindest cop Chicago had ever seen, frowned and stopped Norman when he tried to explain to him how the process of insemination worked.

"Whatever happened to romance?" he'd asked Norman. "Worked for me, and it's free."

This, of course, was a lie. Norman himself was a product of chance and desperation. The whole family knew it had taken years for him to be conceived. His father in one of his many last-ditch efforts had even gone to the length of filling up ice trays with his own seed and making his mother melt the small clouded cubes inside her while she went about daily chores. This was the same man that had given Norman a gun on his eighth birthday. The same black .38 special he'd carried on the streets of Chicago during his forty years on the force. For three long nights, he stayed up filing down the pistol's hammer so it wouldn't shoot before he wrapped it in white butcher paper and tied it with red twine. His father was a living, breathing hero. Back then, being a cop was the best job in the world. People tilted their hats when Norman's dad was in uniform. When his name came up, everyone smiled. But then the city started changing. By 1961—the year Norman graduated high school—Englewood was no longer for the whites. His mother wanted to move to the North Side like everyone else, but his father wouldn't budge. As soon as Norman turned nineteen, he enrolled in the academy. He thought his father was naïve, too forgiving and trusting of the blacks. Norman's father retired early from the department. The city started drowning. The longhairs and blacks blitzed the city worse every month. In one year—1965—Norman lost two friends—cops—killed in the city and then two more and a cousin killed in Vietnam. He cracked heads all night, every night, but it didn't matter. The next week, there was a new crop of assholes waving signs, shitting in the parks, calling him "pig" wherever he walked.

Then the world turned upside down.

No one cared who was good and bad, just like now. In 1968, people walked around stabbing each other, fucking in the streets, threatening to drug the city's water. The blacks got organized, powwowed with pawn-shop pistols and stolen hunting rifles like a Goddamned jigaboo army. It didn't matter. Norman broke them all down. He crushed their fingers in his father's table vice, cattle-prodded their shitholes and nuts. He cuffed the tough guys—the big ones like Lee—to the radiators, and let the steam melt their stiff lips. For the crybabies, it was the shock box, an old army field phone rigged to zap a man's dick. He loosened them up with telephone books, put the screws to them with red-hot razor blades that only left scars the size of his thumb. Back then, he was a flood, a maelstrom clearing out every junkie and ruthless spade in every alley and apartment from Midway to the Loop.

Norman made the sign of the cross.

He pushed himself back into the pew, and opened his eyes. The church was empty, the Mass done. The smell of smudged candles filled the air as a lone altar boy in dirty sneakers walked around the church carrying a brass snuffer. Norman checked his watch. It was just past ten; he'd been at St. Pat's for almost four hours. He wondered if he should skip his lunch, sit in the chapel for the rest of the day. He'd done it before—not at St. Pat's—but at St. Mary's, his old church in Evanston. Sometimes, he'd sit in the chapel for hours watching folks come in and out of confession like a drive-through. Some left in tears; others walked away just happy to have the weight of their sins off their chest. Norman watched them all from the back pew, rolling his rosary for Georgie's soul, doing his acts of contrition until the words vented out of him in a long whispering drone.

He'd come to church that morning trying to make sense out of Georgie's death, but even after four hours, he was still angry, so angry at Georgie for leaving him too soon. He wasn't done. He knew Georgie would've come around. He would've given him everything and his heart. If offered by the Lord Jesus Christ, he would gladly switch places with his bloated, decaying son. Norman grabbed the pew in front of him and pushed himself to his feet. He walked slowly to the center aisle, letting his hand graze the 150-year-old wood. He wouldn't stay. He was tired. The answers he wanted weren't coming, at least not today. His new family—God, Jesus, the Holy Ghost— was as silent as his old family dead in the ground. He put his trench coat back on as he walked to the giant oak doors. He pushed them open, stepped outside. The rain felt like tongues—hot tongues licking his cheeks like all the pictures he'd seen from the Bible. He put one hand over his head and trotted to his truck, pulling out his keys with his other hand. His phone buzzed, groaned like a tiny mule in his pocket. He pulled it out as he opened his car door, flipped it open as he ducked his head and sat down.

"Hello?"

For a long moment, a hum of silence said nothing back; then a throat cleared, a heavy breath drew in, and Lee's deep voice gave him the address to the veteran's hospital across town.

They'd stolen him away. As soon as they saw him, the four masked nurses grabbed Pap's wet groaning body, lifted him onto a gurney, and snatched him away like his liver-spotted skin, and tumor-ridden body, were a 150-pound bag of leopard rubies and chunk of tarnished gold. And then nothing. And then more nothing. For hours, Amanda sat with Stefy and Chance in the waiting area. Sometime in the afternoon—when the clock looked phony—Stefy produced a full hot bag of Taco Bell, and Amanda realized she didn't even know how long her sister had been gone. Chance ate loudly, smacking his mouth together and crushing the paper wrappers one after another like he was playing a game. Amanda sipped on a soda that tasted flat and sour and stared at the windows near the ceiling that ran the length of the intensive-care ward.

They were too high. All they allowed was a hand-size slat of Chicago's gray sky that as the day drew on turned dark gray then a pink-tinted black. When the clock claimed it was 9 PM, Amanda decided she was going to stand on a chair to see why the windows were installed so high—what exactly the hospital was hiding. Just as she stood up to move her chair, a young doctor in green scrubs made his way out from a pair of swinging doors at the middle of the hallway. His curly hair glistened like he'd just stepped from the shower, and the skin on his face and hands didn't have a scratch, not one faint healing bruise.

"Beaumont?" he called out to them.

Amanda, Stefy, and Chance walked over to the doctor. He examined his hands, closed his fingers over and over into a fist, and flipped his thumb like he was flicking a cigarette that wasn't there.

"How are you?" he asked.

No one answered. Amanda was cold. Her jean jacket was still damp from the rain. Under her crooked glasses, her eyes burned and itched from crying. Stefy stood beside her in a pair of torn jeans and a black hooded sweatshirt. Her skin was transparent under the stark hospital light. The bags under her eyes were a hot pink, and Amanda could make out threads of purple and red veins trawling across her cheeks. Dried spots and specks of vomit splattered Chance's shirt and the collar of his jacket, and the corners of his mouth were still splashed red from taco salsa that he'd missed.

"I'm sorry to say that your grandfather's passed—"

Before he could finish, Stefy left. Her head dropped to her chest, and her shoulders shuddered on each step as she walked down the long hallway of intensive care towards a blurred figure pushing a gurney towards them. Amanda squinted her eyes, but still couldn't make out one feature on the figure's face.

"Why?" asked Chance.

"There's any number of reasons," said the doctor. "For whatever reason, the embolism didn't respond to the heparin fast enough—"

The doctor stopped himself, spoke in slow careful words to Chance.

"I'm sorry. Are you a member of the immediate family?"

"Why's my grandfather dead?" interrupted Amanda.

The doctor's cell phone rang in his pocket. Distorted techno music exploded over and over. He moved to pull it out, but Amanda grabbed his arm.

"Why?" she asked again.

"Please let go of me."

"Answer her question," said Chance.

The cell phone's music continued, bouncing around them like a carousel.

"Do you mind if I shut this off?" asked the doctor sharply.

The doctor yanked his arm out of her grip and gave a nervous smile to the black porter pushing the same empty gurney past them from the other end of the hallway. Amanda tried to swallow, but her mouth was hot and dry all the way down her throat. She pulled on Chance's arm, turned him from the doctor.

"Can you get me some water?" she asked.

"Sure."

"Straight past the nurse's station," said the doctor. "Where your friend went."

"*My sister?*" said Amanda.

"I'm sorry—where her sister went."

Chance's work boots knocked like hollow wood blocks on

the speckled linoleum as he walked away. The sound echoed up and down, bounced back and forth from one end of the empty hallway to the other. The doctor watched him leave, waited for him to get out of earshot before he asked his question.

"Do you know if your grandfather drank this morning?"

"What? Like booze?" said Amanda.

"Or beer. I only ask because my initial diagnosis is that alcohol aggravated his stroke. We won't know for sure until we see the blood tests, but something inhibited the drugs from taking effect. The first thing we did was pump his stomach, and by then—"

Music burst again from the doctor's cell phone. He held it up so Amanda could see the call was from home.

"I have to answer this. The head nurse on duty will be able to answer more of your questions . . . I'm sorry."

Before Amanda could stop him, the doctor turned and walked the other way. He answered the phone and the rest of his words trailed off, dissolved into the smooth painted cinder blocks, sucked into the foam ceiling panels, swallowed by the linoleum, her body, the sharp scents of medicine and death. Her heart collapsed the farther he got away, and once her tears overtook her and turned life into a blinking, shaking blur, she dropped to the ground and let out a long wail like she'd been stabbed. She held her hands to her face and felt what it is to be robbed and have nothing left, to suddenly be completely alone in a blinding hallway where you're unable to see or hear anything outside. She swore she was dying, and she didn't know why. That's all Amanda asked as her body folded on the ground, and she brought her knees to her shivering chest.

"**F**olks are grieving in there, you know? People's fathers, brothers, mothers, sons—people's *sons,* Norman. I don't see why we can't wait out here until—"

"Till when, Paul?"

"Until they come out—why can't we wait until they come out?"

"You want to sleep in my truck tonight?"

"Or come back in the morning. We don't have to go in there and give these people hell right now, Norman."

"I don't know what you had in mind, but I wasn't planning on giving anyone hell. I just want to talk to the kid."

Across the parking lot, Lee's long gray Lincoln pulled into the hospital. The rain had stopped, but the streets were still wet and under the white streetlamps; the huge car looked like it was gliding across a long, black quivering pool. Norman flashed his brights, and slowly the car floated around the perimeter of the empty lot and parked in front of Norman's truck. Paul zipped up his big Bears parka, pulled on his Bears beanie, checked his watch.

"Sheila's gonna kill me."

"I'm gonna kill you, if you don't stop whining."

Norman reached across Paul, pulled his revolver from the glove box, and stuck it into the holster at his waist.

"You don't need that," said Paul.

"Tell him that."

The two men got out. Norman put on his trench coat, and they walked to the front of the truck. After a moment, the Lincoln's growling engine quieted, and Lee stepped from his car in his huge black Carhartt. He gripped a small thin cigar between his teeth, and when the wind picked up, the sweet heavy smoke gusted into Norman's and Paul's faces. Lee dug his hands into his jacket pockets; his long beard flipped back and forth in the cold wind.

"What the fuck is this?" asked Lee. "I called you this morning."

"I want it to be a surprise."

"Then go surprise him. They're still inside."

"No, you don't get it," said Norman. "You're the surprise."

"Get fucked."

Lee puffed one last time on the cigar before he threw the butt at Norman's and Paul's feet, turned to get back into his car.

"Lee, either we can pick up Chance or my partner can make a call for all of them. Your choice."

Lee stopped, shook his head back and forth, and gripped tight on his car's door handle before he started across the wet parking lot to the hospital's entrance. Norman and Paul followed him, struggling to keep up. Paul pulled up on his pants, breathed heavy while Norman walked as fast as he could, watching his steps on the wet asphalt. When Lee disappeared through the automatic glass doors, both the men broke into a trot after him. By the time they got inside, Lee was already at the information desk, talking to a lone security guard who was sipping at a tall thermos of coffee. Norman and Paul stopped just inside the entrance, catching their breath. The lobby of the hospital was quiet.

Two living-room sets—couches, chairs, and coffee tables—sat on opposite sides of the lobby, and tall fake potted plants ran up and down the walls.

"They're on the third floor. Cafeteria's down the hall," said Lee, walking over. "I'll go up and bring Chance down."

"No," said Norman. "I'm coming with you."

"The girls don't have to see you."

"But I want them to. That's the surprise, Lee. I want them to see me and you together like the old friends that we are."

"Fuck you, Norman."

"You still got my number now, Lee?"

They walked towards the elevators. Paul took off his beanie, nervously rolled it in his hands. Norman fixed his eyes on Lee's back and straightened his holster at his side. They stepped into a waiting elevator. The motor popped and moaned until the doors opened onto the third floor. Paralyzed fluorescent light flooded the car. Amanda stood alone in the center of the floor's small waiting room staring at a small TV. The local newsman chattered quietly, smiled at her blank face.

"Baby girl," Lee called out.

She turned, stared at Lee, confused, unsure if he was really there. Then a small hurt smile gave way across her lips; her cheeks flushed red and tears filled her eyes. She went to Lee; he wrapped her in his arms, kissed her on top of her head.

"How is he?" asked Lee.

Amanda shook her face back and forth into Lee's jacket, then pushed off, raised her head to speak. That's when her eyes met Norman's as he stood by the elevator. She squinted, wishing she didn't recognize his shiny slicked-back gray hair and his gold-rimmed tinted glasses that in the bright light looked reddish pink, the shade of washed-out blood.

"Lee . . . what is this?" asked Amanda. "Why is he here?"

"Where's Chance, baby girl?" asked Lee.

Behind the men, the elevator's doors rolled closed. Its muted bell rang out and faded away as it went back to the first floor. Norman opened his hands, stepped towards Amanda.

"Amanda, I don't know if you remember me—"

"I remember you," said Amanda.

"Good. I remember you too," said Norman. "I don't want to trouble you, so if you can just tell us where Chance stepped off to—"

"Go fuck yourself," said Amanda.

Norman reared back; blood rushed his face and neck. Paul quickly stepped in front of Amanda, trying to calm his old partner down.

"Norman, let's get out of here," said Paul.

"Go ahead. I'm not done."

"*Let's go, Norman*," repeated Paul. "Ain't no good gonna come of this."

"You should listen to your friend," said Lee.

"Who the fuck was talking to you?!"

Norman jumped, hands clawing for Lee's neck. Paul wrapped him up with both arms and held him tight. Again, the elevator rang behind them. The doors opened. Stefy and Chance stepped out carrying Styrofoam takeout boxes.

"Chance, run!" shouted Amanda.

Stefy froze, looked at Amanda and Lee, completely lost. Chance dropped the food and jumped back into the elevator, smashed on the buttons until the doors closed. Norman ripped himself from Paul's arms, rushed towards the elevator but was too late. He jogged down the hallway towards the stairs. His trench coat, a black flag, flared behind him as he passed the nurse's station. Paul straightened his parka down, zipped it back up. He started to leave, but then stopped and turned to Amanda. His little bit of hair shot in every direction off his head, and his eyes were wide, serious, scared.

"Look, I don't know what this kid is to you," he said quickly. "But you need to ask yourself if he's worth it. Because Georgie's dead, and Norman ain't going to stop—I'm sorry for your loss."

Paul pulled his Bears beanie back on and started after his old partner. Amanda glared at Stefy and Lee, who both stood motionless. Amanda's hands closed into fists.

"Are you fucking kidding me?" asked Amanda. "Now. You guys decide to do this shit now. How long have you known about Georgie, Stefy?"

"Whoa, hold on," said Stefy. "I didn't know about this. I didn't know anything about this, Amanda."

Both the girls turned to Lee, demanding an answer. His giant boots shifted in place, shuffled back and forth on the shiny linoleum. He pulled a hand through his beard. The tops of his cheeks—below his eyes—turned the color of shame, a shocked rose. His eyes overflowed.

"I'm sorry, baby girl—"

"Quit fucking calling me that."

She refused the ride. She wanted to be alone. The last day of his life was the worst day of her life, and it seemed every hour another person she loved was dying, disappearing, or revealing that they weren't who she thought they were. And even though it would have been faster just to have ridden silently in Stefy's Toyota, all Amanda wanted was to sit on a city bus by a window and drift off to strangers' conversations. She'd let the overflow of headphones put her in a trance, buzz her to sleep. But as soon as she stepped on the empty 82 bus at Roosevelt, she was reminded that it didn't matter which way she got home. Her worst day wasn't done. As she reached for her CTA card, the driver—a pale, skinny white kid geeked on coffee—covered the machine, gave her a creepy smile.

"Fare's on me," he said. "Where you going?"

"Logan Square—Diversey."

"I'll get you there."

The driver waited until Amanda was in her seat, and then winked at her in the giant rearview mirror.

"Hold on."

The kid must've thought he was doing her a favor by whipping the bus around like a bull. He skipped stops all the way up

South Homan, and when it turned into Kimball, he ran reds for miles. Amanda's stomach lurched while the city blurred into lines of brick, steel security gates, and homeless on the sidewalk like litter from a war.

"Told you I'd get you there quick. So you live around here?" said the kid, smiling, impressed with himself.

The bus idled in a roar. Amanda ignored him and stepped off holding her stomach. She walked fast down Diversey, trying to make it home. The driver yelled something after her, but she didn't hear it. She replayed it in her head as she got sick in front of that Greek mini-mart on Lawndale. The younger son—she'd forgotten his name—was manning the store by himself. He waved from inside as vomit spilled from Amanda's mouth. He ran out to see if she was all right, but Amanda was already half a block up. She raised her hand straight into the air, too exhausted for anything else. She recognized this feeling; she'd felt it once before. It was the same mixture of fatigue and nausea that had swallowed her on the last day she'd spent with her father. On that day—just like this one—he was awake like she was awake, both of them like burglars cursing dawn.

"The car's warming up. It'll be just like old times," he had said. "We'll be out there before anyone else—find a good spot."

The hallway light had poured into her bedroom from behind him. He was tall and black in his rubber hip waders. His fly rod looked like a whip in his hand. She got up, pulled his old barn jacket from the front closet. It still smelled of the last year, outside, and must. Before she walked out the front door, she grabbed two fresh packs of Parliaments from a carton that Stefy had sent for her nineteenth birthday. Her sister, knowing their father and his drunk hands, had taken the time to inscribe every pack in permanent marker: AMANDA'S SMOKES. GET UR OWN, LOUSY.

That morning, they drove the Old Columbia Pike to Church Road. The Chrysler's heater burned the top of her jeans. Her father breathed heavy the whole way there. A flask of brandy stuck out from under his leg. She didn't say anything. She was tired of fighting and stared out the window, wishing on the slick morning asphalt, the dripping telephone wires, and Maryland's turning ash trees. She wished Wayne weren't her father, and she didn't care.

"This is just like old times," he said. "Do you remember the first time I took you and your sister out here? You tore through the creek like a couple of bats. Sorry I woke you up. I know it's early. I just thought—what's on the radio? Go ahead. Find something good."

He was tired by the time they got to Patapsco Creek, but didn't let on. He still smiled, but now his face was strained, admitting his drunk sham. He parked the Chrysler half on the shoulder and half in the street. When he shut it off, the engine turned one more time and hocked a blanket of white soot into the air. He swigged the brandy, offered it to Amanda. The bottle shook in his shaking hand.

"It'll keep you warm until the sun comes up," he said.

Amanda waited for him to get out before she drank. She lit a cigarette to hold the shit down. She watched him in the rearview mirror assembling his fly rod, pulling his tackle out of the trunk. It had been two years since he was discharged, but he still kept his gray hair high and tight. He said it made him feel young. His square shoulders that used to block the sun had disappeared. All his warring muscles had dwindled to ordinary stock.

"You ready?" he asked, tapping the window, forcing another smile.

"I'll come down in a minute," she replied.

"I want to walk with you, Amanda. I mean, we drove all the way out here."

They climbed over the guard rail and found the trail in breaking light. The forest was wet, charged with morning. Her sneakers fell silently on the ground. He walked in front of her, humming a song she didn't know. His waders squeaked, and then everything mingled and conceded to the rush of the stream ahead.

"This look good to you?" he asked.

His face flushed; his chest ballooned with every breath. She sat on a fallen tree, smudged her cigarette between the rocks. Wayne waded into the water in loud, unsure steps. Before he cast the rod, he winked at her like when he was young. Then he smiled, and Amanda realized she hadn't seen her father smile in a long time.

"I sent the papers along to your mother, Amanda. I'm tired of begging. The divorce is really just a technicality at this point."

"You could still clean up," said Amanda. "We could move into Baltimore like we talked about. I can get a job."

His line tangled in a tree behind him. He yanked on the rod trying to free it. Birds scattered overhead.

"Goddamnit—that's the thing. I talked to Pap . . . I'm selling the house."

"What?—*why?*"

Amanda pushed herself forward on the rotting tree. The bark ripped away like a scab. Wayne dropped his rod in the water, walked to Amanda on the bank.

"You got an extra smoke?" he asked.

Amanda held out the pack of Parliaments. Wayne pulled one out, set it between his teeth. His lips curled back as he lit the smoke. Amanda watched the burning match drop from his fingers. It died before it hit the stream.

"You shouldn't have to be a nursemaid to me, Amanda. Your mother says that, and she's right. I want you to go to Chicago. I got some money together. Stefy says you can stay with her."

"What about you?"

"I—I got some work lined up. A friend of mine—an army buddy—he says he needs someone."

"Where?" asked Amanda.

"Oh, you know, we'll see—a few things have to come together."

He was lying. They both knew it. He just didn't have the energy to say anything else. Wayne took a long drag and flicked the cigarette into the puddle of water at his feet.

"I can't stop, Mandy. I don't know how. I wish I could take it back—all of it. I should've never gone to that fucking desert. You know what I thought? I thought I could have you all back if I won. Sounds silly now, doesn't it? I made mistakes with your mother—same ones that got me discharged. You shouldn't have to make peace with them—not for me."

They left his rod in the stream, their cigarettes jammed in the rocks. As they walked back, his car keys sounded like bells against the trees. They rang a small, unchanging song. Now she heard it clearly as she opened the door to the apartment. It bounced through the quiet space—another ghost doubting its home. The apartment was silent for the first time in she didn't know how long. The TV didn't rattle with voices. Pap's voice didn't sing through the air. There were no scents—only a slight cold draft from the shoddy bedroom windows. If she inhaled deep, she could still smell the street below—wet leaves, garbage clogging the gutters, the fryer burning tortillas at the Mexican restaurant next door.

"Chance, are you here?"

She knew he wasn't, but she asked the question to the empty rooms anyway. She dropped her jacket on the floor, went to the kitchen, filled a dirty glass with water. She drank it, filled it again, and carried it to Pap's recliner in the living room. The threadbare armrests revealed yellow stuffing, crumbling glue, and wood.

She'd known Pap was going to die. Like all her dreams, the thought had haunted her the most in the mornings, when her head was just clear enough to picture Pap passing in his sleep, slipping in the bathroom, or falling down the stairs. It was never like this though—never this quiet. Her father was supposed to have shown up on the doorstep, clean-shaven and sober in his uniform. Stefy and Lee would be taking pictures of Amanda as she modeled all her old teenage punk getups from the back of her closet—torn black jeans, faded black shirts. Pap's funeral was supposed to be in the spring, not in this wet shit start of winter. She was going to write a letter and place it in his coffin. A long goodbye, a thank you. She never thought she'd have to make arrangements to have his body carted to a funeral home. The hospital would call if she didn't. They'd make sure everything was thrown away. It was somebody's job like emptying ashtrays or shaking dust from rugs in sand.

She pulled her legs to her chest and leaned back in the recliner. Its hinges and springs creaked before it clicked into its laying position. It felt unsafe, like it wasn't built for her. Same with the apartment—everything was his. The room lacked its host. She was hungry; her body felt tender and swollen. She didn't know how to find Chance, where to look. She didn't know if she wanted to find him or was better off sleeping alone. Her eyes felt heavy. The glass of water dropped to the floor.

A warm morning sun shot through the bare windows of Terry Novicki's office in the Nineteenth Police District. Norman and Paul sat silent in front of his desk, watching him make his way through the district's long, stretching headquarters. At fifty-seven, he was only a few years younger than Norman, but he was still trim and fit from working every day as a police commander. The short sleeves of his uniform pulled tight over his muscled arms, and his hair was cropped short in an old man's flattop. He talked and laughed with a group of young uniformed officers near the front desk before he weaved his way through the station's bullpen of desks, stopping to talk with two detectives filing reports just outside his office door.

"Fucking Terry, still a prima donna," said Norman. "Belle of the fucking ball."

Norman sat forward in his seat, lifted his suit jacket, and rubbed on his lower back.

"You okay?" asked Paul.

"Yeah, fine. Just tweaked it chasing that piece of shit."

"I didn't think you still had it in you," Paul said, smiling.

"I still got a lot in me, Paul. I got everything."

The office door swung open. Terry came in, covering his tie as he downed the last swallows of his protein shake. He sat down across from Norman and Paul, set the plastic bottle on his desk, and calmly wiped his moustache. He opened his huge hands and spread them wide over the open police report in front of the two men.

"So have you looked at it?" he asked.

"Yeah, I looked," said Norman.

"So you understand the position I'm in?"

"No, I'll be honest, Terry. I don't."

"Norman, the report is right there in front of you. Your boy was found pants down in the bathroom of a shithole bar. We interviewed everyone—the bartenders, the drunks. They all said the same thing: Georgie was assaulting a girl when her friend came and saved her. *His pants were down, Norman.* Do I have to spell it out for you?—Paul, can you talk some sense into him please?"

"I don't give a shit what the report says," said Norman. "You're the Goddamned commander of the district where a fellow officer's child was killed—"

"Norman, you're retired," said Terry.

"So what? My life's work—my thirty-six years on the force—doesn't count for anything now? Is that what you're saying, Terry? Is that how it goes? Christ—"

Norman slammed his hand on Terry's desk. His neck swelled, threatening to burst the double Windsor on his herringbone tie. Paul put his hand on his old partner's shoulder, trying to calm him down. Terry got up from his desk, closed his office door.

"Take it easy, Norman," said Paul. "No point in getting worked up."

"Tell that to Georgie," Norman barked.

"You want the truth, Norman?" Terry said calmly. "I'm doing you a favor right now—"

Terry pulled his keys from his slacks' pocket and unlocked his bottom desk drawer. With both hands, he lifted out a thick yellow file folder and threw it open in front of Norman and Paul.

"Pick a card, any card—that's your boy's fucking rap sheet."

Paul sat forward and immediately started shaking his head as he flipped through the pile of arrest reports.

"Norman, you should take a look at this," he said quietly.

"Don't need to," muttered Norman.

"No, you should," said Terry. "You really should before you come in here and shoot your mouth off. Do you have any idea what Georgie was into? Multiple accounts of possession with intent to sell—meth, coke, you name it. I can't even count the fucking restraining orders."

"He's right," said Paul.

Norman grabbed the folder, scanned the pages. His lips pulled tight and thin as he read.

"That's what I've been doing since you retired," said Terry. "I squashed every single one of these while the two of you were down at the RCPA running your mouth on me."

"Terry, that's not fair."

"Shut up, Paul. You think you're the only one with friends? How many times do I gotta hear, 'Oh, you should've been down at the Lone Tree. Norman and Paul were banging you up again.' But you know what? It's easy to talk that crap from the sidelines. I'm still out here—*working.*"

Norman shoved the file folder back across Terry's desk. He stood up, buttoned his suit, and lifted his trench coat from the rack near the door.

"Norman, I'm sorry," said Terry. "What does he want me to do, Paul? Georgie was a dirtbag."

"Watch your mouth," snapped Paul.

"Are you kidding me?! You think I made all that up? You read it yourself."

"You haven't changed one fucking bit, Terry," said Norman. "You're great behind a desk, but when it comes to doing the work—*the real fucking work*—you're on the bench."

"Yeah, well . . . Go fuck yourself."

In a blink, Norman pulled his pistol from his holster, held it on Terry's face.

"Say it again. Say it again, you pussy sack of shit."

"Go ahead, shoot. They'll bury you right next to your crackhead son."

"Terry, shut up!—put it away, Norman," said Paul.

Terry pushed himself back from his desk, leaned back, crossed his hands at his waist. The revolver stayed steady in Norman's hand.

"Paul, you remember when Terry pissed himself in interrogation?"

"What?" said Paul, his eyes fixed on Norman's gun. "I don't know."

"That's right, you weren't transferred down yet. It was just me, Terry, and that spade—those were some times, weren't they, Terry? See, Paul, this college girl had been stabbed up and left for dead down on Roosevelt, and Daley was getting killed in the papers over it. So, of course, Burge comes down hard on us. He had us filling the wagons for three days straight, putting the screws to everyone on the South Side trying to smoke out a suspect. But Terry here didn't like the work. Oh, he didn't mind taking the credit when we closed the case, but when it came time to do the *work*—"

"Torturing people isn't police work," said Terry. "Beating confessions out of innocent people ain't police work, Norman."

"Ha! Says the *commander*—what a riot. So there we are in interrogation, Paul, and I'm doing my best with this black. Just the usual stuff too, tearing into him with the phonebook—nothing fancy. And *Detective Novicki* is in the corner shaking—white as a ghost. I'm thinking he must've ate something lousy, a spoiled red hot or something. So I keep swinging like Billie Williams on this sack, when all of a sudden, I hear water hitting the floor like a damn pipe's busted in the ceiling, but there wasn't any leak in the pipes, was there, Terry?"

"Get the fuck out of my building. Both of you—"

Without warning, Norman backhanded Terry across the face.

"My partner said watch your mouth."

Terry closed his eyes, swallowed the sting. He stood up, took the two steps around his desk, and opened his office door.

"Get him out of here, Paul, or I'll have you both arrested."

"I'm going to take care of this myself," said Norman.

"Good luck. I'll save you a spot in lockup."

The entire Nineteenth District watched Paul drag Norman out of Terry's office. Fingers stopped tapping on keyboards. Phones rang without getting answered. Every conversation reduced to hissing whispers. Men and women officers sipped at their coffee, pet their guns, and watched Norman strut behind Paul, holding up his middle finger to anyone with eyes.

"I feel sorry for all of you," Norman announced. "The department used to take care of its own. Now all the rats and pussies are in charge."

Sweat poured from Paul's brow as he yanked Norman past the front desk through the front doors. He didn't let go until they were deep into the parking lot surrounded by cars. He bit his lip, wiped his forehead—did it back and forth searching for the words. His whole face rattled. His cheeks quivered like two fleshy bombs ready to burst. Then he raised a finger at Norman's face, cursed under his breath, and started across the parking lot to the street.

"Paul, where are you going?" Norman said after him. "The truck's over here."

"Forget it. I'm taking the bus."

"That'll take you all morning. C'mon, lemme give you a ride."

"You can't do that, Norman!"

Paul exploded, whipped around waving his arms up and down in the air. His voice tremored. His whole body shook. He tore his parka off, wiped the pouring sweat from his forehead on the top of his arm.

"You can't pull a damn gun, Norman!" he shouted. "You can't talk to people like that!"

"So you're defending that asshole? He owes me—*he owes us, Paul.*"

"For what?! What, Norman?!"

"For towing the line. For keeping our mouths shut while that coward got promoted on our work. He didn't do the work, Paul. That should be you in there with the bars on your arm."

"So what are you going to do? Shoot him? Are you outta your mind?!"

"Chicago problems. Chicago solutions. You know how it goes."

"*You're retired!*"

A police cruiser pulled out of the parking lot, turned on its sirens as soon as it hit the street. Norman watched it speed through the intersection of Belmont and Western. The entire city stopped for its flashing lights. Paul threw up his arms and headed towards the bus stop still cursing. Norman watched his friend, made sure he made it across the street before he fished his keys out from his pocket like he always had—jingled them out by one key, shook them in the air the way Georgie liked when he was kid until all the keys fell back except the one. He walked through the service lot of police cruisers letting his hands graze the shiny white paint, the silver stars, and thick sky-blue lines that striped every vehicle. When he got to his truck, he stepped back and, with all his strength, kicked a crater-size dent into the driver's door. He opened it, got in, and his life went quiet. The passing cars and city racket diminished to murmurs, drifting noise. As he turned the ignition, he met his eyes in the rearview mirror. His pupils were dull, full of black.

Boiler steam and puffs of exhaled air rose in the cold morning as the staff of Cathedral Shelter stood outside the loading dock at the back of the kitchen. They huddled together in the few patches of sunlight, sipping coffee and tea while Mary, Father Dunne's assistant, mingled through the small crowd with a clipboard in hand taking a head count. When she was done, she pulled off her gloves, wiped her nose with a balled-up tissue, and ran down the list one more time with her pen before she went to Father Dunne.

"We've got twelve right now, Father," she said. "But Julio and Caren called and said they're running late."

"Better than we had last year."

Father Dunne tucked her blonde hair under a Sox cap and clapped her hands to get the staff's attention.

"Alright, everyone—good morning. Thank you all for showing up early. I know it's cold so I'll make this quick. It's that time of year when we have to clean out the kitchen and pantry. For all the new people, just ask one of the veterans what happens if we don't—"

"Rat shit!" a man's gruff voice hollered out.

"That's right. We get rats, roaches, all of God's blessed creatures invading our building. It's bad for us and the clients that live here. We're going to split you up into teams. Check with Mary to see what you're scrubbing out. Eddie's got all your cleaning supplies together, and if we finish by noon, lunch is on me."

"No more Subway!" another voice hollered.

"How's pizza sound?" answered Father Dunne.

"No thin crust."

"It's going to be stale crackers if you guys don't finish. Let's get started. Don't forget to check in with Mary."

Father Dunne knocked hard on the loading dock's steel-slatted door. After a moment, the door slowly rattled up. Eddie stood inside organizing buckets of cleaning supplies and garbage bags. Parts of his cheek and brow were still a dark purple bruise.

"How's it going in here, Eddie?" asked Father Dunne.

"We're short on mops, Father, but we're always short on mops. Folks might have to get on their knees and get down to it," said Eddie, laughing.

"Nothing wrong with a little elbow grease."

"You said it. When I was carrying on, my mother used to have me scrub the toilets with a pipe brush. You ever had to do that, Father?"

"No, but I've cleaned out my fair share of bed pans, Eddie."

One by one, the staff climbed into the loading dock and started picking up their allotted buckets and bags. Mary walked quickly through the crowd, biting her lip and holding her clipboard tight at her chest until she was right next to Father Dunne.

"Father, Chance is here to see you," she whispered.

"Where?" asked Father Dunne.

"Just outside. He must have walked around the building."

Father Dunne looked back, checked on Eddie, who was busy handing out supplies.

"Mary, I want you to take Eddie inside right now. I don't want him seeing Chance after what happened."

"Yes, Father. Right away."

Mary started off, but Father Dunne grabbed her, pulled her back.

"And Mary, be ready to call the police—just in case."

Mary nodded her head, went to Eddie. Father Dunne waited until she got him inside before she hopped down from the loading dock. Chance was at the other end of the alley standing next to the dumpsters for the block. When he saw her, his shoulders dropped, and a relieved smile broke across his face.

"They wouldn't let me in the front," he called out.

"When you left the shelter, you lost your bed, Chance. You know how it goes—everyone stays on property until they're placed."

"I know, but I was just dealing with some personal stuff."

Chance looked past her, peered into the loading dock. He hadn't slept. His eyes were wired—bloodshot from no sleep. His skin was gray. He was hungry, dehydrated. She'd seen it all before.

"Chance, I talked to Ellen," said the father.

His eyes turned to panic. His face quivered trying to hide his fright. Chance stared at Father Dunne, unsure of what to say next.

"Your mother's a good person. She loves you a lot."

"How did she find me?" asked Chance.

"I called."

"But you promised you wouldn't do that—that's the policy, isn't it? 'Call when you're ready.'"

"You disappeared, Chance. When you came here, the rules were explained to you. No using, no lying, and no leaving the shelter without an approved pass."

Chance wanted to scream; his mother was never supposed to know. His father was never supposed to know. All those people—his home—none of them were supposed to know he was homeless. He had a plan. He was going to get a place. He just needed time, a little bit more time. He banged on the dumpster with his hand. A heavy hollow ring carried down the empty alley. Chance wished it shook the earth, the concrete, the bricks of every building until they toppled down and crushed him right there. But instead, after only a moment—a single echo into the cold morning—the sound fell flat, deadened into the aged dark bricks of Cathedral Shelter.

"What did you tell her?" he asked.

"The truth," said Father Dunne. "You left the shelter and quit the program."

"But that's not true. I snuck out a few times, but I was gonna get a job. I was checking in."

"And then you stopped, Chance. You gave me no choice. We always call emergency contacts when a client quits—it's an *emergency*. That's why we take the information. You were told all of this at intake."

"Can I come back then?" he asked.

"That depends—who's Norman Quinn, Chance?"

"I don't know."

"You're lying," said the father. "What about George Quinn—you know that name, Chance?"

Father Dunne took a step closer. Chance tried to remain expressionless, but his eyes and lips shivered. Father Dunne stared him down, her blue eyes still, her pale cheeks already red from the cold.

"Did you kill him?"

"No," said Chance, stumbling back. "No, Father. *Who told you that?* That's not true."

"It is true, Chance. It's very true. Do you really think I can do this work without having some contacts of my own? You killed that man."

Chance dropped to the ground, covered his mouth and eyes. His breath drew short. He panted, gripped at the rutted cement, the washed-out asphalt, searching for something—anything—to hold on to.

"You know, I bent a lot of my own rules to let you in here," said Father Dunne. "When the staff told me you were taking off at night—coming back drunk and high—I looked the other way. I thought once you got settled, you'd realize that you had a real opportunity to start over here. But you're not ready. You're not ready to be honest with me or yourself."

Father Dunne turned, started back to the loading dock.

"I didn't know I killed him. I swear, Father. You have to believe me. He was attacking someone I cared about—"

Father Dunne didn't stop. She walked faster, vaulted herself back onto the loading dock, and grabbed the chain that lowered the door.

"Did you hear what I said?!" Chance shouted. "I'm trying to tell you I didn't know."

Father Dunne tightened her grip on the chain; her knuckles popped and cracked before she reluctantly let it go. In front of her, the staff rushed in and out of the kitchen's swinging doors, throwing more and more refuse into a growing pile. Vegetables spoiled black rotting in plastic bags. Meat expired to grayish-white grease. Then two volunteers wearing disposable masks rushed out carrying a large collapsed cardboard box. When they dropped it on the pile, the side split open. Those that were there laughed and gasped. On top of it all, a tumbling mass of dead instinct—so many mice crushed in traps.

Stefy was late. Amanda had been at the funeral home since it opened, waiting at the front door for her sister to arrive. The whole building was unbearably hot. Over the past hour, she'd slowly removed two layers—her jacket and her hat, and then her red hoodie. She thought she might be crazy—just imagining the stifling heat—but then she noticed the wallpaper falling off the walls and the bottom of all the windows fogged with steam. The only bit of relief she'd found was a finger-wide slat of cold air rushing through the gap between the front doors. She stood right in front of it, the tip of her nose brushing the cold metal.

The funeral director, an older Jewish man with curly hair, had come out of his office twice. The first time he was dressed in his regular clothes—pressed navy-blue slacks and a starched white shirt with a matching blue tie. He had offered Amanda a chair, told her she was welcome to wait in one of the viewing rooms, but when Amanda pulled open one of the heavy oak doors her stomach turned. She ran to the bathroom and dry-heaved over the toilet. She cupped her hand and drank from the tap, trying in vain to rinse the stench of formaldehyde and Lysol from the back of her throat. The second time, he had changed. He wore a wrinkled black suit with a thin red silk tie. His little bit of hair was slicked back; he appeared taller, like a butler from a movie, but all of his courtesy had disappeared.

"If your sister's not here soon, then we'll have to reschedule," he said dryly. "I'm sorry, but I have other clients."

On cue, Stefy's Toyota swerved into the parking lot. She jumped out of the car, jogged to the door, holding her jacket closed with her backpack slung over one shoulder.

"What happened?" asked Amanda.

"What do you mean?"

"Our appointment was at eleven. It's almost twelve-thirty."

Stefy took off her huge sunglasses. Her puffy bloodshot eyes matched her reek of hangover and cigarettes. When she dropped her hand from her coat, Amanda could see she was wearing a tattered black T-shirt and red Adidas track pants—her pajamas.

"I have everything ready," said the owner. "We just need to settle up, and you can be on your way."

The man turned around, led them quickly past the viewing rooms and down a short dark hallway to his small office near the back entrance of the building. Inside, framed celebrity headshots covered the white-painted brick walls. Black-and-white photographs of Jack Palance and Michael Douglas smiled next to color glossies of Stockard Channing and Carrie-Anne Moss.

"Have all these people been here?" asked Amanda.

"No, no, of course not," the owner replied, laughing. "I wish— I collect the autographs, like stamps."

A white file box sat on the center of his desk next to an open laptop computer. He lifted the top and waved inside as if he'd just executed an illusion.

"You'll see everything is here: your grandfather's ashes, of course, and his personal belongings—his clothes, etcetera, from the hospital."

Pap's silver Casio, brown corduroys, and vomit-stained shirt lay neatly folded inside the box next to a large Ziploc bag of dark-gray gravely ash. The funeral director slid a handwritten invoice across his desk and gestured gently to the total with an open hand.

"Nine hundred thirty-six dollars. I itemized it all from his time of arrival at our facility—preparation . . . Cremation, of course . . . "

"Do you take cash?" asked Stefy.

"Of course, of course," said the owner, his eyes brightening. "We are like the bank."

Stefy pulled a thick fold of hundreds and twenties from her pocket and flipped the bills onto his desk. The money piled next to the box like the whole transaction was a back-alley board game.

"Keep the change," said Stefy.

The man smiled, pulled his own gold money clip from the pocket of his slacks, and folded the money in.

"There we are," he said. "I don't know your plans, but I know some beautiful places in the city. Some of our clients, they take pictures and—"

"We're good," said Amanda as she quickly closed the box and lifted it off his desk.

"Fine, of course. I put my card in the box if you need anything else."

The girls left without saying good-bye. Inside Stefy's car, everything still felt hot on Amanda's skin—her jean jacket, her glasses, the box on her lap. Sweat collected at the bottom of her nose. She wanted to tear off her clothes, dry the wet from her neck, back, and between her breasts. On the dashboard in front of her, the plastic shined where Pap had gotten sick. At once, she smelled fake mint, acrid lemon, and a medicinal evergreen.

"Did you get the car washed?" she asked.

"Yeah, yesterday. I had to. It was everywhere."

They drove east through the city; nothing seemed right. The midday sky was overcast. People walked down the street carrying wet umbrellas, but there wasn't any rain. All the bus stops were empty. Every cab had on its brights. Amanda refused to blink or close her eyes, scared that every single thing would disappear.

"I'm sorry I was late," said Stefy.

"It's alright. I probably got the times mixed up."

"No, you didn't."

They stopped at the big intersection of Clark and Diversey. All the giant stores were closed, their lights dimmed or off. Their windows were blank—clear of displays and advertisements—and all their electronic signs read CURRENT TIME. Crowds of people stood at all the corners waiting to cross. When the light changed, a bus lurched into the middle of the street blocking all the traffic.

"Fuck me," said Stefy. "Where are we supposed to go now?"

Away, thought Amanda, *far away*. They could take a right—right this minute—turn the car south and speed past the miles of Lincoln Park's yuppied perfection, the last two good bars left in Old Town, and end up on the West Side of the Loop at Union Station. They'd done it once before. It had brought them close. They could leave with just the clothes on their back and nothing else—just their clothes and this heavy bag of ashes.

Horns beeped behind them. Stefy cracked her window, lit a Parliament. Cold air rushed into the car, mixed with smoke, and dried the sweat on Amanda's lip.

"Thanks for doing this," said Amanda.

"What do you mean? It's Pap—we have to."

Amanda was nineteen when they ran away. She had been in Chicago for a month. They had been living in Stefy's one-bedroom apartment, two sisters fighting, drinking, and passing out. Back then, Stefy kept getting fired from bars. After two weeks or ten days on the job—whichever came first—every bar manager figured out that Stefy had never thrown drinks in her life and, more important, wasn't twenty-one. Stefy said she didn't care, but when she was drunk, she cried and told Amanda she felt retarded—like she hadn't learned something that everyone just seemed to know. Amanda would try and make her sister laugh. She'd run off, steal dollar flasks of After-Shock, and they'd chase it with strawberry pop that was supposed to taste just like Big Red. Their father didn't call, and their mother's letters piled up on the tiny kitchen countertop with statements of collection and giant envelopes from Publishers Clearing House. It had been an afternoon just like this when, on a whim, the girls took all the money Pap had loaned them for rent and hopped a bus to Union Station. The city was damp. Heavy fog wouldn't quit from the lake. Union Station looked like an ancient Roman capital to Amanda. From the outside, towering stone columns guarded the entryway, and inside, the windowed ceiling curved in a dome. Tired commuters and wide-eyed bums filled the lacquered benches in front of the Amtrak ticket windows.

People eyed each other back and forth, comparing their lives, thanking their gods.

"We need two tickets," Amanda had said.

The older Mexican man working the window folded his newspaper and set it aside. Amanda remembered his eyes—deep brown pupils that were as warm as the polished wood throughout the station. His graying hair and mustache were trimmed handsome, and his uniform—a dark blue Amtrak blazer and blazing white shirt—made him look like a president.

"And where would you like to go, ladies?" he replied quietly in accented English that made every sound a mystery.

"Fuck if I know," said Stefy. "It was her idea."

The man smiled, slid a glossy Amtrak pamphlet under the window. The girls opened the map across the counter. Amanda ran her finger along the winding lines trying to make sense of it.

"Looks like a pile of snakes," said Stefy.

"If you don't mind me asking," said the man, "will the trip be for business or pleasure?"

"Pleasure, definitely," said Amanda.

"In that case, I'd recommend the *California Zephyr*. After all these years, it's still my favorite. There's a train leaving in thirty minutes."

"How much is it?" asked Stefy.

"For two round-trips? Let's see—you know, if you young ladies were students, I could give you quite a discount."

"Yeah, we're students," said Amanda. "I'm going to be a teacher."

"And I'm a doctor—well, I'm gonna be," said Stefy, smirking.

Amanda looked at Stefy, laughing at the thought.

"A doctor, Stefy?"

"*A teacher, Amanda?*"

The man scanned a price chart taped to the counter in front of him. He ran his finger from left to right across the columns of colored boxes.

"For one doctor and one teacher—*in school, of course*—that'll be $267 round-trip."

They shoved cash under the window, and for six days the girls rode the train west. They ate dinner, shared a hamburger, on Seminary Street in Galesburg, Illinois. While they slept, the train chugged through Iowa. Dawn broke on their faces in Nebraska; Stefy cleaned their window with the arm of her jacket. For hours, they stared at the rolling plains and golden spring fields. Amanda said she'd never seen anything that ran so far in her life. The train didn't stop. They smoked in the smoking car and yelled over the pounding tracks. They bought a disposable camera in Colorado and burned up all the pictures before the train left the state. Rain blanketed the mountains in Utah, and the Nevada desert looked like the Bible to Stefy. They didn't stop, sleep, or fight in Emeryville, California. They got back on the next train home and did it all over again. The route was the same, but it didn't matter. For one short week, everything was calm and new. When they got back, Pap picked them up from Union Station. The money he had loaned them was gone, but he didn't ask a question. He let the girls tell their story—how they snatched booze from the liquor car, how much their necks hurt from sleeping in the seats. It all made Pap smile. Stefy fell asleep before they got back to the apartment. Amanda stayed awake and walked to a Walgreens six blocks away. She remembered dropping off the camera to be developed. The photos would get labeled UNPAID/UNCLAIMED.

Horns squeaked and boomed into a mash of tone. Amanda squinted her eyes, massaged her temples.

"Are you okay? You look pale," said Stefy.

"I'm fine," said Amanda.

"Have you eaten today?"

The bus rolled slowly out of their way. Stefy gunned the car through the intersection just as the light turned back to red.

"We'll get something to eat before I drop you off," said Stefy. "We can go to the market."

"You don't have to do that."

"Yeah, I kinda do."

Stefy parked the car at the end of Diversey. Amanda gave her the last of her change for the meter. They walked across the park towards the lake. The harbor was empty. Rows of vacant docks spread into the black water like bone ladders. Amanda clutched the Ziploc bag of ashes under her arm. She looked at Stefy, the bare trees, the sidewalk edging the brown grass and tried her best to imprint it all in her mind. She wanted the day to stain her thoughts and be close at hand, waiting and doting on her just like Pap. As they crossed under Lake Shore Drive, her breath caught in her chest. Tears filled her eyes. Stefy walked behind her through the underpass. Their steps clattered against the walls. When they reached the other side, the wind off the lake slapped their faces. Amanda buttoned her jacket to her throat and checked to make sure her sister was still behind her.

"Jesus, it's fucking cold!" Stefy yelled out.

Amanda stepped down the giant concrete steps to the water. Stefy followed, pinching another Parliament between her teeth. The cigarette burned bright in the wind; sparks and ash swarmed through the air.

"Do you want to say something?" asked Amanda.

Stefy took off her sunglasses and shoved them into her pocket. She spoke out loud and clear to the water.

"Pap, we love you. We'll miss you. You made it easier. Thanks."

Amanda crouched down and opened the bag. The cold wind grabbed her tears as they fell. Below her, Lake Michigan pressed at the stone walls, licking at the concrete and rusted ties.

"Don't you want to say something too?" asked Stefy.

Amanda shook the bag, spilling the ashes into the water. She wished for a prayer, even a short fitting lyric from one of Pap's favorite songs. But nothing occurred to her. Nothing was good enough.

Three weeks later . . .

he day couldn't beat the cold. Chance stood up and closed his eyes to a bright afternoon sun. Two hot beads of sweat that somehow managed to break from his temple instantly turned to a single numbing drop as it swiped by his ear. He zipped his jacket to his throat, slapped his bare hands together, and ripped apart another cardboard box with a box cutter and threw the pieces into the alley. That morning—before dawn—a truck had dropped off three palettes of damaged goods from supermarkets all across the city. Father Dunne explained to him that the delivery happened twice a month. Without it, Cathedral Shelter couldn't go on. It was Chance's job to unpack and unload every single thing. Some of the food went straight into the dumpster—a case of canned peaches infested with ants, two crates of milk curdled and separated into whey. He carried five boxes of mouthwash straight up to the office. In the shelter, the clients weren't allowed near the stuff; the older booze-hounds couldn't resist the taste.

Chance did all the work without saying a word. He didn't stop for lunch because at some point, he stopped thinking about Amanda, Pap, and Norman Quinn. He forgot about the painful phone call that Father Dunne had forced him to make to his mother the week before. The way her voice cracked with relief and anger when she heard his voice—she'd thought Chance was dead. When he told her he'd decided to stay in Chicago, she broke down. His father picked up the phone and only asked one question before he hung up.

"So you're going to live with bums?"

Chance could still feel the warm plastic of the receiver in his hand, and whenever he had long enough to think, the click of his father hanging up banged in his ears. Chance didn't know how to put it into words that his parents would understand. For the first time in he didn't know how long, he felt safe. Father Dunne, Cathedral Shelter—it was as close to a home that he'd felt since the murder of Lonnie's mom. Yes, sweat soaked his clothes from the hours of work that the father was making him do, and sharp pains did pinch his entire back from sleeping on a roll-up on the ground because he'd lost his bed. But every day since he'd come back, his shame and worry for destroying that woman's life, his parents' life, his own, were gone. Today, he had shelter and food and a day of work in front of him. Today, he was surrounded by people who truly didn't judge him and cared for him. *Today.*

"You should've given me a call. That's gotta be a bitch with a busted hand."

A large house of a man stood in the alley. Chance hadn't even heard him walk up. His long hair spilled out from under a black beanie stretched tight over his huge head, and thick dense stubble cratered his cheeks, turned them into fleshy gravel. If it weren't for his huge Carhartt jacket, Chance wouldn't have recognized Lee.

"It's healed," said Chance. "Works fine."

Chance held up the box cutter, flicked the blade in and out with his right thumb. Lee took out a box of Swishers from the front pocket of his jacket, pulled a cigar out with his teeth.

"There's no smoking back here," said Chance. "No smoking within twenty-five feet of the property in fact."

Lee shook his head, pulled out his Zippo, and lit up his small cigar. Chance threw a flattened box out the loading dock, nearly hitting his face.

"Your buddies around the corner ready to bust me, Lee, or are they just waiting for you to give the call?"

"Chance, I came here to talk."

"Fuck your talk."

Chance dropped the box in his hand, sleeved the cutter in his back pocket. Lee puffed deep on the little cigar. The smoke curled, took life in the cold air like five gray snakes dancing, tangling into knots. With a groan, he crouched down and began sorting the flattened boxes into a pile at his feet.

"I stopped giving a fuck a long time ago, Chance. I got sick of people looking at me the way you're looking at me now. The truth is, I've done some horrible things to get where I am, and for that, I've got debts to people like Norman Quinn. I'd give it all back in a heartbeat if I could, but for me, it's too late."

Lee pulled an envelope out of his pocket, set it on the edge of the loading dock, and then went right back to work. He yanked another tall stack of boxes off the dock and began ripping them apart with his huge hands.

"I'm sorry I gave you up, Chance. I've realized my debts are mine to square, not yours or the girls'. There's seven grand in that envelope, enough for you to get out of town and get a start somewhere. If you love Amanda, you'll go."

"Keep it," said Chance. "I'm staying and working the program with Father."

"Goddamnit. This isn't a fucking game, Chance. Norman Quinn ain't forgetting, and he ain't screwing around."

Chance kicked the envelope off the dock and jumped down to the alley. As soon as he clenched his fists, Lee grabbed the back of his head and slammed his forehead into his nose. Chance wobbled back, covering his eyes—blood instantly dripped from his nostrils in fat drops.

"You telegraph your intentions, son," Lee said calmly. "We don't fight country in the city."

Chance held his hand at his face, catching the thick stream of blood in his palm. He threw it off, pulled the box cutter and rushed Lee, slashing wild at his face and gut. The corner blade caught Lee's side—Chance dug in, ripped down.

"Goddamnit, Chance!"

Lee dropped to the ground, fell to one knee. Chance stood over him, face bleeding, eyes crying, chest heaving up and down.

"I'm sorry about your past, Lee, but you said yourself they're your debts to square, not mine. Norman Quinn doesn't know me. He doesn't know a damn thing about me. Let him come. I don't scare. I'll beat him down like I did his son, and if you want to push, you can have the same."

Lee let out a wincing laugh as he fished a black bandanna out of his back pocket and held it to the bleeding gash on his side.

"You little shit. How am I supposed to drive with this?"

"Take the bus. That's what I do."

"Take the bus . . . I like that—Chance, if you don't leave town, Norman is going to come after Amanda and Stefy to get to you. He will make their lives even more hell than it already is. He'll have them arrested. He'll have them locked up—"

"But they didn't do anything."

"It doesn't matter!" Lee shouted. "That's what I'm trying to tell you. Norman's a cop—*a lifer*—his friends are cops. He's chief dick number one over there! Are you hearing me now? He'll ruin you, and if he can't get to you, he'll ruin the girls. He hurts people, Chance. That's how he works."

Chance stared at the envelope of cash on the ground. Lee got up, stumbled towards him, hand clutching his side. Chance took him by the arm and helped him to the steps of the loading dock. The soaked bandanna trailed Lee's blood, mixed with the splatter of Chance's on the ground.

"You shaved," said Chance.

"Once a year," said Lee.

"Looks like you're going to need stitches."

"I'll be alright," said Lee. "But if you stay, the girls won't, and they're all I got."

Lee groaned as he shifted his weight back on the stairs. He stared out past the potholed alley, the rusting dumpster, and all the two- and three-story brownstone rooftops that spread across Chicago, the only place that he had ever called home. Chance picked up the envelope, tore it open, and flipped through the crisp hundred-dollar bills.

"What's it like in the country?" asked Lee.

"Everywhere smells like cow shit, and at night, the sky curves like a bowl."

"Sounds like heaven right about now."

Without Pap's VA check, Stefy couldn't afford the rent. After only eight delinquent October days, Pap's landlord, a short, fat Armenian woman, knocked on the door. Amanda knew who it was before she opened it; the woman had been taping handwritten invoices to the door since the evening of the first, but Amanda hadn't expected the woman's teenage daughter to be with her. The girl stood in front of her mother with a hand on her upturned hip like the whole building was beneath her. She twirled her hair with three fingers; her glittering silver nail polish looked like sequined lice tumbling through her thick black curls. She gave Amanda a pained snobbish smile and batted her glued-on eyelashes. Amanda hadn't showered or slept in days; a sheen of dirt, oil, and sweat covered her skin. In that moment, she wanted nothing more than to grab the girl by her crusted sprayed head and use her caked-up face like a Brillo pad on the bathroom floor. Her mother must have sensed it, because just as Amanda's hand tensed into a claw, the woman shoved her daughter in the back and grunted, "Tell her."

The girl rolled her fat shadowed eyes at Amanda then crossed one foot over the other and asked in a surprisingly deep voice,

" . . . Do you, like, have the rent yet?"

Amanda, unmoved by the display of parental guidance in eviction, simply shook her head.

"Okay . . . Alright . . . Well," stammered the girl. "You have one week to move out."

"Two days," her mother clarified, smiling at Amanda. "She take over. She still learning."

Amanda shut the door on their faces and listened to them argue in Armenian as they left. The girl's voice pitched up, threatening to break into a crying tantrum as she whined. As they walked down the stairwell, her mother cut her off in a booming guttural tirade that echoed so loud Amanda thought they might be coming back. But then their voices faded, and the metal gate to the street slammed shut. Amanda dropped to the floor and pushed her back against the door. She pulled out her last cigarette and lit it with her last limp match. The apartment was cold and smelled of garbage. Every room looked like a botched robbery, as if everything of obvious value had been taken and the criminals were stopped just as they had upturned every shelf and drawer. Piles of Pap's clothing lay up and down the front hallway. In the living room, stacks of books and loose papers covered Pap's recliner and the couch. Old family photos lay bare in liquor boxes that Amanda had taken from behind the corner store. In the kitchen, all the cupboards were open and empty. Two dirty glasses and a half-eaten can of tuna sat dry in the sink. A stain of brown evaporated water spread out from under the fridge—the freezer had melted off one week before.

She hadn't wanted to move over to Stefy's, but when the electricity was cut off, she had no choice. Since then, she'd been coming back to the apartment in the mornings and working until the sun set or until her back gave out—whichever happened first. She filled black trash bags until they were too heavy to carry. She tore them back open, unable to part with anything that was left—wallet photos of their parents on their wedding day, Grandma Sara's costume earrings and fake pearls, Pap's unused colostomy bags, his pomade and aftershave, two of her father's army medals inside that black velvet case. When she hurt, she popped the last of Pap's medication. No one was there so she didn't have to crush up the pills. When they were gone, she took ibuprofen eight at a time for her blinding headaches. Her stomach burned so bad it kept her awake.

"You need to get better, baby. You shouldn't be out."

That's what the lady at DHS had said the day before when Amanda went to register for welfare and stamps. She took one look at Amanda and gave her the address to a free clinic across town. Amanda hadn't gone, and now as her body flashed hot, she wished she had. Amanda stubbed out her cigarette on the wall and flicked it down the baseboards. She grabbed the door handle and pulled herself back up. As she got to her feet, she heard Stefy's boots stamping down the hallway. Amanda quickly unlocked the door and held her stomach as she ran the six steps back to the couch. After two knocks, Stefy opened the door.

"Amanda, you here?" Stefy called inside.

"Yeah . . . "

Amanda pulled a half-filled garbage bag of Pap's sweaters to her feet and sat forward on the couch as if she was just filling it up.

"Jesus, it smells like a sewer in here," said Stefy, taking off her jacket. "I'm going to open a window."

"No, don't!" said Amanda.

"*Whoa*, relax, I was just going to crack it open."

"Don't. It just warmed up. It takes forever."

Amanda wanted to stand up. She wanted to go to Stefy and collapse into her sister's arms, but her stomach kept turning. She pushed herself down on the couch and closed her eyes. She swallowed, trying to wet her throat.

"Let me open the front door," said Stefy. "Come on."

"Just for a little."

Stefy went back down the front hallway and cracked open the door. Amanda exhaled; for the moment, her stomach had calmed. She felt blood coming back to her face, and the cold sweat on her brow dried, pulling her skin tight.

"I'm sorry it took me so long to get over here," said Stefy. "Lee hasn't been around. I've been working the shop by myself."

"It's too much . . . "

"Tell me about it. I have to open and close the shop, deal with the walk-ins. We need someone to handle the front. I've been telling Lee that for months."

"No, this—it's all too much," said Amanda, kicking the garbage bag away from her feet. "I just want this to be done with."

"Fine, it's done," said Stefy. "Fuck it. Let's go."

"We can't. If we throw it away, it's gone—*everything*. Pap kept so much. He's got one of Dad's uniforms here. I thought they all got thrown away when he sold the house."

"Honestly? I wish he had, because I sure the fuck don't have the room for it."

"Of course you don't."

Amanda's fought off her nausea, pushed herself to her feet. She ignored Stefy's open-mouthed scowl and went back to work pulling the last of the photos from their frames.

"What the hell does that mean?" asked Stefy.

"You never have room for it—with Dad, with Mom, with Pap—it's always the same: You don't want to deal, so it falls in my lap."

"Are you serious right now, Amanda? Did you forget that I've been paying the rent on this shithole for the past five years? Buying you food, taking Pap to the doctor—because hell if you have to work—*if you have to hold a fucking job for once in your life.*"

Amanda dropped the empty frame in her hand. The thin glass shattered into a puddle of shards at her feet.

"You couldn't stand to be in the same room as Pap. 'It's embarrassing'—that's what you said, Stefy—"

"You're going to throw that in my face, now?!"

"Who had to stay with Dad 'cause you *couldn't take it*? Who went to the fucking hospital for Mom?"

"That's not fair, and you know it, Amanda! I'd just started at the shop. I couldn't go—"

"Bullshit. You didn't want to go. So I *had* to."

"Oh God, here we go—"

"It's always the same—you don't have the time, but somehow I do. You get your perfect fucking life, and I get the shit."

Stefy grabbed her jacket from the floor, threw it back on.

"You know what, Amanda? You better start coming up with some better excuses for why you're a fuck-up. Because Pap's dead, and you're running out of people to blame."

The door slammed shut just like it always did when they fought, but with the apartment empty, the walls bare, and every piece of the family's belongings on the floor, in trash bags, and collapsing food-stained boxes, a deafening ring filled Amanda's ears. Her stomach turned one last time, and without her sister to witness, Amanda dropped her head and walked to the bathroom. With every step, shame swallowed more of her body, and as she pushed open the bathroom door, she wished it were night so she could ignore the tall scraped-up mirror hanging above the sink. She dropped her pants and tore the cover off an old waterlogged issue of *Time* that Pap had left on the counter. She wiped at her ass and legs. She turned on the hot water in the shower knowing that now it only ran cold and lifted her shirt above her waist before she stepped into the tub. The freezing water was chains; she shivered as she waited for the brown to run clear. She got out, left the water spraying, and walked half-naked across the apartment to get a clean pair of Pap's pants. She knew which pair she wanted. She had put them in the garbage bag closest to the door. Water trailed off her body down the front hallway and collected at her feet as she opened the garbage bag and tossed out Pap's shirt with the pearl buttons, two pairs of elastic-bare boxers, and a knot of polyester striped ties. Near the bottom, the pair of herringbone wool slacks were folded neatly with his brown blazer. As she dried her body with a pair of the tattered boxers, she remembered the last time—six years ago—she'd seen Pap wear the slacks.

He'd driven her and Stefy to the airport in the middle of the night. Stefy was in the front seat of his Fairmont, and Amanda was drinking a warm Pepsi in the backseat trying to sober up. Pap had shown up at Stefy's apartment at three o'clock in the morning and banged on the door loud enough and long enough to wake Amanda from her drunk dreams. She'd gotten up, unlocked the door, and as soon as she cracked it open, Pap pushed himself in. He turned on the lights before she could, and when her eyes adjusted—when the glowing white spots faded away—Amanda remembered thinking that Pap looked like he was dressed for church. Before she could slur out her question—ask him why he was in his jacket and slacks—he grabbed her by the arm and made her wake Stefy up. He sat between them on Stefy's bed like when they were children, like he was going to teach them how to sing a song. But this time when he tapped on their hands three times, his eyes swelled. His voice retreated to a whisper.

"She's dying, girls. Your mother's dying, and she needs you."

On their way out the door, Amanda grabbed a can of Pepsi that had been sitting out all night. On the highway, the tires sounded like they were tearing apart. In the front seat, Stefy and Pap spoke, argued, and cried. Amanda fought to stay awake. The car was a hummingbird. The city was a cave. When the car slowed, Amanda's eyes opened as if her body knew they had arrived at the airport. It knew she had to run to the ticket counter, through the terminal. The gate numbers bounced up and down to a shitty slamming techno song that had been plaguing her head all day. She'd never flown before, and Stefy wouldn't come. Pap pulled a wad of Kleenex from the pocket of his slacks and wiped at his mouth and dabbed at his eyes; he was irritated, then angry. *Why in the hell did Stefy let him buy the ticket if she wasn't going to go?* Stefy couldn't. She just couldn't—her job, her job. Amanda jogged down the gangway alone. The people on the red-eye to Baltimore didn't care. No one got up to help. She was trash. Her lips were sticky from the soda. Her mouth tasted like cat shit. Her crooked hacked hair matched her crooked smudged glasses. Everything looked like soup. The jet engines sounded like they did in the movies—just louder, deeper, like a giant drill. When the plane rose, her ears stuffed with pressure. She popped her jaw over and over all the way to the hospital to see her dying mother. She popped her jaw over and over to make sure she was awake.

"Come here. Gimme a hug. I missed you."

Her mother's body had felt like an empty costume, as if her bones were wire hangers, and if Amanda squeezed too hard, they would bend. Her breasts were gone along with her gorgeous brown hair. Her scalp was warm, dry like an elbow.

"That was your first time on a plane, wasn't it?"

Amanda couldn't speak. Caroline's condition stole all her words. She wanted to say, *I can't believe a few hours ago I was 700 miles away. I saw dawn in the air.* But instead, Amanda just bit her lip and nodded "yes."

"I thought about that when I got off the phone with Pap," said Caroline. "He said he was going to buy you and Stefy tickets, and it occurred to me—that's going to be Amanda's first time on a plane."

Flowers filled the room—reds and yellows on the windowsill; blues, greens, and purples on the bedside table. Bouquets of orange and blooming deep-green plants covered every surface.

"Did you get my letters?" Caroline asked. "Did you read them?"

Amanda's palms became wet. Her mother's letters were in the kitchen on the counter nearest to the door under a pile of old magazines and a small pamphlet titled *Guide to Better Living*, left by a Jehovah's Witness. On the front of the pamphlet was an illustration of a black man and white woman holding hands on a pastel-green hill. An orange sun shined on them, and a family of horses stood at a wooden fence in the distance. Underneath that were copies of issues of whatever magazine Stefy had stolen from the neighbors—*People*, *Glamour*, a single volume of *National Geographic* with a cover of swarming bees. And underneath that soaking up beer and splashes of dirty dishwater were Caroline's seven letters, each personally addressed to "Amanda and Stephanie Beaumont" all unopened, touched only once when they were put in the pile of junk mail.

"No," said Amanda.

Her mother took it in stride. Like always, she didn't let on that it hurt. She did what she always did, turned it into a joke.

"You're probably better off. Some of them are really depressing."

"Why didn't you call?" asked Amanda.

Caroline rubbed at the bed remote in her hand and repeated Amanda's question back to her, as if saying the words herself would conjure the short, honest satisfying answer that she owed her daughter.

"Why didn't I call? Why didn't I call? . . . Can you pour me a cup of ice?" she asked, pointing to a sweating plastic pitcher on a rollaway table just out of her reach.

Amanda flipped open the top, filled a plastic cup with half-melted ice. She handed the cup to Caroline. Her mother picked out a sliver of ice and rubbed it on her lips.

"I always used to do this for patients, and they loved it. Now I know why."

Caroline closed her eyes and rolled the ice around the inside of her mouth. Amanda immediately regretted asking the question; she didn't even know why it had come out of her mouth. She hadn't planned on it. She hadn't planned anything. She was just going to show up. But now that she had asked it, part of her wanted to hear the answer more than anything else in the world even if it troubled her mother—even if it was the last thing her mother ever said. Caroline opened her eyes, sat up as much as she could. Every inch of motion came with wincing pain.

"When your father came back from Iraq, he was different. He would say things to me—when he drank, he would threaten me, us, Amanda. I tried to get him to see the doctors, but he wouldn't. All that bullshit they brainwash them with before they go. He didn't want to be seen as hurt. But they broke him, Amanda. He looked the same, walked the same, but it wasn't him. I wasn't planning on leaving you. It was just supposed to be for a little while. But then I got away, and I was happy, and it was the first time I was happy in a long time, and I kept saying next month will be better and then Stefy moved away and—"

"Stop. It's okay."

"No, you need to know. I know you hate me. Stefy hates me—I didn't call because I was scared, Amanda. I was scared to say all of this. I failed you two."

Amanda sat on the edge of the bed, took the remote from Caroline's hand, and replaced it with her own. The scent of iodine and medicine rose from Caroline's body and mixed with the stale stench of bars and cigarettes off Amanda's clothes. Caroline wiped her eyes, caressed Amanda's face.

"You look so much like your dad sometimes. Thank God you got his hair."

"I hate it," said Amanda.

"At least you have some," Caroline said, laughing. "You know, there's a salon I used to go to before work. It's only a couple blocks away. You should go—my treat."

"No, I didn't come for that," said Amanda.

"Yes, I want you to. I'll rest for a little while, and when you come back, we'll eat. I have a friend in the cafeteria, and I asked him to make enchiladas because I knew you were coming—hand me my purse."

"Some other time, Mom."

"Mandy, *let me do this.* I want this to be happy. I've watched so many families fall apart in here. I promised myself I wasn't going to let that happen. I thought Stefy was going to come, and we'd all eat lunch together—"

Caroline smiled, opened up her purse, held out her credit card to Amanda.

"There's a guy there. His name is Caesar. Just tell him you're my daughter, he knows all about you. Go. I need to rest. There's no point for you to stay here and watch me sleep."

"We'll call Stefy when I get back," said Amanda. "She wanted to come, Mom."

"Then that's what we'll do. We'll put her on speakerphone."

Amanda bent over, kissed her mother's gaunt cheek. She smelled musty—sour like cheap cheese.

"Take your time. The salon's on Chester just past a big ninety-nine-cent store, two or three blocks down. It doesn't look like much, but Caesar's great. He's a friend."

Amanda walked to the hair salon just like her mother had asked. Amanda remembered the front of the building was fuchsia pink with silver-flecked paint bordering the windows. The sign above the door read SIMPLY VOGUE, in hand-painted black cursive. The first thing Caesar did was take her hand and walk her to the washbasins at the back. He sat Amanda in a chair and laid her head into a black sink. He hummed a song as he adjusted the temperature of the water. He massaged her scalp and worked the shampoo and conditioner into her skin. She closed her eyes and listened to her breath fill, then empty her chest. He sang a lilting lullaby in Spanish behind the rush of water. She couldn't wait to tell Caroline that she was proud to be her daughter. She was going to promise to visit more, fly on more planes. No matter what it took, she'd convince Stefy to come; they'd drive back before the end of the next week. When she got back to the hospital, she felt like an idiot. Like she was wearing a short-cropped wig when they told her Caroline was dead. Like a shoplifter busted in a cheap disguise, they took her by the shoulders and pulled her into a strange room. Amanda didn't hear any of their words after "We're so sorry . . . " All she wanted was to strip naked, burn her clothes, shave her head.

Amanda folded Pap's slacks over at the waist. They fell as she walked back into the trashed living room so she stopped, folded them over again. Just then, a dusk sun stretching across the city broke the crest of the living room windows. The dirty glass turned orange, and shadows of forgotten water stains, smudged cigarettes, and dried puddles of spilled beer became apparent on the rutted hardwood floors. Amanda took the broom from the wall. Her wet hair pasted to her naked back as she swept up the broken picture frame in front of the couch. She knew she should work faster. In twenty minutes, the sun would be gone; the apartment would go dark. Her bare feet could get cut, her hands slashed. And then once again, she'd find herself hurt, naked, blind.

Paul banged again at the front door. He'd been there for an hour; he knew Norman was home. Even if Norman wanted to, he couldn't let his old partner in. His house was a mess. Weeks ago, he'd brought in all his old case boxes from the garage. He'd kept everything—the good and the bad. Every murder he solved and every crime he fixed. Thirty years of investigations jack-scratched longhand stacked three high up and down the front hall. He'd been working around the clock just like the old days. He closed the blinds, forgot the sun, ignored the moon, and got back to counting time in pots of coffee and quarter-bottles of Tullamore Dew. A few nights, he even took a cigar in the house. Something he hadn't done in years. He was never much of a smoker to begin with; he only ever partook when he was coming home late, when it was so late that it seemed it was the only correct thing to do. He'd be driving on the empty city streets, swerving drunks and delivery trucks guiding him home. He'd turn on WMAQ on low and let the replay of the day's Morton Downey Jr. radio show soothe his pounding head, his swelling knuckles, and get his mind off the fresh blood he seemed to smell everywhere. For eight minutes, the cigar overpowered the black coagulated corpse blood under his fingernails and the mist of beaten suspects' blood that covered his neck. If he couldn't breathe, he couldn't think, and sometimes the stench was so bad and he was so tired that he'd roll up the windows, light the cigar, and let it burn like incense in the ashtray. He'd roll his neck from side to side, inhale the scorching tobacco, and work his index finger inside his nose trying to clean out a twelve-hour shift's worth of shit coffee, cheap aftershave, bus exhaust, city garbage, bad breath, dirty pussies, convenience store candy, warm beer, dead bodies, and hot spit and tears from the assholes he arrested and interrogated every single day. Over thirty-six years, he tried everything and could honestly say it was the only thing that worked.

But this past night, it wasn't the same, not like how it'd been. He'd been up for a day going over all his cases, annotating, celebrating his life's work. He set up his coffee table just like his old desk. A corded phone, a small Bible, and whiskey all in arm's reach. Three boxes of blue Bic Cristal pens. Coffee cooking on the hot plate. He even put one of those giant red dicks of garlic bologna in his fridge that he used to leave at the station and eat off for weeks way back when. He used to hack off chunks with his pocketknife, shove it inside his cheeks, and suck on it until it dissolved back to paste. Paul always hated it, but Norman always loved it, and part of him wanted to jam a thick slice through his mail slot right now just to see the look on Paul's face when he got a whiff of those sour green olives that infested the length of meat like a bunch of gorging termites on a log of wood.

"Norman, I'm sorry about what happened at the station," Paul said outside. "You're right: Terry's an ass . . . Come on, open the door."

He'd had to stop. He was overcome. He'd been flipping through cases all night when he came upon a large yellow envelope holding a case specifically relevant to his present state of life. At first glance, it was nothing special—one of the hundreds of robberies and assaults from early in his career before he worked homicide. The numbers were faded on all the addresses and times, and what was left of the barely legible letters were ghosts on the old onionskin paper. When Norman brought the pages too far into the light, everything disappeared; words became translucent, leaving only black ledger lines running crooked to the margins. Only the single suspect's name, LEVI VERBOSA, stayed fresh, looked barely dry as if Norman had just scrawled it out a few hours before. As soon as he read it, his breath shortened, knowing what was in the bottom of the envelope. He carried the envelope to the kitchen, set it on the counter, and pulled an old single-wrapped cigar from the back of the same cupboard that held all the telephone directories that he couldn't bring himself to throw away because it seemed like so much waste. He tore the package open with his teeth, bit off the end, and lit the cigar over the stove. He inhaled deep as he upturned the envelope, and when the blood-blackened straight razor fell onto his countertop his throat closed out of fear just like it had the night he pulled up to the back of that building— the same building he'd found Lee in barely a month before— and saw the door cracked open. As he approached, he heard screaming—a man begging not to die. At twenty-eight, Norman wasn't any greenhorn; he'd already been on the force ten years. But he still recalled having the distinct thought that he'd never heard anything like that in his life, the splash of guts, the almost womanly scream of the man's pleas, and then silence. Silence like he'd never heard. So silent his knees got weak as he opened the door. So silent he nearly passed out when he looked down the stairwell and saw a river of dark red blood streaming across the bare concrete floor.

"Okay, I'm gonna leave, Norman," Paul said through the door. "But I want you to call me. Sheila wants you over for dinner. You shouldn't be alone right now, you hear me?"

Two bare light bulbs dangled from the basement's low ceiling. A tall, hulking Levi Verbosa—Lee Verbosa—stood motionless, his torn white T-shirt covered in blood. His whole body dripped sweat, even his arms that appeared painted in the dead man's guts. His terrified eyes shook scared as he stared at the mutilated black body sprawled across the yellow couch in front of him. He didn't fight. He didn't run. Norman remembered Lee calmly kneeling, raising his hands as soon as he saw Norman's gun, and as Norman cuffed him, he realized that Lee was as shocked and scared as he was, as if even he himself couldn't believe what he'd done. Norman was so struck by Lee's state that instead of calling for backup, he went upstairs into what was then an old barbershop and drew two glasses of water from an old iron utility sink and brought it down to Lee. The men drank the room-temperature water in silence while they stared at the dead black man lying in a mixture of his own intestines and gold chains at their feet. And after what seemed like a long night of talking and confessing but was actually a short thirty-minute chat, Norman made the first and last deal that would eventually buy his home, fill his jewelry cabinet with solid gold watches, and keep his closet filled with the kind of expensive off-the-rack suits he liked.

In exchange for more of Lee's stolen gold untraceably pawned into the form of cold hard cash, Norman made the body of Cupid Calloway—a founding member of the Almighty Vice Lords, the city's most notorious gang—disappear. The agreement would be indefinite and binding as long as Lee wanted to stay away from a murder charge. Once agreed, Norman picked up the bloody knife from the floor and rolled it in newspaper. He uncuffed Lee and together the two men put Cupid's body in the back of Norman's cruiser. They even shook hands once they were done, as if both their hands stained with the same blood didn't bind them enough. That very same night, Norman dropped the body in a junkie shack across town, and for another fifteen years, Lee dutifully delivered white envelopes of cash every other month. By the time Norman was working homicide, Cupid's murder had bought him his house, a car, and the expensive in-vitro treatments that gave him Georgie, his one and only son.

When Lee finally got arrested on a separate assault charge years later, Norman's conscience was wiped clear. The scales righted themselves like they always do; one way or another, justice got served. The end had truly justified the means because by then Norman was after the real bad guys who were doing the real murders. Over the years, he beat, twisted, and burned out enough confessions to literally fill his house, and now as he cracked open the blinds and watched Paul's Nissan trail white smoke down the block he asked himself the same question that used to keep him up at night for years on end:

Why?

Why of all the criminals he'd met over his entire career did he let Lee go? Was it pity? Greed? Did his young conscience get the best of him? Was that young version of Lee so much more cunning and shrewd? He remembered seeing past Lee's long hair and devil goatee that hung from his chin like a long dirty sock and recognizing that he wasn't a liar; he hadn't intended to kill Cupid. Norman believed Lee when he told him that he'd brought the box of gold chains in good faith to purchase the building, and it was Cupid who'd gone sour. Cupid tried to rob him, and Lee just did what came natural to him. He defended himself. He killed the man because he knew that Cupid wasn't going to let him just walk away. Even retelling it to himself now, Norman still nodded his head in agreement. He still could see how something like that could go down. So what was the big deal? One time a long time ago he gave a guy a break? One time a long time ago he took a little bit of money from a dirtbag so he could make his wife happy? One time a long time ago he helped the asshole who helped the cocksucker who murdered his only one true gift from God—his son?

Norman screamed, flipped the coffee table in front of him. The phone, a half-tumbler of whiskey, and his Bible danced in the air with hundreds of pieces of paper from his cases. They fell on top of his lap as he sobbed into his hands. Paul's old transfer papers dropped into his lap. He'd become Norman's partner a week after Eileen, Norman's wife, had passed. Years after, at Norman's retirement, Paul said when he started Norman didn't speak to him for nearly three months. Norman didn't remember it like that, but he took his old partner's word. Paul had the memory of an elephant and the heart to match. Norman pulled one of the few items Georgie had left for him to find—a red nylon duffle bag—through the tossed mess on the floor. He was glad Paul was gone. He'd been putting off going through his son's things. He wanted to do it alone. When he unzipped the bag, the stench of Georgie's BO filled the room. He threw two pairs of his son's slick dirty jeans and a tattered black T-shirt on the floor. At the bottom of the bag, an object sat wrapped in a black towel. As soon as he picked it up, his eyes streamed with tears. He slowly unwrapped his first revolver—that perfect toy gun his father had given him and that he'd given to Georgie lay in front of him. The handle was still duct-taped, and the barrel looked like it'd seen a war. But it was still as heavy as he remembered. The weight made it real.

Norman set it on the coffee table and picked up the last thing from inside Georgie's duffel, a crumpled brown paper bag. He squeezed it, knowing what was inside. If he opened it, would that be breaking his son's trust? Like reading his diary or opening his mail? He ripped open the bag; cash and pills spilled onto the floor. A sticky, brown bottle—Norman's own prescription cough syrup—rolled onto the table, and a small clear red baggie of crystals, like ice shavings, dropped next to the gun. He'd seen it all before. Baggies just like this clenched in the hands of the dead— the dearest thing in their murdered world. Norman opened the baggie and dipped his fingers inside. Bitter, like bleach and salt, attacked his tongue. He poured a line onto the coffee table—just like he'd seen in the movies—straightened it with his fingernails and inhaled.

"Medger . . . Fontez. How do you say this? I can't say this—"

"Fuentes."

It didn't matter how many times the ancient white receptionist got up from her desk and croaked out a name in her cigarette-burned voice, the waiting room stayed full. Amanda had watched it again and again: One person went to see the sole doctor down the hall, another came in from the line outside. There were thirty-five coveted chairs; Amanda knew it because she'd counted them eight times over the past four hours. She'd gotten to Community Health Clinic that morning, just before they opened. The line moved fast at first. It only took her forty-five minutes to get inside. But then it slowed—she imagined the doctor arriving eager, clean-shaven, and then after each deteriorating patient, becoming more and more disgusted with Chicago, the people, the cheap liquid pink soap that dried his knuckles raw.

A stack of out-of-date magazines sat on a foldout table near the door next to a messy pile of worn-out *Chicago Reader*s and an old Mr. Coffee that hadn't dripped a cup all morning. The TV mounted on the wall had been turned on and off several times. Each new person that came in stared at it wondering why it wasn't on—why it was so quiet, stuffy. After eleven minutes like clockwork—Amanda had timed it—they stood up, walked across the room, and turned it on. And each time, the old receptionist waited until they were back in their seat before she pulled a remote from her desk and clicked it off.

"Nothing but crap," she said each time.

Everyone had laughed the first time she said it, but after the fourth or fifth time—Amanda couldn't remember which—the joke got old. The new guy from outside sat down in the empty seat next to Amanda. He stank of cheap incense and menthols. He took off his jacket, pulled a black Bulls beanie off his head. He was a young black guy, but his bloodshot eyes and gold-capped teeth made him look old.

"DHS send you over here?" he asked Amanda.

"Yeah," said Amanda. "They told me about this place, but I didn't know about the wait."

"I thought I recognized you. I saw you over there the other day. What shelter you at?"

"Excuse me?"

"*What shelter are you staying at?*"

The man asked the question loud, over-pronouncing each word. The whole room stared at Amanda waiting for her answer.

"You at Interfaith or Deborah's?" asked the man.

"I'm not—" said Amanda. "I'm not at a shelter."

"Oh . . . Well, Deborah's is good if you need a place. It's safe. They only let in women."

Amanda wished there was a mirror close so she could see what the man saw. Were her eyes as sunken as they felt? Was her skin a sallow green and her lips dry and cracked like his? Did she stink? She didn't remember the last time she'd washed her clothes. She didn't remember the last time she'd had the energy to do anything but wake up, walk, and try to stomach mouthfuls of bread and instant noodle soup. Amanda wanted to run home, wash her hands and face. She wanted to tie back her hair, squeeze the blackheads out of her nose, and paint her lips shiny like when she was twenty. She'd dig through the two boxes that she'd brought over to Stefy's and find her one pair of jeans that lifted whatever was left of her ass. She'd put on one of her old T-shirts—a tight one—and then come back and see if the man still thought she lived on the streets. He'd want her; every man in the city would want her. She wanted to believe it as she cleaned the crust of sleep from her eye. She needed to believe it as she felt her clothes soft and filthy on her skin.

"Lucia . . . Men—Manon—I can't say it," the old woman blurted out, struggling with another name.

"Menendez," a voice called out.

Across the room, a Mexican girl got up and walked to the old woman at the desk. She scowled at Amanda as she passed, tapping her bottom lip with her fist.

"You know her?" the man asked Amanda.

It was the girl from the bus stop—the one that asked Amanda to buy her fare. She didn't look the same. She didn't have on her pink jellies or tight T-shirt that made her tits look like water balloons. Under a red jacket that went to her knees, the girl's stomach was huge. The bump was so round it looked fake, like she had a giant basketball under her shirt. Amanda broke the girl's stare and flipped the page of the year-old *Cosmopolitan* in her lap.

"No, I don't know her," she said.

"She definitely knows you."

The man groaned in pain as he pulled up the left leg of his sweatpants and gently squeezed his bulging calf. Even with his dark skin, the muscle appeared red and tight like it was going to explode.

"I took some medicine, but it don't help," he said to anyone that was listening. "It feels like it's on fire."

"Get the fuck off me!"

Yelling came from down the hall. A door slammed shut. Everyone in the waiting room froze, looked at the hallway entrance. The Mexican girl—Lucia Menendez—stomped out followed by a hapless security guard, a tall black kid who couldn't have been older than seventeen. He tried to gingerly hold her arm, walk her into the waiting room, but she threw him off and pushed him into the wall.

"Get the fuck off me, *mayate!*"

The girl's face was red—hot pink from crying—and when she felt the thirty-five sets of staring eyes, she shrank just like Amanda had a few moments before. She slammed open the front door, pushed past the next freezing person outside.

"Bement . . . Amanda," the receptionist announced.

Amanda got up, walked past the young security guard who was still standing in the middle of the waiting room, looking for someone to tell him where to go. At the other end of the hall, a middle-aged doctor stood by an open door. He looked exactly as Amanda had imagined. His thinning early-gray hair was in every direction as if he'd been pulling his hands through it all morning, and the lenses of his glasses were covered in fingerprints on his stressed face.

"Right this way," he said, ushering Amanda in.

A large examination table covered with butcher paper sat against one wall of the small room. On the other wall, clear jars filled with butterfly bandages, long cotton swabs, and rolls of gauze were lined up on a counter. He closed the door, sat on a low rolling stool. He straightened his glasses and scanned the intake form that Amanda had filled out in the line outside that morning.

"When's the last time you saw a doctor?" he asked.

"It's been a while . . . Probably—I don't know—a long time," replied Amanda.

He threw the folder on the counter, looked Amanda in the eye.

"So what's wrong?"

"I'm tired all the time. I've been sleeping just about all day. I'm not hungry, but I eat—ya' know—because I have to, but then I get sick."

"You vomit?" asked the doctor.

"Yeah—right after—like twenty minutes later."

The doctor stood up, pulled a pair of blue rubber gloves from a box, and put them on. From his breast pocket, he pulled a small flashlight and shined it into Amanda's eyes.

"Are you on any drugs? Legal, illegal?" he asked.

"No."

"I can't stress this enough, I can't help you unless you tell me the truth. So are you on any drugs?" he asked again.

"No—I mean, I took some hydrocodone, but that was weeks ago for my stomachaches, and I had these headaches."

"You're having headaches?"

"I was, yeah," said Amanda.

"Open your mouth."

The doctor pressed on her tongue with a depressor, shined the light down her throat.

"Can you sit up straight for me and lift up your shirt? You don't have to take it off."

His cold gloved hand ran across Amanda's lower back, pressing on her sides.

"Does that hurt?" he asked.

"A little . . . It's sore."

The doctor snapped off his gloves, wrote into Amanda's file. He pulled open one of the cupboards under the counter and took out a small pink box.

"Do you know how to use one of these?" he asked.

"What is it?"

"A pregnancy test—you just pee on it."

"I can't get pregnant," said Amanda.

"Sometimes it's not up to you."

"No, you don't understand. I'm not able to have children. My uterus was damaged . . . I was—I've been—"

"Hey, it's alright. I don't need to know. Let's just take the test so we can rule it out, and if you can't, you can't. And then we'll move on and figure out what's going on with you. Please—"

The doctor opened the door, pointed down the hall.

"Right down there. Don't put it in the water, just hold it in your stream."

Amanda took the box in a daze. She felt cold, lightheaded as she replayed the last times she had sex with Chance. Then she

remembered Georgie—his hand over her mouth, his body convulsing against her when he came.

"C'mon, we gotta do this fast," said the doctor.

The security guard led her down the hall and unlocked the
bathroom with a set of keys at his waist. Amanda stepped inside,
flipped the deadbolt. She opened the box and looked at the direc-
tions but didn't read a word. Her heart raced. Sweat drenched her
armpits and dripped down her side. She unsheathed the stick,
unbuttoned her jeans, and sat on the toilet. She had to go all
morning, but didn't bother asking because of that crotchety old
woman at the desk. Amanda held the stick between her legs. At
first, her piss only trickled because of nerves, and then it came on
full. Her hand shook; she wasn't sure if it was from fear or if she
was going to faint. When she was done, she put the stick back in
its plastic case and set it on the edge of the sink. She buttoned her
jeans, washed her hands. She unlocked the door and walked back
down the hallway. The doctor stood waiting at the door, his head
buried in another file. The floor fell as she walked, warping down
and down. Her legs felt long and useless like a spider walking on
ice. Amanda handed him the test stick and sat on the exam table.
She picked up her jacket and nervously folded it over her arm.
She squeezed the denim as hard as she could. The doctor stared at
the tiny window on the stick, bouncing his head to a silent song.

"These things are fast, but I bet not fast enough, right?—
wait—you're pregnant."

She was tall. She was on a building looking down. She saw her
mouth moving rapidly questioning the doctor. Her eyes blinked,
squinting as if they were standing in a blinding sun.

"Are you sure?" she asked.

"*It's* sure—they're rarely wrong. We can do it again if you want," replied the doctor. "Do you know how long it's been?"

"Since I had sex?"

"Well, yes, but more importantly, the fatigue. How long has that been going on? I'm just trying to get an idea."

"I don't know. Maybe a month—since my grandpa died."

"We're going to need to get you back in soon—tomorrow, even. I want to schedule you for an ultrasound, see how far along."

She wanted to die. She wished closing her eyes would kill her—that just by shutting them tight like she was doing now would stop her belting heart and the plummeting fear that she instantly recognized would not have any immediate end. As she walked back into the waiting room, the thirty-five sets of waiting eyes turned to her and tried to gauge the gravity of her condition by the numb expression on her blank face. Amanda didn't see them. She was already into the next day, and the day after that, and then the following week all the way to the end of the month. And in every single circumstance, no matter the time of day or night, presence of sun or close to freezing rain, Amanda was just as terrified as she was now. This was impossible. She didn't close her jacket in the freezing wind. Back on the street in the rushing crowd of muffled and bundled bodies, she felt like an anomaly, a damned aberration.

eorgie's speed cleared his eyes. Like long straight lines dissecting the city from north to south and east to west, Norman now recognized the order of things, how the scale would naturally balance. Time had expired. It was no longer his choice. He'd fulfilled his obligation, done his due diligence, dutifully gone up the chain of command. Terry's refusal to take action was Providence. He saw now for the past few weeks he was only doing what his soul had already known. God had guided his inaction, wisely forced him to wait until he was another dot in Terry's rearview mirror before he pulled out his old opera binoculars that Paul used to give him shit about and followed Lee to Cathedral Shelter that afternoon. From fifty yards back, he watched Chance say his good-byes to that almighty, all-dyke priest and her step-it-fetch-it black—the same one Norman shook down. The man's face was still busted up, and with his cheap oversized suit, he looked like a clown. Norman laughed so hard, he almost got made. All the crocodile tears back and forth, that little dyke hugging that dirtbag, Lee, like he was a saint—it was all too much.

The two of them were looking to skip town. Norman watched them pack all sorts of weird shit into a U-Haul parked in front of Lee's condo—fish aquariums, velvet paintings of Elvis, a bar made out of railroad ties, and what looked like a safe door. For a few hours, Norman thought they might be opening up a store, but then the regular shit started coming out, crap that people needed to live—suitcases, an ironing board, a mattress and box spring. When they were done, Norman tailed them to a shithole Mexican bar on North. Three hours later, they stumbled out sailor drunk, maybe even high. He thought to kill them right then. He could've rushed them like a freezing gale, blasted them both in the face. But he decided it would've been too fast. He wouldn't have enjoyed it. They wouldn't have recognized him. All day—since he'd tried Georgie's drugs—he'd been working on what he was going to say. He hadn't decided on how it ended, but he was going to start by reminding them about heaven—a glorious place they'd never see. He'd tell them that he made a pact with the archangel, Michael, and his army of potentates. Once he ended them, Michael would command his soldiers to tear off their limbs and send them hurtling to hell. Norman didn't know how he was going to put it all in words, but he wanted to make sure they understood that he'd prayed, made special requests.

When the clock hit three in the morning, Norman pulled his Explorer behind the building and turned off his lights. He left his truck running and double-checked his revolver to make sure it was loaded. He straightened his tie, made the sign of the cross, and got out of his truck. He walked slowly across the gravel parking lot, enjoying the night's passage to dawn. The neighbors' VW hatchback was parked next to Lee's Lincoln. That day, he'd seen the couple almost more than he'd seen Chance and Lee. The man looked like Georgie but without all the dope. He had nice thick black curly hair that he wore a little long just like Georgie used to. Good teeth. Tall solid frame—probably played a little high-school ball in his day. JV linebacker or fullback just like Georgie. His wife was in her late forties; Norman knew it because she'd let herself go. She was ugly and fat with splotches of freckles and wiry red hair that didn't look soft how women's hair was supposed to. She never wore makeup, seemed to always be in sweats or pajamas. That poor man—her pussy was probably corn beef after she jammed out that big-headed baby. For the life of him, Norman couldn't figure out if it was a boy or a girl. Either way, it looked like the mother—like an old man.

When the man had gotten home from work late in the after-noon, the couple held hands and pushed that little tumor around the block. The stroller was the size of a grocery cart—practically a wheelbarrow. They lived on the first floor, and Lee was on the second. The top condo was empty. The building was one of those new constructions—brushed metal and dark red brick all around. Norman took each step admiring the craftsmanship, all the smooth seamless welds. Everything was clean. This is exactly what he had wanted for Georgie; he would've cosigned a note for something like this.

On Lee's balcony, the blinds were drawn closed. Norman cupped his hand and pressed his ear against the glass. He couldn't hear a thing. Triple-paned insulated windows—of course, they hadn't spared a dime. No drafts in winter, probably kept out all the street noise too. He was willing to bet that Lee even had that radiant floor heating that Norman always saw on TV. The same stuff Norman almost had installed at his home in Evanston. It was after a blizzard. He told Georgie he'd pay him good money to do the work. Thank God, he didn't buy everything. He only got as far as pricing it all out—the wiring, the special mats. He would've needed a new thermostat and a bigger breaker for the box. It was a small fortune. He couldn't admit it at the time, but the truth was he didn't want to spend all that money to just have Georgie let him down again. He would've ended up doing it himself or gotten bilked by a Russian or a Mexican, and then had to pay top dollar to get it fixed and redone. The floors would never have been the same; he'd see mistakes everywhere for the rest of his life.

Norman pulled out his gun, turned the handle of the door. One of them had left it open. Most people do; Georgie told him that. The living room was as big as a warehouse. It had tall ceilings and acres of space. Stale cigar smoke filled the air. Light spilled from the kitchen ahead. A flat-screen TV sat on the hardwood floor; a cooking show played to the empty room. The host, a fat Jewish woman, was pulling a crown roast from the oven, Norman's favorite. He'd had one at his retirement party, but it didn't look nearly as good as hers. Her voice bounced off the bare walls and echoed like she was talking in a well. Shadows moved back and forth in the kitchen. Meat was frying in a pan.

"They have liquor stores in the country?" asked Lee.

"Yeah, of course, it's not Mars."

"What about bars?"

"Don't worry, there's a couple," said Chance. "But it's a small town. You can't go around pissing everyone off. Why? You getting cold feet?"

"Yes. No. Chi's been good to me," said Lee. "I don't know anywhere else. What's important is the girls will be safe—that's all I'm thinking about right now. Stefy's gonna be happy once it's all done."

"Lee, if you're going to make sure, I keep my word. You don't have to. You can stay."

"You know, I hate when people say 'Everything happens for a reason.' But I guess it does. I want something else, Chance. I want family. Kids. And from where I'm standing, Missouri is as good as any."

Lee's deep quiet laughter echoed through the entire space. The fridge opened. Two beers popped and cracked. Norman cocked his revolver at his side. The hammer clicked into place.

"You hear that?"

"What?"

"Quiet."

A drawer slid open. Boots shuffled on the floor.

"Run," said Lee.

Norman raised his gun, stepped from behind the wall into the light. Chance ran—a blur across the kitchen. Norman shot at his back, missed. The two bullets exploded into the plaster of the far wall in clouds of white dust.

"Get the girls!" Lee screamed after Chance.

Norman let off a wild shot at Lee's head. Lee ducked behind the kitchen island as a cabinet door blasted apart. Lee jumped out, rushed Norman with a butcher knife slashing at the gun.

"I bring you psalms from Asaph," said Norman. "'At the time that I appoint, I will judge with equity.'"

Norman shot again, hit Lee in the shoulder as he drove all

his weight into Norman's gut. The two fell to the ground. Lee reared back, drew the knife at Norman's neck. With one hand, Norman locked his arm and held Lee's wrist. Lee pushed down with all his weight, but Norman's arm didn't budge. He looked dead into Lee's eyes.

"I found something, Lee—" Norman croaked out. "I want to give it back."

Norman dropped his revolver at his side, pulled the blood-stained straight razor from his pocket, and flipped it open on Lee's cheek.

"St. Michael is going to rip off all your limbs, Levi Verbosa."

Norman bent the blade into Lee's skin. The corner of the blade dug into Lee's cheek. Lee grabbed at the gun on the ground. Blood dripped onto Norman's face. Lee's eyes widened; his jaw clenched as Norman cut deeper down his face.

"Do you hear me, Lee? It gets worse. I made sure of it."

Norman pulled the blade back, jammed the razor deep into the bullet hole in Lee's shoulder. Lee screamed, fell back. Norman picked up his revolver, got up from the ground.

"Please—" said Lee.

"I've been praying for clarity, Lee, and now I know I was wrong. I should've killed you in that basement all those years ago, let you die swimming in that black's blood. Georgie died because of my mistake. I can admit that now."

"Fuck off."

Norman pulled the trigger.

First thing in the morning, she went to the Walgreens two blocks away from Stefy's apartment. She had to make sure. The doctor wanted her to come back, but she got scared—scared to hear the news all over again, scared to hear the details, scared to find out what she'd have to do. So she ignored it, acted like the pregnancy wasn't there, and for all of twelve hours it worked. Her stomachaches stopped. Her energy came back, and she actually kept down solid food. But it didn't last. In the middle of the night, her cramps came back and worsened by the hour. Her body was a furnace—hot flashes, choking heartburn—she'd pour sweat if she thought of the sun. When she couldn't bear it any longer, she forced herself up on Stefy's couch, pulled on her dirty jeans, and snuck out the front door.

As soon as she left the building, she wished she'd worn one of Stefy's jackets. She had enough of them—a whole closet full. She didn't know what she was thinking. She was sweating but freezing, and the pockets in her jean jacket barely held her hands. When she got inside the Walgreens, she walked up and down the tampon aisle three times. The cashier watched her in the fish-eye mirror in the corner of the ceiling. The woman looked like a hungry cat. Her cheeks bloated, spread across her bowed reflection;

her eyes shrank to tiny stalking gems. When another customer went to checkout, Amanda crouched down and ripped open one of the pregnancy tests. She slid a testing stick into her back pocket and put the box back onto the shelf. The cashier stared her down as she walked to the front. Amanda picked up a Caramello from next to the register, set in on the counter. The woman squinted at her body, inspecting it up and down before she ran the candy bar across the scanner.

"That's going to be $1.07," said the lady.

Amanda dropped a handful of pennies on the counter, grabbed the chocolate, and walked out.

"Hey, this isn't enough," the woman yelled after her. "Come back here!"

It was into November now. The real cold was here; the city moved faster. Two city buses sped by like huge steaming bullets. When they stopped, the people in their winter jackets shoved each other on and off like they were fighting for their lives. Amanda walked as fast as she could without running. Partly trying to stay warm, partly trying to get back to the apartment before Stefy woke up. For a moment, the clouds cleared and a white morning light broke in every direction. Amanda tried to enjoy it; she closed her eyes waiting for a small hand of heat to brush against her cheeks. But instead, the city got colder, the wind stronger, and Amanda felt her eyes water as she held her jacket closed and ran the last block to Stefy's apartment.

"Where were you?"

Stefy was on the couch watching Pap's old TV. It was one of the few things they had brought from his apartment. She'd just stepped from the shower. Her red hair was slicked back, and she had on one of her many oversize black sweatshirts with another pair of her favorite red potato-sack track pants. She tapped her cigarette into a cup on the ground next to Amanda's pillow. Ash sprinkled onto the blue pillowcase.

"The drugstore," said Amanda. "You're up early."

"I have to open the shop, and the weather report says it's gonna snow."

"Have you heard from Lee?" asked Amanda.

"Nothing. I left messages."

Amanda took off her jacket, went into the kitchen. Dirty dishes were piled up on the small counter next to an empty box of Lucky Charms.

"Are you hungry?" Amanda asked.

"What do we got?"

"Some Hamburger Helper and mac 'n' cheese."

"Do we have any meat?"

"A little bit," said Amanda. "It has to defrost."

Amanda opened the freezer, pulled out the frost-covered package of meat, and put it straight into the tiny grease-stained microwave.

"What'd you need at the drugstore?"

"I was craving chocolate."

Amanda pulled the Caramello from her pocket and set it on the counter. She pressed start on the microwave. It whirred to life; the frozen square of beef pirouetted under the flickering light.

"Were they hiring?" asked Stefy.

"I didn't ask."

Stefy came into the kitchen, hovered in the doorway while Amanda washed their one pot in the sink. She'd been doing it since they were kids—when she wanted to confess, when she felt guilty, when she lied or destroyed something of Amanda's—she just hovered, watched Amanda for a long time.

"I think you need to find your own place," said Stefy.

Amanda shook her head, avoided her sister's eyes. Her anger boiled. She scrubbed harder at the pot. Burned eggs and hardened cheese came off in black and yellow specks.

"Are you kicking me out?" she asked.

"That's not what I'm saying," said Stefy. "You don't have to move out right now. But I think you should start looking . . . Maybe by the end of the month?"

"That's two weeks away."

"Two and a half. I can help you with the deposit."

Amanda wiped her hair from her face with her wet wrist. Warm soap suds dripped down her forehead, caught at her nose. Again, nausea gripped her body. Her throat swelled, got fat. Her tongue was choking her. Her heart raced. She'd never lived alone in her life.

"That's not it—I can figure that out. But Pap just died—I mean, I haven't—I don't know, Stefy—"

"You staying here isn't good for either of us, Amanda. You gotta learn to take care of yourself."

She hadn't expected that—to be judged, called helpless, even worse: incapable. Anger stilled her stomach. Anger calmed her breath.

"What are you talking about? I can take care of myself. Christ, I took care of Pap for five years."

"You know what I'm talking about. Pap's gone. I can't support you. It's not fair to you or me—"

"First off, you don't *support* me, Stefy. If it wasn't for me, there wouldn't be any food in the house. I fucking cook and pick up after you like a maid."

"But you're not, Amanda! That's my point. You're not a maid. You're my sister."

"Stefy, can't we just talk about this? I have something I need to tell you—"

Amanda dropped the sponge, took her sister's hand, but Stefy pulled away and walked back into the living room.

"No, I told you—no more excuses."

Stefy picked up her pack of Parliaments off the ash-spotted carpet and put her jacket on.

"I'm gonna go get some breakfast. Do you want anything?"

Stefy stood by the door waiting for Amanda's answer but none came.

"Suit yourself."

As soon as the door shut, Amanda ran to the bathroom. She sat on the toilet and held the testing stick in her piss just like the doctor had said. She set it on the counter and watched it as she pulled up her jeans. The two blue dashes appeared before she reached the top button. Uncertainty and doubt dragged her down to the carpet of the tiny bathroom. Her knees came to her chest. She cried, then prayed, then wished to feel Pap tapping on her palm just one more time.

The air smelled of fire. Burning metal and rubber had choked Chance as he sprinted down Ashland Avenue just before dawn. There was an accident. A car blocked the street. Red sirens flashed into orange flames. Everything multiplied as he got closer. All the scrambling black forms became people running from the fire and firemen struggling to save the driver's life. He wanted to turn back, try and save Lee. But he'd heard Norman's final gunshots from the street. They rang in his ears, repeating like a string of Black Cats set off in a drum. It all happened so fast. He didn't even see the gun. One moment, he and Lee were fighting behind the shelter, and in the next, they'd already finished packing the truck. The whole time, he didn't think Lee was serious. He figured at the last minute, he would've dropped him off at the airport in the middle of the night. But then in one afternoon, Lee told him the truth about Ghost Town, and made arrangements for the building with an old black lawyer that Chance didn't trust. The more they packed, the more excited Lee got. He said it felt good like they were at a casino and he was winning back everything he'd ever lost.

More than anyone, Lee understood the exact shame Chance carried around. Its weight, its needs, how it could spend all of you in four swallows of a beer or hold you like a spot of warm in a giant cold lake. Lee knew it would all work out. They'd say their good-byes to the girls, and for two days they'd drive south back to Missouri, laughing and fighting like only true kin could. Together, they'd found the kind of soul that would disappear if they ever gave it a name. They saw the best and worst of themselves in each other. Lee showed Chance that life remains after disaster, and Chance reminded Lee that fears and regrets left unattended can spoil to a willful suffering that never shakes on its own.

But he didn't listen—like Lee said, he had hard ears. Lee couldn't have said it any clearer—*you have no idea what you started*. And he hadn't. He didn't. Like a bad night of tequila, he thought the whole mess with Georgie's father would get killed off by the sun. Naïve? Lee would've called him "stupid," and he was right. He didn't know where to go or what to do. Lee told him to go to the girls, but if Norman followed, they'd be killed too. So he went to the only place he knew, to the only person who could help, and as Father Dunne stood in her bathrobe looking out her kitchen window at the sun rising behind Cathedral Shelter across the alley, Chance waited in her kitchen, drowning in dizzying fear and guilt—white as a sheet.

"I'm sorry, Father," said Chance. "Sorry for waking you up. I shouldn't have come."

Chance got up from her small kitchen table and started towards the door.

"Stop . . . Don't go."

Father Dunne took her dented kettle off the stove, filled it over the sink. Its light blue paint was chipped and scratched all over. It had been with her around the world. She couldn't count how many times she'd confided in its scarred steel and cracked wooden handle. Likely more than her pearl rosary and silver crucifix that she'd had since she was eight. She turned on the stove, sat at the table, and pulled out the other chair.

"Sit," she said.

Chance slowly sat down. She took his hand. Her skin was more calloused, rougher than his. Thick veins twisted over her bones.

"Chance, I don't know if you believe in God," she said. "To be honest, I really don't care. But if you want my help, you'll try right now. You'll try and pray. You'll close your eyes and ask for mercy from God."

The kettle hissed on the stove as Father Dunne made the sign of the cross and closed her eyes.

"Dear Lord, we pray to you for guidance. We ask that you welcome Chance's friend, Lee, into heaven with open arms. We don't know why you've set this trial before us, but we trust that you will provide us the means and the path to find our way out. Please give us strength in our time of need. Help us protect the ones we love. Amen."

Without pause, she dropped Chance's hand and went to her bedroom. He heard her pull open drawers; her closet light turned on.

"We'll need to bring your friends—the girls—to the shelter for their safety."

Chance nodded his head. The kettle whined softly. Father Dunne came back out, her hair under her White Sox hat, wearing a thick gray sweater and jeans. She pulled the kettle off the stove and filled two mugs.

"Do you want coffee?" she asked.

"Yes. Thank you, Father."

She heaped Folgers into both of the mugs, stirred it in.

"Once they're here, we'll need to call the police."

"No, we can't—"

"I'm not finished."

Father Dunne tapped the spoon on the lip of a mug, set it on the counter.

"Let me make this clear, Chance. If you want my help, we'll be doing this my way. I'm going to pick up the girls and bring them back here."

"I should go with you."

"No, you're going to stay here, and you're not going to move. And when I come back, we're going to call the police, and you're going to tell them everything—*everything*."

"They'll arrest me, Father," said Chance. "This guy—Norman—he knows everyone. He's like a hero. Lee told me—"

"Lee's dead, Chance!"

Father Dunne slammed the mug in front of him. Hot, steaming coffee splashed out over her hand, but she didn't wince.

"He's dead, and I'm accepting that I'm partly to blame for that. It's time you do too."

"What are you talking about, Father? You didn't kill him—*we didn't kill him*. That fuck, Norman, did—"

"And I should've called the police when he came to the shelter. I shouldn't have ignored it."

"And then what? What would've that done?" Chance insisted.

Father Dunne went to the front door, grabbed her black peacoat from the coat rack, and pulled it on.

"Your friend would still be alive," she said. "And there wouldn't be another dead man right now. We're going to call the police, and after that, you'll make amends."

"With who?"

"Everyone—me, your parents, the man you killed—*the man you killed, Chance!*"

Father Dunne froze, became still. She took a long deep breath and closed her eyes. All of her—every drop of hot blood tightening her hands, drawing them into fists—wanted to take Chance by the shoulders, punch him in the face, and rattle him until his eyes cleared, until something broke. But instead, her words came out slow and quiet, her voice steady.

"You can't live like this, kid. Life always gets its due. Like it or not: When you killed that man, you put everyone you love in danger. That is yours to atone for, Chance. I will love you and help you, but you need to understand this. Do you hear me?"

Father Dunne took a long sip of the pale coffee and buttoned up her jacket.

"I'll need their address," she said. "Where I can find them."

"Okay—"

"Stop letting me down."

er life was on her desk. Amanda saw the birth of the woman's first and second child, their baptisms, and how much they'd grown over the years. A framed report card and finger painting hung on the painted brick wall beside a large inspirational poster. Four children, two white and two black, held hands as they walked up a grassy hill. They smiled under a warm glowing sun. A quote in cursive scrolled beneath them. Amanda squinted to read, *Your love, O Lord, reaches to the heavens.*

"So congratulations are in order."

"Excuse me?" said Amanda.

"Your baby. Congratulations on your pregnancy. I got my two boys—"

The woman turned one of the pictures on her desk towards Amanda and pointed to each of her children. They were beautiful, smiling like the children in the poster. The older one had a Bulls shirt on, and the other—clearly styled liked his brother—did too.

"That's Fashawn—he's twelve. And Derek—he's nine. How far along are you?"

"I'm not sure," said Amanda. "I think about seven weeks."

"You wouldn't know it. You're thin as a rail, girl. Let's see what we got here."

The woman scanned Amanda's application up and down over a pair of small, red-framed reading glasses that looked like two dollhouse windows on her round face. As she read, her braided black hair scratched at the papers in front of her. She pulled them back behind her shoulders with one hand, and immediately her perfume—a potent bouquet of rose and vanilla—filled the room. She was older, but Amanda didn't see one wrinkle. Her black skin was smooth, perfect.

"Are you my caseworker?" asked Amanda.

The woman looked at Amanda over her glasses, smirked.

"Are you pulling my leg?" she asked.

"No, I've been waiting for two hours and I—"

"That's not my problem. We work as fast as we can."

"I'm sorry. I didn't mean it like that," said Amanda. "I just wasn't sure if you were who I was waiting to talk to."

"You've never done this before?"

"No."

"*Never?*"

"No, I've never been here," said Amanda.

"Okay, okay—you look so familiar. I swear I've seen you in and out of here."

The woman put on her reading glasses from around her neck and flipped Amanda's application to the first page.

"So just to clarify: You've never applied for any kind of public assistance?" she asked again.

"No," said Amanda.

"Because I'm going to tell you, we've got people who go office to office trying to file claims under different names, and we catch them every time, young lady."

The woman stared cold at Amanda, waiting for her to flinch. When Amanda didn't move, she set the application down, took off her glasses, and leaned forward on her desk.

"Okay, okay. Sorry. I have to be careful," she continued. "Okay, Amanda—let's start over. My name's Dorothy—Dorothy Coates—and yes, I am going to be your caseworker."

Dorothy held out her hand. Amanda shook it; her skin was even softer than it looked.

"So you were saying, you're about seven weeks along?" asked Dorothy.

"I think so, that's what I figure."

"Have you seen a doctor?"

"Yeah, I went to Community Health," said Amanda.

"On Chicago Avenue?"

"Yeah."

"They're good people over there. Have you been back?"

"No, not yet."

"Okay, you're gonna need to do that. Is this your first time being pregnant?"

"Yes."

"No abortions or miscarriages?"

"No."

"Are you lying?" asked Dorothy.

"No, this is definitely my first time."

"I know. I can tell."

Dorothy put her glasses back on, picked up Amanda's application again, and continued scanning as she spoke. Amanda's mouth was dry. She wanted a soda, something sweet and cold.

"And the father—do we know who he is?"

"Yeah, I know him."

"Is he around?"

"No—yes—he doesn't live with me, if that's what you mean."

"Does he know about the pregnancy?"

"No."

"Are we gonna tell him?"

"I . . . I don't know. I don't know," said Amanda, her voice trembling.

"Okay, okay, that's alright. I'm just trying to get a picture, Amanda. Sometimes it ain't worth it to tell the dads. I know plenty of girls who wish they hadn't. Where are you living right now?"

"With my sister."

"Does she know?"

"No."

"Have you told anyone in your family? Anyone that can help?"

"It's just me and my sister," said Amanda.

"What about your mom or dad? Are they not around?"

"My mom's dead, and I don't know where my dad is."

"What about grandparents?" asked Dorothy. "Extended family?"

"Like I said, it's just me and my sister."

"Okay, okay, that's okay."

Amanda didn't feel like she was crying, but her cheeks were wet, and tears dropped from her chin. Dorothy slid a box of tissues across her desk, turned to her computer, and began typing Amanda's information into a copy of the application on the screen.

"Amanda, from what you've told me, it looks like you're going to be eligible for the state TANF program—*temporary assistance for needy families.* We can get you registered on Medicaid, get you a SNAP card, but housing is going to be a separate application."

"What? That's why I came here," said Amanda. "I need somewhere to live."

Dorothy pushed the keyboard to the center of her desk. She turned the pictures of her children back around to face her, dusted them off with her hand.

"Are you sure you want to do this, Amanda?" she asked. "You know you got plenty of time."

"For what?"

"To terminate."

Amanda's throat went tight. Her heart pinched inside her chest.

"I'm looking at your situation," said Dorothy. "You've got a high-school diploma—which is good. But you've got almost no work history and no family to help with this child. I can qualify you for the program, but I'm not gonna lie to you—this money ain't gonna go far. It's temporary. If you came back to me without the baby, I could set you up in a work program—maybe get you some assistance for continuing your education—community college or a vocational school. There's plenty of clinics available. I could get you in this afternoon."

She wanted to slap Dorothy across her perfect face. She'd come looking for somewhere to live. She'd answered all her questions. She hadn't stuttered or blinked. Didn't this woman see she was trying? Wasn't it good enough that she'd laid it all out? Checked the boxes and eaten her pride like a rotting shit sandwich? Now, after all that, she was going to ask if she was sure? Like she'd fucked all night, wiped her legs, and sucked every cock for bus fare to the human-services office across town. Two hours in that ear-splitting waiting room wasn't enough? Being spoken to like an idiot wasn't enough? Getting accused of being a criminal when she walked in the door didn't cut it? Having all these pictures stare at her, judge her with their high Christian smiles—didn't count for anything?

Amanda bit her tongue and crushed the tissues in her hand. She worked them in her palm and imagined the damp thin paper was a stone. A warm sharp stone like a freshly born diamond.

"Okay," said Amanda. "What time? Where?"

Dorothy picked up the phone, and with three fingers quickly tapped in a number.

"Do you have a car?" she asked Amanda. "That'll help."

"I know someone."

Father Dunne cupped her hands on Ghost Town's front doors and peered inside. It was just after ten in the morning and the shop was still dark. Lee's barber chair sat empty in the shadows. She could just make out the cracked red leather on its armrests and back. At the center of the shop, the brass antique register glowed. It looked like a storybook treasure, shining and reflecting the sunlight stabbing through the front. She was ready to leave. For the past hour, she'd sat in her car waiting for the shop to open up. She needed to go to the bathroom, call the shelter, make sure Mary knew where she was. She didn't know who she was looking for— what the girls even looked like—and the longer she waited, the more she believed that whoever they were, they were possibly already dead.

"Shit . . ."

The word came out in a sigh. Father Dunne watched her breath condense and dissolve in front of her. Again, she cursed herself for forgetting her phone. Chance had caught her off-guard; she'd left in a rush. Since she'd got back to the States six years ago,

Cathedral Shelter had been her life. People misunderstood, always thought her heart brimmed with healing love—like every day was Christmas to her because she was supposedly closer to God. Like she had a special tea she sipped while she said a special mantra that turned on a special light inside her chest that made it that she required no sustenance besides the satisfaction of bringing homeless men and women into a twelve-week program and convincing them to reenter society before they died. Like convincing adults to abandon their addictions, secure employment, and seduce skeptical landlords and managers of halfway homes to give them a spot on a waiting list for a sinking mattress in a room the size of a large closet was so fulfilling that it actually lengthened her life, helped her sleep, and was free of any ulcer-inducing anxiety or cancer-causing stress.

If she was honest, she was stunned, in a daze. The whole thing—the murder, Chance coming over at the crack of dawn, his face and body struck with terror—was like she was trapped in a memory that wouldn't end. She was back in Nyarubuye when things were at their worst. Near the end after three years of missionaries, she'd finally gotten used to the work. She'd stopped shrinking at the gang rapes and the gaping cracked skulls. Exposed bone and organs no longer made her wince. Some of the other priests went cold. Their hearts died at the sight of children with minced limbs—their white tendons dangling like bloody fringe on the ground.

But she'd witnessed something else.

It took her two years after she'd left to recognize it for what it was. Until then, she'd believed life and faith were companions—

one heightening the other in a single ballad to heaven. But there—day after day—life made its case under that damned sun on that parched starving ground. Life argued in slaughter, and faith replied in joy. Like two hyenas, life cackled at the mass graves reminding her of everyone's end, and faith snapped back with the velvet songs of survivors, their laughter and gracious prayers to God. It was there in a makeshift school under a plastic blue tent with the soles of her only pair of shoes worn slick, threadbare, taking on water in the chicken coops or flooding with urine from the clinic as she ministered to the dead. There, she had finally realized the stakes of the fight. The people came to her, and she armed them with orisons she had composed herself. While the other priests ran away, she stayed and fought. Militias and legions killed everything around her, but her devotion screamed like a million raptors delivering her barbed pleas to God.

"Hey, what are you doing?"

Father Dunne turned around. One of the sisters—she didn't know which—stood in front of her. She had sunglasses on and a set of keys clenched in her fist.

"Are you Amanda?" asked the father.

"We don't open for another hour."

"Do you know Amanda? Amanda Beaumont? I'm a friend of Chance's."

The girl hurried, putting her key in the front door, turning the lock.

"I don't know who that is," she said. "Please leave."

"Are you Stefy?" asked Father Dunne.

She pulled open the door, dropped her purse inside, and whipped around.

"Did you hear what I said?! Get the fuck outta here or I'll call the cops."

"Stefy, my name's Sara Dunne. I'm a friend of Chance Pritchard. He's in trouble and asked me to come—"

"Look, lady, I don't give a fuck who you are. I'll say it again, *please leave.*"

"Stefy, Lee is dead."

Stefy took off her sunglasses, eyeballed Father Dunne up and down.

"Bullshit."

"Chance asked me to come here to make sure you're safe."

"Is this some kind of joke? Where's Lee?"

"My name's Sara, Stefy. I'm a priest. I work at an organization called Cathedral Shelter downtown. Here's my card."

From her wallet, Father Dunne pulled out her business card and handed it over. Stefy flicked the paper in her hand still looking past the father, searching for Lee.

"You, a priest? Okay, seriously, where's Lee? I really need to talk to him. This isn't funny. Lee, get your ass out here! You got me!"

Stefy laughed, shouted down the sidewalk. At any moment, Lee would peek his head from around the corner or knock on the window from inside, laughing, probably still drunk. Father Dunne stood still. She waited for Stefy's eyes to calm and her nervous open-mouth smile to fall away. Then like a reflex, the father drew closer, held out her hands, and tilted her head just slightly— all the same gestures she used all those years ago when she had to tell a young mother that her sick child wasn't coming back. Stefy stumbled back. Her knees buckled and she fell to the ground covering her mouth. Father Dunne dropped down, wrapped her in her arms.

"We have to find your sister. You're not safe."

The 82 bus stumbled through traffic. These were the worst rides, when for no apparent reason—it wasn't even rush hour—the bus stopped at every single stop, went nowhere. The ride was so horrible that Amanda was actually happy she felt the Mexican girl's eyes boring through the back of her head. *Lucia Menendez.* Amanda was surprised she even remembered the girl's name. Just like at the other clinic, she was leaving the DHS office as Amanda was going in. Amanda avoided her eyes like she had before, thinking she would be long gone by the time she was done. But now they were both on the same southbound bus, heading the same way home. This time it didn't bother Amanda, though, not like before. This time she was almost thankful for the clawing thick tension. It gave her something to do—took her mind off the fact she had exactly one hour to get across the city, get Stefy, and explain to her sister that she needed a ride to a women's clinic in Oak Park for an abortion of a pregnancy that wasn't supposed to be possible.

"I told you I see you all the time."

Lucia stood over Amanda, holding the handrail above her head. The bus swayed back and forth. Her pregnant belly pushed out from her red jacket right into Amanda's face.

"Don't worry, white girl, I ain't gonna jack you," she said. "But that's pretty crazy we keep seeing each other. I told you."

Lucia smiled. Her black hair was pulled back in a tight ponytail. Sweat shined off her forehead as she struggled to keep her balance. Amanda picked up her bag from the empty seat next to her.

"Do you wanna sit?" asked Amanda.

Lucia took a deep breath, held on to the rail, and lowered herself down. Immediately, she dug through her giant purse in her lap and pulled out a large rubber-banded bag of Doritos.

"You want any?"

"No, thanks," said Amanda.

"You gotta eat for that baby, *mija*. Can't be starvin' the little motherfucker."

"I'm not pregnant."

The girl laughed loud as she snapped the rubber band off the chips. Crumbs sprinkled onto both their laps. Embarrassed, Amanda closed her jacket. The girl tilted her head back and dropped a pile of chips into her mouth.

"You can't fool me, white girl. Your titties are starting to swell, and I know you don't got no money for no boob job—what'd they tell you?"

"Who?"

"Your caseworker—what'd they say?"

"Nothing," said Amanda nervously. "I've gotta go back to the doctor and then make another appointment—"

"Good luck. Those *putas* take forever. Did they try to get you to kill your baby?"

Amanda could have gotten sick right there. Her stomach

flipped; she pinched her leg, took a short breath, and fought the faint. Lucia straightened out the Doritos, poured the last of the chips into her mouth. Bright orange specks dusted her cheeks before she crumpled the bag and kicked it under the next row.

"Relax, they always be doing that. They just don't want to fill out the papers. Half of 'em can't even have babies, that's why they get so mad. Fuck 'em."

"How far along are you?" asked Amanda.

"None of your fucking business."

Lucia wiped her mouth. Her eyes dropped, went cold, and she looked at Amanda in the same scary way she had before at the bus stop and at the clinic—like she was going to rip off her face and eat it.

"I'm just playin'," she said, laughing. "I'm, like, seven months."

Lucia opened her jacket; her belly ballooned from under her huge breasts. Her T-shirt bunched up above her belly button, exposing her stretch-marked skin.

"I think I'm having twins—that's what my mother says. Is this your first?"

"Yeah," said Amanda.

"Boy or girl?"

"I don't know."

"How long has it been?"

"About seven weeks—maybe eight weeks . . . I think," said Amanda.

"Yeah, you'll know in a minute—like another month. Boys be wildin' out in there, feels like cats all inside you."

"How many do you have?"

"Just the one—a boy. These are gonna be two and three. Do you wanna touch 'em? They're kicking hard."

Amanda bit her lip, rubbed her sweating hand on her jeans before she reached out. The girl's skin was tight, warm, almost hot. At first, there was nothing, but then a patter tapped at the skin, and then a fist—maybe a foot—punched against the flesh wall. Amanda smiled.

"They hate the bus, and they hate spicy food. So right now, they're pissed like a motherfucker. But I didn't eat breakfast, ya' know? What do they want?"

"What does it feel like?" asked Amanda.

"It's like—"

Amanda leaned forward; she wanted to hear every word. A grin broke over the girl's face.

"You know what? I ain't gonna tell you. But it's good, you'll see—white girl, you gotta name or what?"

"Amanda."

"Okay, Amanda. My name's Lucia. You got a phone?"

"No—"

"*You don't got a phone?!* What's wrong with you?"

Lucia pulled down her shirt, leaned over, and pulled the stop cord on the window.

"This is me—don't let them fuck with you."

"Who?" asked Amanda.

"All of 'em! Haven't you been listening? The social workers, the doctors. My mom always says, 'You're the only one who knows what's good for your baby.' And she's right—you staying with your man?"

"No."

The brakes groaned, and the bus came to a bouncing, jerking stop. Lucia braced herself on the seat in front of them and grunted as she pushed herself up.

"Then fuck him too. He should be coming with you. They're all the same, you know that, right?—bunch of fucking dogs."

"You need any help?" asked Amanda.

"No, I got this."

Lucia heaved her bag over her shoulder and pushed into the people crowding the door.

"Excuse me, can you get the fuck out of my way, please?" she announced. "I gotta get the fuck off."

She stepped off the bus slowly and vanished into the rush of bodies on the street. The last thing Amanda saw was a red patch of Lucia's parka flashing behind a swarm of legs. As the bus rolled forward, a stranger took the empty seat. His bag hit Amanda in the neck, but she didn't turn from the window. She slipped her hand under her shirt, felt heat spreading inside her own body. She tapped at the skin trying to send a message through her blood.

He could take his blade to Chance's neck—cut his dirty cracker skin from ear to ear. Or he could just shoot him—smother his pretty white head with that pillow he was sleeping on and crack a bullet off. There wouldn't be no mess. Yeah, Father might have to buy a new bed, a new pillow. She might want to move but he could help her with that. The point is: The boy wouldn't know what hit him.

Like always, the police were the problem. Either way—blade or gun—they'd cuff Eddie, put their knees in his back, and try to drive his face through the concrete. He'd been through it all before—too many times. He'd have to fight to speak, beg them to listen, because they wouldn't take his word that Mary sent him to check on the father. He'd have to stay pinned to that dirty alley until Mary told them herself. They wouldn't believe the whole shelter was worried because Father Dunne had left without a word, that it was unlike her—the woman was never late. No matter how much he wanted to kill this motherfucker, Eddie knew better:

They would never ever believe a black ex-felon killed a white boy in good faith.

But nothing made sense. Father Dunne was gone without a note or a message. And now this motherfucker, Chance, was in her bed, but the doors weren't broken, and the windows were still shut. Eddie was sure the father wouldn't be defiling her bed with this shiftless motherfucker—she liked the girls. And if she was, it sure the hell wouldn't be with this one—this one was no good to the core. Eddie hated white folks like this—little entitled motherfuckers that thought the world sat on their knee. Goddamn, he wanted to kill him. His face hurt just thinking about it.

"Wake up!"

Eddie kicked the bed, shaking Chance's sleeping body.

"I said wake up, motherfucker! Get your ass up!"

Chance rolled onto his back, cracked open his eyes.

"What the fuck . . . Eddie? What are you doing?"

Eddie pulled a pistol from the pocket of his overcoat, cocked it over the bed. Chance shot up, scrambling to the headboard.

"What the hell are you doing, Eddie?!"

"Your ass is moving now, ain't it? Funny how that works—get out there."

Eddie jabbed the gun at Chance, walked him into the small living room of the father's apartment. Two tall bookshelves covered one wall. A TV and a cheap stereo sat on a rolling cart in front of them. The only seats were a small red loveseat and a rickety wooden chair repainted in red. Eddie waved Chance onto the chair, stood in front of him, leveled the pistol on his chest.

"I'm gonna ask you some questions, Goldilocks. And you better be straight with me unless you wanna bullet, alright?"

"Eddie, I can explain—"

"*Alright?!*"

"Yeah . . . Alright," said Chance.

"Where's the father?"

"Out."

"Don't get smart."

"She's helping me out. You don't need to know anything else."

"I'll decide what I need to know—where did she go?"

"To pick up some of my friends."

"Who? That big motherfucker, Lee?"

"No . . . Lee's dead."

Eddie shook his head, scowled at Chance. He knew the answer to his next question, but asked it anyway.

"That old pig killed him, didn't he?"

Chance didn't move. He grit his teeth and fixed his eyes at the two windows in the living room behind Eddie. Through the scratched paint-splattered glass, he could see gray smoke rising from the ash-stained chimney of the building next door.

"What'd you do to that man?" asked Eddie.

"None of your business."

"Actually, it's a whole lotta my business, Chance. *When I got beat down for your ass*, it became my business."

Chance leaned forward; he couldn't look at Eddie. He kept his eyes on the smoke rising thick and dense like a long, patterned scarf into the sky.

"I killed his son," Chance said quietly.

Eddie lowered the pistol, paced back and forth. His old scuffed Florsheims clapped up and down on the hardwood as he cocked his head, burned a nasty stare into Chance.

"You know, I knew it'd be some shit like this. Father said, 'Nooo—he's a good kid.' But I knew it. She doesn't see shits like you for what you are."

"And what's that?" Chance fired back.

"Selfish, son. Sinful. Hurtful—you want me to go on? You should be ashamed of yourself."

"Don't worry, I am."

"Well, obviously not enough, motherfucker, because your ass is sitting here like you're somebody—like you're some God-damned little prince—while Father's out there right now—*right now*—risking her life for your deadbeat ass—it's a girl, ain't it?"

"What?" asked Chance.

"Father's gone to find your girl, ain't she?"

"Yeah but—"

"I knew it! Your little dick got some pussy, and now you put another person in front of the devil. She pregnant?"

"No—"

"C'mon, now, get the shit out! He already knows," said Eddie, pointing to the sky. "You can't hide—that's the shit you don't get."

"Who the fuck do you think you are talking to me like this? You don't know me!"

Eddie stopped, crouched in front of Chance. He leaned in close so Chance could feel his spit, his burning breath.

"See, that's where you're wrong. I know all about you, Chance Pritchard. You got locked up. You thought you were gangster, and then you got shook when that woman got killed. Oh, I read up on you, but it didn't tell me nothing that I didn't already know. I met you so many times before, it makes me sick. I got locked up with folks like you. I maybe even killed one of your dirty sinning cousins. And you're all the same—don't matter if you're black, white, Chinese—all you care about is yourself, and you wanna know how I know? 'Cause I used to be the same way, son—the same fucking way."

Eddie stood up, put his pistol back in the pocket of his overcoat, and buttoned it up.

"Where'd she go?"

"A tattoo shop on Damen. I can show you where," said Chance.

Eddie slipped on his leather gloves, wrapped his red wool scarf around his neck and tucked the ends inside the lapel of his coat. He still wanted to strangle the boy. He wanted to feel Chance's throat crack and collapse in his grip. Right then, Eddie was sure that he'd never wanted anything more in his life. He raised his shaking right hand from his side and pointed his gloved finger at Chance, imagining it was the barrel of his gun.

"I'll tell you right now, Chance. If something happened to the father—as God is my witness—I will extract a pound of flesh from your ass. I owe that woman my life, and I will go back to prison happy knowing one less of you are in the world."

They were holding something back. There were too many pauses, glances back and forth. While Father Dunne spoke, Stefy stood at the living-room window biting her thumb. She hadn't moved since Amanda walked through the door. Amanda had seen her sister scared before. Brief patches of panic had seized her face when she taught Amanda to drive or anytime Pap had fallen. But not like now—Stefy was terrified. Her already pale skin was faint, almost transparent, and her eyes snapped back and forth involuntarily from the front door to the window overlooking the street. A packed backpack was at her feet—the same one she'd used when they ran away on the train and that Amanda had never seen again—and she had on that black winter parka with the hood. Years ago, Pap had bought one for both of them. Amanda had worn hers out two winters before, but Stefy's still looked brand-new. The waterproof black was bright and crisp like it had never seen wet.

"We need to leave right now," said Father Dunne. "I'll explain everything when we get to the shelter."

"I can't," said Amanda.

"You can't what?"

"I can't go. I have to see a doctor. I have an appointment in Oak Park."

"You have to go to the doctor, now? *Right this minute?*" asked Father Dunne.

"No, but later, I do."

At a loss for words, Father Dunne got up, took Stefy by the arm, and walked her to the small kitchen. Amanda couldn't make out the exact words Father Dunne spoke, but they were strong enough—serious enough—to have a sob well up and spill from her sister's throat. Father Dunne wrapped Stefy in her arms and walked her back out to the living room.

"Amanda, Lee's dead," said Stefy, quietly through tears. "Norman killed him."

She had been working on a speech all the way home. She was going to come clean, tell Stefy about the pregnancy. She knew Stefy would freak out at first, but Amanda was going to tell her plans—that'd she'd gone to a doctor, met with a social worker, and decided to have an abortion. After she got better, she was going to get her own place, a job, maybe go back to school. None of it would be easy. But more than anything, she wanted to tell her sister that she'd listened to what Stefy had said. She'd thought about it, and Stefy was right—she had to make her way on her own.

Now the whole thing sounded stupid, like she'd gotten drunk, written down her fever dreams, and thought they were reasonable plans. It was the exact same feeling she'd had when they told her their mother was dead. She shook her head, bit her tongue. At least this time, she looked like herself—no expensive haircut, just her own dull limp hair—no dumb smile holding her face, just her same daggered stare. Christ, she almost forgot. She should've known better. She lived on the bias. Her life was one-sided, always leaving her with dead loved ones or abandoned by people she thought cared. She swiped the brimming tears from her eyes, shook her head trying in vain to stoke her anger, burn out her fear.

"Chance is at the shelter?" she asked quietly.

"Yes, he's there waiting," said Father Dunne. "We're going to call the police once you guys are safe."

"Did you hear what I said, Amanda? Lee's dead," Stefy repeated.

Tears broke from Amanda's eyes. Her cheeks vibrated. Her legs drew heavy. Her hands opened and closed, wanting to cover her face, but instead she forced herself up, grabbed an old canvas bag from under the kitchen sink, and picked up her only other pair of jeans and a sweater from the living-room floor. Stefy followed her to the bathroom, hovered silently as she opened the medicine cabinet and grabbed her toothbrush.

"That's it," said Amanda. "Let's go."

They left through the front door, took the stairs down to the street. Amanda carried her bag over her shoulder, and Stefy dragged behind her lugging her backpack in her hand. Both their faces were still, both their eyes emptied by shock.

"The car's at the end of the block," said Father Dunne, walking ahead.

"We're right behind you," said Amanda.

Amanda took one of the shoulder straps from Stefy's hand, and together they shared the load. It was the weekend so the street was packed with cars; kids played in empty driveways. People, families were home. Lights were on in all the apartments, and the popping mutter of TVs blared behind windows and bled through the bricks to the street. At once, Amanda realized why Stefy lived here, why she had never moved. The block, the neighborhood, was full of life. Everything felt related—even the bare trees and cold freckled cement.

"Maybe I can get an apartment around here," said Amanda. "Somewhere close."

"What?" said Stefy. "Oh . . . Yeah . . . Maybe."

When they got to Father Dunne's small SUV, she had the back open and was moving poster boards and boxes of brand-new socks from the backseat.

"Take the front. I'll sit in the back," said Amanda, stepping out into the street.

"Lee—" said Stefy, looking past her.

"Move!" screamed Father Dunne.

Down the street, Lee's Lincoln tore towards them. The engine roared in a long volcano of sound. Father Dunne ran around the side of the car and grabbed Amanda by the arm. With both hands, she shoved her back onto the sidewalk, sending Amanda to the ground. As Father Dunne turned towards the street—checking for the car—Lee's Lincoln dipped, jabbed to the left like a plunging boat and caught her at the waist, launching Father Dunne like a ragdoll into the air. Her arms flailed like they were filled with water. Her legs—two thick black strands—flapped in the gray sky. Her body flew over two cars before it landed, collapsing the trunk of a third. Stefy exploded into a long crying scream. Amanda rolled on the ground, covering her face, blinding herself from the steel crater filled with the father's broken body, a spineless mess of blonde hair.

t took them all afternoon to get inside. Eddie insisted on parking one street over, four blocks away. He said if shit went down, he didn't want to get his car towed and impounded. He said it had happened to him too many times before.

"I'll tell you how they do it, Chance—police beat your ass on the way in, and the city robs your ass on the way out. You know they charge *you* every day they got *your car*? So you're locked up, your car's locked up, and the whole time, you're paying money you don't got. Which by the way—*nine times out of ten*—is why you're doing the devil's work from the start. No thank you. You can get fucked with all that."

It took them a half an hour just to walk to Ghost Town, and then once they got there, the spare key wasn't where Lee said it would be. They had to walk all the way back to Eddie's car to get a crowbar. Chance begged Eddie to drive back, and after twenty minutes of arguing, Eddie finally relented and moved the car two blocks closer. As soon as they got back the second time, Chance took the crowbar to the lip of the steel back door, and he and Eddie took turns kicking and prying. In a last-ditch effort, Eddie made them hold hands and pray before they stood together and leaned on the bar with all their weight. The steel frame groaned as it bent back, and finally, the door opened with a pop.

"Ain't nothing stronger than prayer," said Eddie, pleased with himself.

They walked into the back of the dark shop together. Eddie felt up and down the walls, looking for the light switch while Chance immediately went down the creaking wood stairs to the basement.

"Yo, where the fuck are you going, Chance?" Eddie called out. "I can't see shit."

"The switch is by the door on the left—up high, close to the top," said Chance.

Just as Chance reached the bottom of the stairs, two bare light bulbs flickered on over the middle of the basement. Chance stopped and stared over the bare, pitted concrete floor. This is where it had happened, just like Lee said. Chance hadn't believed him, but as he followed the black, forty-year-old blood stains around the floor, he saw Lee killing Cupid the Vice Lord. Before Ghost Town was Ghost Town—before Chance was even born— Lee had splattered the man's blood across the basement like paint.

"Where your peoples at?" asked Eddie as he came down the stairs.

"I don't know," said Chance. "It doesn't look like Stefy came in today."

Large dust-covered mousetraps were strewn around the floor like Lee had stood at the bottom of the stairs and tossed them randomly in every direction. The two light bulbs hanging from the ceiling were just bright enough to light up white-and-green mold growing on the brick walls.

"I hate it down here. Why don't we wait upstairs?" said Eddie.

"We will in a minute."

"Ain't shit down here. Let's go."

On the far wall—just like Lee had said—a set of chairs, a couch, and two old school desks sat half-covered with a tarp. Chance started unstacking the chairs and setting them at the other end of the basement.

"Eddie, can you gimme a hand?" asked Chance.

"You must got me fucked up," said Eddie. "I didn't come here to work. Let's go check upstairs."

"Please, Eddie, it'll just take a sec."

Chance threw the tarp off the furniture while Eddie carefully took off his overcoat and hung it over the stair's railing.

"We shouldn't be messing with this man's stuff," said Eddie. "Didn't anybody ever tell you don't trade with the dead? You can't pay them back. I don't like it down here."

"I just need help with the couch, then you can go," said Chance.

The couch cushions were stained deep with blood. The yellow embroidered flowers were crusted black like they were painted with burned oil.

"How long you been friends with this guy?" asked Eddie.

"A while. Like six months," said Chance.

"Were you close?"

"Close enough," said Chance. "Get the other end."

They both crouched down and dug their hands under the bottom of the couch. Eddie winced, struggling with the weight.

"You okay?" asked Chance.

"Must be a damn foldout," said Eddie, trying to catch his breath. "My uncle had one just like this."

They moved the couch to the center of the basement and dropped it on three empty mousetraps. Two of them snapped off with muffled pops. Eddie dusted his hands off on his pants while Chance squatted down on the patch of floor where the couch had sat. He swept his hand back and forth on the ground, clearing away the thick grainy soot.

"I don't got time to be cleaning out this bum's basement," said Eddie. "If these girls ain't here, we need to be finding them and Father Dunne. Are you listening to me?"

The safe was set into the concrete just like Lee told him. Chance rolled the dial; after two gritty rotations, it glided smooth and silent. He put in Lee's birthday backward: right fifty—left fifteen—right two. The tumblers clicked into place.

"Did you hear that?" asked Eddie in a whisper.

Above their heads, two sets of muted footsteps went back and forth across the length of the shop. A faucet was turned on. The old building's pipes filled with water, and then the quiet pop of Amanda's and Stefy's voices spitting back and forth drifted downstairs. Eddie pulled his pistol from his pants and peeked up the stairs.

"Put that away," said Chance. "It's them."

Chance rushed past Eddie and took the stairs two at a time. He ran through the back office, pushed through the set of heavy drapes into the front of the shop. Stefy jumped, stumbled back. She ducked her head, instantly started shaking, and both her hands shot up in front of her like she was about to be bashed into a wall.

"It's alright. It's just me—it's just me," said Chance, holding up his own hands.

Amanda collapsed in Lee's barber chair, too tired to be surprised. She glanced back and forth at Chance and Eddie, not stirred in the slightest, like she'd known they'd been there the whole time.

"What are you doing here?!" asked Stefy. "How'd you get in?"

"Through the back," said Chance.

He went to Amanda, wrapped her in his arms. She didn't move. Her body was stiff like a chewed, hardened paper doll.

"I missed you," he whispered into her ear. "You okay?"

"Where's the father?" asked Eddie. "Ain't she with you?"

Stefy locked eyes with Amanda, unsure of what to say. Amanda pushed Chance off and got up from the chair. Dark pink bags hung under her eyes. She took a deep breath and when she spoke, her voice cracked out quiet like she'd just been woken up from the fat of the night.

"Who are you?" she asked, straightening her glasses.

"That's Eddie. He's from the shelter," said Chance. "He came to help."

Amanda nodded, taking it all in. She had nothing left. She was thirsty, hungry, and her saliva covered the inside of her mouth like drying glue. As she gazed at Eddie in the darkened shop, her bloodshot eyes glowed, pounded in her head. She pursed her lips, trying to wet her mouth, and prayed for the appropriate words to arrive, to make themselves apparent. But again, just like when she spread Pap's ashes, nothing occurred to her. She realized she was useless to this man. She was a fraud, an imposter of the person who should be bringing him this news. The refrigerator rattled on in the back office. A wash of cars sped by on the street. Amanda's breath became louder. Eddie nodded as she turned back to Lee's empty barber chair. His breath joined hers, and together they exhaled, began to sob.

A full moon rose early, hung low in the pink and black sky as Norman parked Lee's long gray Lincoln in front of Paul's house in Lakewood. Whereas Norman had grown up in Englewood most of his life, Paul had been born and raised on the North Side of the city. His and Sheila's house was the Kowalski family home—the same four-bedroom house Paul had grown up in as a kid with his younger brother and sister. The property was huge, hard to maintain, but Paul had always done a decent job, especially now that he was retired. Norman got out of the car, let the door swing wide and hang open as he stomped through a string of freshly planted flower beds and tracked muddy footprints up the clean white steps to his old partner's front door. He knocked twice, and then quickly started knocking again until he heard Paul's heavy footsteps tromping across the old hardwoods towards the door.

"I was in the neighborhood," said Norman. "Thought I'd stop by."

Norman's usually pressed and starched button-down was open, untucked, revealing a dingy wife-beater hanging from his shoulders like a stained drape. His gray hair was a matted mess of pomade and cigar ash, and his unshaven skin that normally shined because of his religious application of aftershave and Oil of Olay looked like used sandpaper under Paul's front porch light.

"Whose car is that?" asked Paul, looking at Lee's Lincoln parked on the street.

"Aren't you going to invite me in?"

"I can't—Sheila's resting," said Paul. "Where'd you get the car, Norman?"

"A friend of mine, a good old friend of mine."

"Where's your truck?"

"We traded," said Norman.

Norman shifted back and forth; his face twitched and contorted like he'd been pepper-sprayed in his eyes. Paul stepped outside, closed his door. He pulled a dishtowel from his shoulder and dried his hands.

"Why don't we go get some beers?" asked Norman. "That bar still down thereabouts? You know the one I'm talking about—"

"Forget it. It's filled with kids now. You look like hell, Norman."

"You look like shit, Paul. You look like a steaming pile of horse scat, you fat fuck."

"That all?"

"What do you mean, 'Is that all?'"

"I gotta finish up inside," said Paul.

"What the hell's your fucking problem? What am I, a leper?"

"Norman, I haven't seen you going on a month. You don't call. I come to your house, and you don't answer the door."

"What are you, my fucking keeper now?"

"No, I'm your friend, asshole—"

Paul caught himself before he unloaded; his neck turned beet red as he pushed his anger back down. Norman scratched at his crotch, pulled up his pants. He clapped his hands, faked a punch into Paul's gut.

"You're right," said Norman. "You are my friend, and my partner. We need to talk. Let's go."

"I can't. I told you, Sheila's resting."

"You can't or you won't, Paul?"

"You know what you need, Norman? Sheila and I been talking—we're looking at one of them senior cruises up to Alaska. You should come with us. I know you got the money—"

"Paul, I've done some bad things."

"So you shot your mouth off at Terry? Big fucking deal. He'll get over it. Norman, you're not alone in all this. I'm sorry about how it went down at the station, but me and Sheila are here for you. You're family."

Paul took Norman by the shoulders, squeezed his old friend tight. Slow tears swelled out and rolled over the swelling purple bags under Norman's eyes. His whole body shuddered; his broad, fat shoulders collapsed.

"You're a good man, Paul Kowalski," said Norman. "I wouldn't want anyone else."

"You're not too bad yourself," said Paul, smiling, patting Norman's back. "But it's time you move on, partner. You gotta accept Georgie did some horrible things—you know Sheila and I were talking, and in a way, Georgie was lucky because you know it was only going to one place."

"You and Sheila were talking, huh?"

"Yeah, I tell her everything, Norman."

"And you two—you two—think it's good Georgie got beat like a dog—"

"I didn't say that, Norman. Don't put words in my mouth. My point is you and me both know *he was sick*—Christ, we locked up monsters like him."

Norman shoved Paul off, grabbed him by the throat. His eyes went wide, the last of white flooded red. He reared back and, with all his fading strength, punched Paul with the same hand-twisting haymaker that he used for thirty years on cuffed suspects, innocent plaster walls, thin steel lockers, and his wife Eileen when she cackled at his fits. Blood poured from Paul's brow, split by Norman's rings, but he didn't stop. One after another, he wailed slow, deep gut shots on his old partner. Paul wheezed between each pounding hit, his body seeming to shrink more and more after each vicious blow.

"Why would you say something like that?!" shouted Norman. "I thought we were family."

"*Norman, stop!*"

Sheila's screaming voice came from inside as she ran down the front hallway of the house. She yanked open the door, jumped on Norman's back, and grabbed his arm just as he was about to drop another fist. Norman whipped around, cocked his pink bloodied fist over Sheila's face.

"Don't you do it, Norman!" Paul shouted. "Don't you dare!"

Down the street, porch lights flipped on one after another. Paul's next-door neighbor sprinted out from his home, holding up a phone.

"I called the cops, Paul!" he yelled from his lawn.

"Ya' hear that, Norman?!" said Paul. "Don't you touch her."

Norman dropped his hands, stared down his old partner. Blood dripped from his raw knuckles and stained rings. He spat on the ground, wiped his mouth. Paul's blood smeared across his face from cheek to lips to cheek. Sheila ran to Paul, helped him up. His right eye was hot pink, already closing shut. Norman waltzed slowly down the sidewalk to Lee's Lincoln. He held his head high in the air and inhaled deep grating breaths like some war-high Hun.

"That's the problem with you, Paul—always has been. You're always taking the other side."

Norman started up the car. From his front lawn—with only one good eye—Paul couldn't tell if his old partner was crying. He was definitely shaking. Norman's whole body vibrated, and his face looked like a fading demon behind the cloud of black exhaust.

She'd never seen a man cry like that. For two hours, Eddie sobbed in the basement. His muffled cries and curses gusted up the stairs through the velvet drapes into the shop. Amanda heard him trying to make sense of it—talking, whispering to himself in circles. But inevitably, his heartache came back. She knew the feeling. It was close to a convulsion or a seizure, like vomiting on an empty stomach while getting hit with a bat. There was nothing she could say, so she didn't say anything. She leaned back in Lee's barber chair, extended the foot rest, and watched Chance and Stefy sleep on the ground.

That woman—Father Dunne—hadn't looked scared. Her face was calm as she turned end over end in the air. Her eyes were open. Guilt and regret didn't possess her last moments. When life left, it rose from her crushed body in a blanket of steam. Amanda and Stefy had run without saying a word. It wasn't until they were in a cab—miles away—that they found each other's hand. They both squeezed the other's tight—another involuntary motion, a reflex to their blood running cold. When Pap died, it had been the same. After they rolled him back into the hospital room—blood and iodine staining his sutured chest—Amanda saw no trace of any hostile dreams. He was empty, like he'd been lured away. She had picked up his hand while Stefy watched from the door. One last time, she tapped his fingers on her arm. She saw him smiling. She felt his laughter, his last telegraph from the dead. It was her secret, like the pregnancy, a fact she wasn't beholden to share. Amanda lifted her shirt and ran her hand in a circle on her stomach as Stefy tossed back and forth on the ground. Chance snored in spurts; air caught at the back of his throat till he wet his lips, slept silent, and did it all over again. She couldn't wait for Norman to come kill her—run her over while she slept in a dead man's shop.

At once, she remembered her father locking up his pistols— the sheriff and the gold—in her parents' closet back in that house in Maryland, where everything smelled of liquor and Stefy sent her cigarettes in the mail. Then she remembered being smaller, younger, sitting with her mother in the kitchen, looking out the screen door to the snow-covered backyard. It was cold, the beginning of winter like now. Her mother bounced Amanda on her lap, laughed, told her she was growing inside her body when her parents got married. She said Amanda punched and kicked—beat at her through her vows—like she wanted to stop the ceremony, start a fight with the entire world. Amanda pulled her hand from her shirt. The chair creaked forward as she got up. Stefy opened her eyes.

"Where are you going?" she whispered.

"To the bathroom," replied Amanda.

"Don't forget to turn off the light. You can see it from the street."

"You're good to me, Stefy. You're a good sister."

"Do you mind if I take the chair?"

"Go ahead. I'll be alright."

She pushed past the drapes and went to the back. Eddie was leaned back in Lee's chair, watching one of the video monitors as a young blonde bent towards the camera showing off her tattoo-covered chest. In front of him on the long steel desk, an old rusted breadbox sat open.

"There's Kleenex in the bathroom," said Amanda.

Eddie jumped, shut off the monitor.

"I was . . . I was—"

"It's okay," said Amanda. "She's pretty."

"Found these in the basement. Your friend liked making videos."

"And you like watching them."

Eddie smiled, closed the breadbox, and turned to face Amanda. He had on his gloves and jacket like he was about to leave. His red scarf was still muffled, tucked neatly into his breast as if he had somewhere else to be.

"That's what we do, isn't it? Watch while someone else gets their hands dirty."

Amanda buttoned up her own jacket, glanced at the back door. Chance and Stefy had wired it shut with a coat hanger.

"It's cold out there, you know that, right?" said Eddie. "You start going that way, and your heart just might freeze up—won't be nothing left."

"I can't just sit and wait for someone to come save me."

"Father used to say the same thing. She'd say, 'I can show you the way. I can give you my love, but in the end, ain't nobody gonna fight for you but you.'"

Eddie nodded his head knowingly and then stood up, pulled his pistol from the pocket of his jacket, and checked the magazine.

"Father wouldn't let you go alone."

"Thanks, but I can take care of myself," said Amanda.

"Oh, I know you can."

Now he knew what they felt. Paul remembered the men crying, crawling to the corners of the interrogation rooms, scared for their lives. Their wrists rubbed raw from being cuffed to those bolted-down tables. Their eyes filled with a mad boiling panic as if at any moment the world was going to explode, and they were the only ones that knew. He and Norman would smoke cigarettes while the men trembled in the corner—a tradition to celebrate breaking their will. He remembered his sore hands—red as a steak—gripping the blood-stained telephone books and slamming them on top of the men's heads. His forearms would be jelly from holding plastic bags over their faces—even the scrawny ones bucked like donkeys when they ran out of air. A lot of the time, they'd pass out, half-suffocated. Their throats gurgled and popped letting out their last breath. He and Norman would bring them back. If you just let them sit, they'd come back to life. They'd return from the dead sucking air like they'd just been holding their breath at the neighborhood pool.

If they still had lip—anything left—he and Norman would make them drop their pants, and Norman would wire up their nuts to that old army field phone while Paul cranked that thing till his hand cramped. The men pissed themselves where they sat.

He could touch the cattle prod to the puddles and wake them up without ever shocking their skin. No bathroom breaks; some of them shit their seats like pigeons. When he and Norman burned their thighs or crushed their fingers in the vice, the men screamed—almost squeaked—like when you drop a lobster in hot water and tamp it down with a brick.

Now he knew their thoughts, what had run through their minds as he tortured them. He always thought they prayed, but it wasn't a sentence or any string of words. It was white. It buzzed. It was sharp and faster than the pain. The pain came after—once you had a moment to breathe. As Norman beat him to a pulp, cracked his orbital socket on his front lawn, Paul finally understood what he'd done to those men in those interrogation rooms. He'd crushed all of them, fouled their bodies with pain, reduced their souls to bleached shadows, not even ghosts. Sheila was right. He didn't have a choice. There was no more talking to be done— no more sympathy for Norman and his dead son. Paul touched his fingertips to his bandaged face as he waited for Terry Novicki in the lobby of the Nineteenth Police District. It felt hollow, numb from the painkillers they'd given him at the hospital two hours earlier. He didn't know how he was going to start. Never in his life had he turned anybody in. He was always on the other end. He'd never been a victim. He'd never been scared for his life. As an adult, he'd never cried from fear till today. He'd never felt this powerless or weak, like at any moment everything could end. He was convinced any moment someone was going to stab him in the chest, and there was nothing he could do.

"Follow me, Paul."

Terry held open the door into the back offices of the police station. Sheila in her pink cloche and matching jacket got up from her seat, picked up her purse.

"No, Sheila. You stay here," said Paul, patting her lap.

"Pauly, you can barely walk," she said.

"I'll be alright, sweetheart."

Paul leaned forward, pushed himself up. Through his good eye, he focused on Terry's blurred body across the lobby and tried to keep his balance as he walked. Terry didn't offer a hand. He held the door until Paul was inside and then pulled it shut.

"Follow me," said Terry.

Even though he could barely see, Paul could still feel the room of eyes staring at him. All the cops stopped what they were doing and whispered back and forth just like the last time he was there. But this time it was worse because he felt shame, embarrassment, and—worst of all—pity directed at his beaten body. His eye welled up as he realized that to them he was just a fat, feeble old man.

"Everyone back to work!" Terry shouted, opening the door to his office.

Paul stepped in, reached out for a chair. A waiting young detective got up and helped him to his seat, then sat down next to him in the same chair that Norman had sat in only a few weeks before. The detective had a close-cropped beard, wore jeans and a Columbia College sweatshirt. His badge was clipped to his belt next to his gun.

"Paul, this is Nick Weiss. He's Harry's boy. Do you remember him? He's homicide—one of my best."

"Nobody's dead, Terry," said Paul. "He doesn't need to be here."

"He's only here to take your statement."

"I told you on the phone. I'm only talking to you."

The young detective got up, picked up his mug of coffee from Terry's desk.

"It's alright," he said. "Why don't I give you guys a minute—Paul, you need anything? Coffee?"

"I don't need nothing from you, asshole, and you can quit with the good-cop bullshit already. I got your number as soon as I walked in."

"Thanks, Nick. Just give us a few," said Terry, waving him off.

The young detective closed the door. His aftershave lingered in the room—a musky maple like scorched coffee cake. Paul clasped his hands over his belly. He rubbed his palms together, and his head rocked back and forth as he stared at the floor.

"You know how it goes. I have to record this," said Terry, pulling out a small voice recorder from his desk.

"My word not good enough?" asked Paul.

"Just procedure."

"Yeah, I remember that."

Terry pressed a button on the hand-size recorder. A tiny red light glowed next to the mic.

"You wanna tell me what happened this evening, Paul?"

Paul felt like an idiot. He wished he'd taken the kid's offer—asked for some water. He licked his lips. His eyes didn't move from the floor.

"Alright, how 'bout I go first?" said Terry. "And then you can decide."

"Decide about what?"

"About how much you're gonna protect your friend."

Terry opened a red file folder on his desk, slid a pile of pictures in front of Paul. There was Norman's truck parked in the back of an apartment building he'd never seen. A dead body—that man, Lee—lying in a pool of blood. Bullet holes covered his chest. A single shot had gone through his cheek, right under his eye. Paul covered his mouth, shook his head trying to wash the photographs away. The deeper he got into the stack, the more the surgical tape tightened on his face.

"Last night, we had a murder, Paul. North and Ashland—just outside Wicker. As you can see, the responding detectives found a late-model Ford Explorer abandoned in the building's parking lot. I don't think I need to tell you that it's registered to Norman Quinn. The neighbors also reported seeing an older man matching Norman's description leaving the scene just after three in the morning. You're police. I don't have to make it any more clear how serious this is. So I'm going to ask you again—*as part of an official murder investigation*—when last did you see your former partner, Norman Quinn?"

hey took the streets. Eddie said it'd be faster than crossing over to Lake Shore. They drove up Damen and took Lincoln north to Western. Block by block, the city's brownstones turned into newly constructed strip malls the farther they got north. All the liquor stores and bars with their Old Style signs became glossy shimmering gas stations that looked like carnival rides this late at night. Eddie's Buick smelled of pine and sweet oranges from the two gold-crown air fresheners on top of his dashboard. He drove slow—not like Stefy. He leaned back in his seat with his hand cocked over the wheel and steered the car with his wrist. Every time he slowed down, the car let out a wailing moan like a beast on its last legs. When Eddie sped back up, the car turned to an earthquake. Amanda's seat shook, and she instinctively grabbed the door handle, ready to ditch out.

"Don't worry. We'll make it," Eddie said with a grin. "This car runs on faith, and I got plenty."

Amanda didn't know what she was going to do. Just thinking about stepping foot in that house and seeing Norman's face made her stomach turn. Wasps swarmed in her chest. She wanted to kill Norman, stomp his throat like Chance had done to Georgie. She wanted to shoot him like he had shot Lee. She wanted Norman to die slowly—for him to contract a deteriorating punishment for all that he'd done.

"You alright?" asked Eddie. "You look like you're fixing to be sick."

"Think I'm just hungry," said Amanda. "I never got a chance to eat with everything yesterday."

"There's a store around the way. We'll stop and get you something."

"I don't have any money."

"I got you."

Eddie took a left into a quiet Evanston neighborhood. Two-story brick houses in red, brown, and beige lined both sides of the street. With their glowing front-door lights, they all looked like toy houses in the dark. After a couple more blocks of homes, a huge brand-new strip mall with a brightly lit Jewel Osco grocery store appeared on their left. Eddie turned into the empty parking lot, cruised slowly all the way to the front doors.

"You want a sandwich?" he asked. "They got some of them in the deli."

"Yeah, that sounds good."

"I'll grab us both one and some pop."

Eddie pulled his pistol from his jacket, stuffed it under the seat.

"Black man cruising this 'hood past midnight? That's one way to get picked up," he said, laughing. "I'll leave the heater on for you. Be right back."

"Wait," said Amanda, taking his arm. "Why are you doing all this?"

Eddie took a deep breath, stared across the sprawling empty parking lot.

"I've been asking myself the same thing since we got in the car. . . ."

Eddie rubbed the black-and-gray stubble on his chin and held his fingers to his lips just like Pap used to when he was putting together a thought.

"How old are you, Amanda?" he asked.

"Twenty-nine."

"Seems about right."

"For what?"

"You ain't a child no more. Your sister and that boy, Chance, they look like children to me, but not you. You understand what needs to be done. Ya' feel me?"

Eddie wiped his eyes. In the dark car, Amanda couldn't see his tears, but his voice cracked, caught in his throat.

"Amanda, my daddy was locked up by dirty-ass cops before I could walk. His daddy was strung up like a dog five miles west of here in the middle of the night. My uncle got stabbed and robbed in his barber shop over nothing when I wasn't barely ten. I promised the father a long time ago I'd never do harm to another man again, but now I see why God put me here, with you, with the father. I know that man, Norman. I know his kind, them of the snake. What I'm sayin' is—"

Eddie turned to Amanda, looked her in the eye. His lips didn't quiver, and his voice stopped shaking.

"You won't have to do a thing, Amanda. You just show me the way."

"Father Dunne was good to you, wasn't she?"

"When I say she was a saint, I mean it in the truest sense of the word, Amanda. She saved me. She set me free."

Eddie got out of the car and headed to the front door of the supermarket. There was a bounce in his step like it was the middle of the day, and he was just running inside to grab them both lunch. For as much as Amanda was exhausted and scared of what the next hours would bring, Eddie was still full of life—joy, even. She didn't understand how he could smile even if it was just an exercise in sympathy for her sake. She couldn't grasp how anyone could after all he'd seen and lost in the past hours. He said it himself: Father Dunne had saved his life, set him free. And now she was dead. Yet, Eddie still walked as if the world played his song. While Amanda was a broken blurred mess, he was sifting through day-old sandwiches searching for the least-handled one for her. Without a second thought, he'd buy it with his own money—probably buy her a soda too, even though she hadn't asked. Then they'd drive together, and he'd fulfill his offer. He'd kill for her this very night.

Amanda didn't understand any of it. She only knew it was cold because she could see her own breath. She only knew she was angry because she felt her fingernails creasing into her palms. She finally knew she was fed up because right then—in Eddie's wailing, bucking Buick with hot Pep Boys coolant piping through the vents in a sweet toxic steam—Amanda finally saw her entire life crystal-clear. She couldn't let Eddie, a stranger, give up his life for her. She couldn't let one more person take responsibility for this mess that she'd started years ago. When Chance had killed

Georgie, she told herself that it was his decision, and when Pap died, she told herself that he was old and well on his way. Every time Stefy had paid the rent, fed her, clothed her, she told herself that one day she would pay her sister back, knowing she never could. Even Lee had tried to protect her. She hated him now, but knew he'd only done what he thought was best. She couldn't let Eddie do this. From the start, it had been her problem to end.

Amanda slid behind the wheel, pulled Eddie's pistol from under the seat. She'd never shot a gun in her life. The weapon felt like an animal—a hand-size statue of a killer—cursed to be enslaved to whoever could clench its frame. She sat forward, pulled the gear shift on the column towards her and down. Three loud knocks, and then the old Buick banged into gear. The motor wound up with a whine and then settled into a shaking, knocking snarl. The brakes hissed as she let off. The tires licked the ground, lapped at the concrete like four dogs on a bleeding sugar leg. She tapped the accelerator; the car jumped. The headlamps brightened. She leaned back, threw her hand over the wheel like she'd seen Eddie. As she gunned the car out of the parking lot, she rested the pistol in her lap and replaced her hunger with the weight of nicked steel.

Stefy brought her knees to her chest, curled up in Lee's barber chair, and watched a homeless man cup his hands to Ghost Town's front doors and peer inside. Snow crusted his beard. A blanket draped over his head. Weak breaths puffed out from his dark hairy face and fogged the glass in vanishing circles no bigger than the size of a thumb. Stefy stayed still as he went down the set of windows looking in, then back up and down the street, searching for someone or somewhere to hide him from the cold. After ten minutes, he pushed on. Stefy zipped her black jacket to her neck and went to the back. The security monitors flickered to Lee's empty office. Cigarette smoke and dim yellowed light spilled up from the basement stairs. She heard feet shuffle. Something dragged across the floor.

"Amanda, you down there?" Stefy called out from the top of the stairs. "Chance?"

"Yeah," said Chance.

"What are you doing down there?"

"Nothing. I'm coming up."

"Where's Amanda?"

Chance walked back up the stairs. His hands and the legs of his jeans were covered in black grainy dust.

"Is Amanda down there?" Stefy asked again.

"No."

"What were you doing?"

Chance went to Lee's desk, flipped open the top of the old steel breadbox. It was empty.

"Did you move all the video tapes that were in here?" he asked.

"Lee's tattoo videos? What do you want with them?"

"Nothing. Lee just wanted to make sure they got to somebody before we left—or before we were going to leave."

"Who?"

"Doesn't matter now. They're gone."

"Where's Eddie?"

Chance untwisted the coat hanger from the back door, stuck his head outside.

"Amanda, you out here?" he called out. "Christ, it's fucking snowing."

"They're gone—both of them," said Stefy.

"Eddie probably went back to the shelter. I bet he went to tell Mary."

"Who's Mary?"

"She's—she was Father Dunne's assistant. She runs the office."

"So where's Amanda then?"

"I don't know . . . Don't worry, Stefy. She's coming back. She didn't go far in this weather. She probably went to get something to eat."

Chance rubbed his head, started shuffling back to the front of the shop.

"Where are you going?" asked Stefy.

"I'm going back to sleep. It's fucking freezing back here."

"*Are you serious?*"

"What do you want me to do, Stefy? I don't know where they are."

"How about giving a fuck? Jesus . . . "

"What do you wanna do? Go drive around the block yelling out the window?"

Stefy shoved Chance out of the way and ripped past the drapes to the front of the shop. She grabbed her backpack from the floor and threw it over her shoulder.

"Stefy, where are you going?"

"To find Amanda."

"*Where?*"

She pulled her keys from her pocket, unlocked the register, and pulled all the cash from the drawer.

"You're acting crazy," said Chance. "Amanda's gonna come back."

Stefy ignored him, went to the front door and held up her keys in the little bit of light searching for the right one.

"When this is done, Chance, if you love my sister—no, I won't even say that—*if you care one bit for Amanda,* you'll leave and get out of her life. You may not be able to see it, but she deserves better than you. A whole lot better."

Stefy unlocked the door, pushed it open. A wave of cold flooded the dark shop.

"Where's the shelter?" she asked.

"Wait, I'll go with you—"

"Just gimme the address, Chance, and then you can go back to sleep."

The house looked the same. It seemed like at any moment Georgie would open the front door and creep towards her. His head would be bald, scabbed-up from shaving with those blue disposables that he always bought by the bag at the dollar store. He'd be wearing that cheap pleather jacket—the one with studs that he told everyone he stole from a Clash concert but that he'd actually bought with the credit card he'd stolen from his father. Sometimes he'd have on a T-shirt underneath—sometimes nothing—but he'd always say, "Good morning, sweet tits," grab Amanda's body, and roll his tongue around both walls of her cheeks. She remembered in the mornings his spit was sour sludge—like a garbage-tightening cement. They'd walk to the bus stop because his Mustang would still be broken down. He'd hold Amanda's ass and tell her that he found a good spot where they could chill. They'd get a motel with all of Amanda's cash. Then they'd get high, smoke speedballs, and he'd fuck at her for two more days. She knew she'd been awake too long when she burned her hands. She would watch the pipe cook her skin, put cigarettes out on her legs, but all she felt was a twinkle like a battery on her tongue. Georgie waited in the bathroom while the men came in and out. The young guys—the scared ones—just wanted to see some tits. Amanda could make them come just by grazing their pants. If they were really sweating, shaking in their boots, she kicked the wall, and Georgie came out with that pistol. All he'd say is, "You shouldn't be here," and the johns would throw their money on the bed and hightail it out. They'd get naked, celebrate with hundred-dollar hits. Georgie would slam at her body. She couldn't sit for days.

As Amanda closed the door of Eddie's Buick, she remembered the day she called Stefy for help. She thought she was going to die; the blood wouldn't stop and she could barely see. She was tied up. Georgie was passed out naked at her feet. He looked like a tiger. Fresh styptic clots ran in stripes over his shaved head. His dick dropped between his leg like a child's, and deep bleeding scratches ran down his forehead onto his cheeks. Wire snakes covered the walls. Dusty boxes were stacked high to the ceiling. Amanda's lone shadow grew off her feet and ended at the blacked-out windows. Her blood tasted like iron candy—like red hots mixed with blood. If she rubbed her eyes, she could see for moments. Extension cords on the ground, needles and pipes on a chair. She tried to take a step but fell. Loose rope tangled her feet. She scrambled, got Georgie's phone from his pants, and then Norman, Georgie's father, opened a door. He was drunk, carrying a plate.

"Tell them to go to the garage," he slurred.

He groaned as he threw Georgie over his shoulder and carried him into the house. The door slammed shut, and the last thing Amanda saw was the ceiling. The light of the garage opener blinked. The filament burned a swarm of gnats. Dust showered from the peeling paint. Her back was wet. A gag hung from her mouth. Yes, the house was just how she remembered it—a damned place disguised in red bricks, peeling white paint, and a growing blanket of the winter's first snow.

Eddie's pistol pinched at Amanda's stomach as she walked. She adjusted it, jammed it snug at her waist. The barrel pressed against her underwear. It felt cold and stupid, like when she used to steal CDs. The front door was cracked open. Through the slit, she could see light from a television flickering on the floor. A speeding voice boomed about car deals in downtown Evanston. Amanda glanced at the sky one last time, pushed on the door. Weatherstripping grazed the hardwood. Cardboard file boxes lined the front hallway in stacks of twos and threes. They trailed into the front sitting room where the TV played the local news to a sinking couch, an ironing board, a jar of olives, three empty bottles of Tullamore Dew, and a tossed coffee table covered with file folders and pieces of white and carbon paper.

She walked slowly down the front hallway to the kitchen. Her hands shivered, but she couldn't tell if it was from fear or the cold. Her breath came out in front of her, dissipating clouds that smelled like nothing because she hadn't eaten in a day. Dirty plates and glasses grew from the sink and spread across the countertops. Three open black plastic bags of garbage sat propped up against the lower cupboards. The coffeemaker was on, the pot empty. Its red light reflected through a half-glass of water. The oven's clock blinked 12:00, repeating like a lone silent alarm. At the back of the kitchen, the open door to the garage made a rectangle of white light on the linoleum. She stepped closer; Norman was singing. He muttered through a melody, stopping every few words to catch his breath. Again, Amanda pressed on Eddie's pistol to make sure it was there. She stepped into the doorway, and at once she smelled everything that she had tried to forget for the past four years.

Norman dunked a sponge into a bucket at his feet. Soapy water splattered on the ground as he scrubbed the front bumper of Lee's Lincoln. He was unshaven, haggard. Patches of gray-and-white bristles covered his cheeks and sprouted wild from his chin. His undershirt was stained yellow at the pits, and his sweatpants were soaked from the knee down. He moved in a frenzy. His slippers shuffled back and forth on the polished cement as he drowned the sponge, scrubbed the chrome bumper, and sang in deep warbling tones. Sweat dripped from his face, fogging the amber lenses of his glasses; they only cleared when he stopped to draw a breath. Amanda shifted in place. Norman's voice trailed off. He wiped his forehead, dropped the sponge into the bucket at his feet.

"I was expecting someone else," he said, chest heaving. "I left the door open, didn't I?"

"That's how I found it," said Amanda.

"Doesn't matter. Heat's not on."

Norman picked up a hose and sprayed Lee's Lincoln down. The garage was larger than she remembered. Power tools, quarts of oil, and gallons of coolant sat neatly on wall-mounted steel shelves. Orange extension cords and garden hoses still hung on the walls, but up against the back wall where Georgie had tied her up, a water heater and matching washer and dryer had been installed. They looked brand-new and out of place, like Lee's shiny Lincoln—only she could tell they didn't belong.

"I painted, can you tell? Got the door changed too," said Norman. "Did it last year. Georgie helped. Bastard was cutting up the whole time."

Norman set the hose down and picked up a towel from a stack on the shelf behind him. He dried his face and arms and then threw it on the Lincoln's long hood. He took a deep breath, leaned over the car, and began moving the towel in huge circles the length of his arm. Water slapped to the ground. Norman panted; fresh sweat broke from his brow.

"I always wanted one of these—1977 Mark Five, V8, two-door, leather. Hell, he even got the color: high-gloss battleship gray."

He stopped, straightened his back again. His skin sagged from his arms, and his gut sucked in and out as he tried to catch his breath.

"I tell you what, though, these old cars are a pain to keep clean."

"What do you want?" asked Amanda.

Norman smiled, leaned into the passenger seat. He pulled a box of Lee's Swisher Sweets from the glove box and lit one with a match. Heavy smoke curled up from the tip and hovered over the car in a gray fog. He shook his head, chewed on the end of the cigar like a savory piece of fat.

"My son, sweetheart. I want my Georgie back."

Amanda tried to swallow the frog growing in her throat. She was scared; she knew it was going to be like this. She stepped forward trying to will out the words.

"Georgie attacked *me*," she choked out. "Your son came looking for *me*. I wasn't following him. I was done."

"God knows he wasn't perfect. You don't think I know what

he did to you? Do you know how many times I tried? His mother said he was a lemon—an asshole just like me—that's what she said. My father said the same thing, called me a 'disgrace.' Who calls their own a disgrace? They're a part of you. You don't just put 'em out, forget 'em. You love them. You try, and when you get sick of trying, and you got pie all over your face—you try some more!"

Norman slammed his hand on the Lincoln's hood. Water splashed over the windshield and onto his chest.

"He was gonna come around. I know it. You have to do the work, and by God, Georgie was doing it. For thirty years, I worked homicide. All those cases in those boxes out there? *That's me!* Everybody came and went, but I stayed. I put in the work. It's in my blood. It was in Georgie's blood. He would've changed. He would've done right."

"He tried to kill me," said Amanda. "Twice."

Norman crumpled in front of her. His one arm shot out, holding him up on the Lincoln; his other took off his glasses, blotted his tears with his fist. At once—just like Pap had—he looked his age to Amanda, a tired old man working alone to stay warm.

"You'll see," said Norman. "You'll see for yourself."

Outside, a car door slammed shut in front of the house. Norman wiped his face with his wet hand and pulled his father's black service revolver from the back of his pants. The handle was still wrapped in duct tape, and the body was scratched to hell.

"Seems fitting it's just you and me, lady," said Norman. "The two people Georgie loved the most."

He walked towards her. With each step, his eyes filled with more hate. Amanda told herself to reach for the gun, but her body froze. Terror robbed her strength. Her heart emptied down her legs—just as it had in that bar's bathroom—and just the same, she struggled to breathe, but this time it was Norman's arm closing around her neck. Her breath turned to a rasp. On the far wall, two rakes, a square shovel, and a green yard trimmer began to dance. Norman twisted his body, yanked her off her feet. He dragged her through the dark kitchen; the stench of the rotting garbage was stronger than it was before. They moved down the hallway bound at the neck and arm. When they got to the front door, Amanda's legs kicked at the file boxes of Norman's old cases; a carpet-cleaning jingle played from the television in the living room as Norman yanked open the door.

"Norman, don't do this."

She heard Paul's voice before she could see him. It was quiet, calm, just like it had been at the hospital. Norman dragged her onto the front steps. She could just make out the bottom of Paul's legs and snow spotting his boots as he stood on the front lawn.

"Where's Terry?" asked Norman.

"They had me there all night," said Paul. "I couldn't cover for you—they found your truck, Norman . . . Did you kill that man?"

"Did they find the priest?"

Amanda strained, got her feet beneath her, and managed to lift her head to Norman's waist. Paul was rolling his Bears beanie in his hands like a rosary. Snow gusted around him, sticking to the shoulders of his blue parka and the fresh bandages on his stunned face.

"*What priest?*" asked Paul. "What are you talking about, Norman?"

"He'll figure it out. Terry's dumb, but he's no idiot."

Norman tightened his headlock on Amanda and pulled up. She felt her face turn purple as he closed her throat. Up and down her neck, her veins throbbed like a mess of gasping snakes. She pulled on his arm, fighting to breathe.

"Remember this one, Paul?" said Norman. "Now I know why Georgie fell so hard for her. This girl has some balls. Came over here by herself. You believe that?"

" . . . Help . . . "

Amanda strained out the word. Her eyes bulged from their sockets. With both hands, she yanked on Norman's arm trying to get air.

"Let her go. She's about to pass out, for Christ's sake!" yelled Paul.

"This ain't my first rodeo, Paul. I do remember how to subdue a suspect. Gimme some credit."

Norman loosened the headlock a hair. Immediately, Amanda got her feet back underneath her. She gasped over and over. Thick saliva drooled from both sides of her mouth, numbing her face as soon as it hit the cold.

"Let me go!" she shouted.

"See, that's why you keep it tight—"

Again, Norman clenched down on her neck. Amanda's knees buckled; she clawed at his arm trying in vain to break his grip.

"You've gone soft, Paul," he barked. "This is Policing 101."

"Norman, you have to let her go," said Paul. "They'll kill you right here."

"If Terry wants a fight, I'll give him a fight. Maybe this time the decorated commander will actually get his hands dirty for once."

Norman held up his grandfather's duct-taped revolver so Paul could see before he mashed it into Amanda's cheek. The steel dug into her skin, forcing open her clenched molars and pressing against her tongue. Her legs scrambled beneath her; she screamed through her spread jaw.

"What are you doing with that?" asked Paul. "That don't—"

"Shhhh—"

Across the street in a patch of sky, the morning sun broke over the rooftop of another two-story Evanston home. Her body relaxed at the sight of the blinding yellow light. Paul stared at Amanda as her scream reduced to moans; his brow furrowed, and his eyes blinked over and over trying to erase the sight. *It's alright,* Amanda wanted to tell him. *This is all familiar, a song I've sung before.* Blood leaked from some fresh wound inside her mouth. She tasted salt, smelled the alewives dying off in Lake Michigan ten miles away. She heard both her and Norman's breath laboring inside their chests. For the moment, their hearts beat together, clicking and tapping like a pair of broken pawn-shop drums. Sirens began in the distance.

"Paul, you should go before they get here," said Norman. "Tell Sheila I'm sorry . . . for everything."

"I'm begging you, Norman. Not like this."

Paul's voice cracked. Tears collected around his good eye before they dropped down his face, dissolving the sticking flakes of snow.

"We had a good run, Paul. We made a difference, right?"

"I don't know what we did, Norman."

"We did. I know we did. I've got all our cases laid out in there," Norman said, motioning inside. "We did a helluva job."

Paul staggered back. His mouth dropped open, and his hands closed to fists at his side.

"Norman, nobody needs to see those. Why'd you do that?—all those cases are closed."

"That's right, and we closed them, Paul—you and me. I'm gonna tell them everything. Everyone will see who did the real work. Let's see Terry make chief after that."

"You can't do that to me, Norman. They'll lock me up," Paul pleaded.

"For what?! For doing your job?"

"For breaking the law!"

Amanda closed her eyes, pressed on Eddie's pistol at her waist. The gun didn't feel stupid anymore. It was warm from her body and heavy—like the baby growing inside her—the weight made it real.

"Why, Norman? Why couldn't you leave it alone?" begged Paul. "I've been nothing but loyal to you."

"Chicago problems. Chicago solutions, Paul. Don't tell me you forgot."

Norman laughed; his arm slacked just enough for Amanda to get one deep breath. She sucked in all the air she could. She wanted to stomp Norman before he choked her dead. She wanted to shoot him before he killed her. Amanda would give Norman what he asked for. She'd reunite him with his family of ghosts. With everything she had, Amanda reached down and shot her elbow up, deep into Norman's gut. Her arm moved like a piston, up and down, as hard and as fast as she could. Norman collapsed on top of her, his grip loosening from her neck. With both hands, Amanda shoved him off and pulled the pistol from her waist.

"Gun!" screamed Paul.

Amanda fell back onto the front lawn, her gun aimed at Norman's chest. He stood on the porch holding his side, coughing, smiling through the pain.

"I was wondering what you were waiting for, lady," he said. "You had me worried."

"No, don't! It's not—" yelled Paul as he jumped towards Amanda.

Norman raised his family's toy sidearm but didn't get it past his waist. Amanda pulled the trigger. The two shots echoed down the street, mixing with the rush of early commuting traffic, the last birds who'd not fled south, and the sirens barely a mile away. Norman dropped to his knees, fell down the steps. His eyes closed. His hand gripped at his chest.

"No, no, no," cried Paul. "His gun's not real. It doesn't shoot."

Paul tossed Norman's gun at Amanda's feet. The broken-down revolver—still hot from Norman's grip—melted into the snow. Norman drew deep, heaving breaths as his face flushed one last time. Streams of dark blood spilled from the holes on his chest. Paul kneeled down and carefully lifted Norman's head into his lap. He cried as he wiped Norman's face with his beanie. The sirens grew louder; they were only a few blocks away. The two men stared into each other's weary eyes. Paul's tears wet his old partner's face.

"I always wanted grandkids," said Norman. "But Georgie got the blanks just like me."

"Just stay with me, Norman. They're coming."

"Don't let them cuff me, Paul. I don't want to die in cuffs."

Amanda was dizzy; the world tilted like she was falling down. She fumbled through her pockets for Eddie's keys and started towards the Buick across the street. Her feet stumbled left and right as she walked. She took a deep breath, willing herself to walk straight.

"Wait!" Paul yelled after her.

Amanda turned around, Eddie's pistol still shaking in her hand.

"Gimme your gun!" shouted Paul.

Amanda ran back across the yard. Wet cold seeped into the holes of her sneakers. Norman stared at her from Paul's lap. He nodded his head; his eyes blinked slowly as he watched her hand the gun to Paul.

"Take care of that baby," he whispered. "Hold 'em close."

"How does he know?—*how do you know*?" asked Amanda.

"He's a detective," said Paul. "Chicago's finest."

Amanda sprinted back to Eddie's Buick and got in. When she turned the key, the car hacked over and over for what seemed like an hour before it rumbled to life. She threw it into drive, pressed on the gas. The brakes bucked as she turned the corner at the end of the block. A single gunshot exploded behind her. Four police cruisers tore by going the other way.

Three days later . . .

A bright noonday sun melted the top of the packed snow, turning the entire cemetery into a blanket of shining white. Amanda and Stefy stood together at Lee's gravesite, watching the skinny, curly-haired funeral director polish Lee's giant red mahogany coffin. When he reached the end, he slid his finger down the length of the casket, and without looking at them, pulled out a small yellow invoice from his breast pocket and set it on top of Lee's coffin. Stefy snatched it up; her eyes went wide as she read the bill up and down.

"Family and friends discount," said the funeral director, smiling. "You and your sister are good business."

"Like the bank?" asked Amanda.

"Exactly."

Stefy pulled out a finger-thick set of crisp hundred-dollar bills from her backpack, counted out five, and handed them over to the funeral director with a begrudging smile.

"Thank you," she said. "We appreciate it."

"You have my card?" asked the funeral director. "The weather is so good, but it changes."

He gave them another counterfeit smile before he turned and sprinted back to his waiting hearse. From a distance, his swinging cash-stuffed hands looked like a pair of squirming eels. Across the cemetery, a stream of cars trickled into the small parking lot. A large group of people stood together hugging, sipping coffee, laughing loud. Stefy dropped her backpack and yanked at the bottom of her black skirt, trying to stretch the sheer fabric over her knees.

"Is there a fucking Bears game or something?" asked Stefy. "And where the fuck is Chance?"

"He said Eddie was picking him up," said Amanda. "You okay?"

"I'm fine. Just feel a little silly in this getup—don't know what the fuck I was thinking."

The day before, Stefy had brought home two black dresses from Goodwill for them to wear to Lee's funeral. She'd chosen the short tight cocktail and given Amanda a draping grown that fell well past Amanda's feet. Amanda knew she looked ridiculous—like some raving goth princess with black lacy taffeta dropping over her sneakers—but now she didn't care as she saw goose bumps orange-peeling up and down Stefy's calves. Because even though a warm December sun beamed across the cemetery, Chicago's freezing wind still didn't quit. Chance and Eddie jogged towards them from the parking lot, zigzagging around headstones and three freshly dug gravesites. They wore matching black suits and purple ties. As he ran, Chance's slacks flooded up, exposing his work boots.

"It's my fault," said Eddie. "I needed him at the shelter. I'm helping Mary, and we got no one to watch the door."

"Where'd you get the suit?" asked Amanda, smirking.

"It's mine—well, was mine," said Eddie. "Looks sharp, don't he?"

"He needs some new shoes," said Amanda.

"One thing at a time, one thing at a time . . . "

Without pause, Eddie pulled a small Bible from the breast pocket of his suit and winked at Amanda.

"Y'all ready to get started? People got things to do."

"Who?" said Stefy.

"All them people right there—"

Eddie pointed behind her. Stefy turned to see the mob of people from the parking lot tromping across the snow towards them.

"Who are they?"

"You want the good news or the better news, Stefy?" asked Eddie, pulling up the sleeve of his jacket and holding out his arm.

A blurred and faded mighty dagger tattoo sat on the inside of Eddie's right forearm. At a loss, Stefy shook her head as she looked closely at the faces of the arriving men who were surrounding Lee's coffin. At once, she recognized them all—even Eddie. When they first came into the shop, they were younger, angrier, ashamed to show their faces, but now all of them were old, some happy. She saw Lee in all of their hardened faces and soft eyes. Stefy ran her hand around the faint but still visible R's across the hilt of Eddie's dagger.

"Regret. Repent. Redemption—that's what we live by. Your friend, Lee, didn't start as a good man," said Eddie. "But he ended his life loved by many who've been inside. You girls were his family, his everything."

Eddie reached into the inside breast pocket of his jacket and pulled out an old wax envelope and handed it over to Stefy.

"Here's the better," he said.

Stefy slowly opened the envelope and took out two crisp, waterlogged pieces of paper. She shook her head back and forth as she scanned down the documents. Tears poured from her eyes.

"What is it?" asked Amanda.

"Lee paid a lot of money to my family for a long time for killing my uncle Cupid," said Eddie. "He made right. Ghost Town is hers free and clear."

With that, Eddie walked to the head of Lee's coffin, opened his Bible, and waited patiently as Amanda took Stefy's arm and pulled her to the side of the grave. Chance stood on the other side with the other men. All their heads lowered, eyes already closed. Eddie held the Bible at his chest. As he began, Amanda noticed his voice sounded different; it was deeper, clear like orchestra horns. The words carried over the cemetery. The wind slowed and allowed the sun to warm.

"It is the same with the resurrection of the dead. What is sown is perishable, what is raised is imperishable. It is sown in dishonor, it is raised in glory. It is sown in weakness, it is raised in power. It is sown a natural body, it is raised a spiritual body. If there is a natural body, there is also a holy ghost."

Stefy had fought it all morning, but now her body sobbed with tears. Amanda took her sister into her arms as Eddie lowered his Bible, closed his hands, and prayed, "Dear Lord, please welcome Lee into heaven with open arms. He was good but imperfect like all your children that walk this earth. Show him the same love that he showed these folks that he cared for. Allow him a seat in eternity with your son, our savior. I ask all this in the name of the Lord Jesus Christ. Amen."

Stefy pulled away from Amanda, hugged Lee's coffin. She whispered, kissed the wood. One by one, each of the men came forward and paid their respects. By the end, everyone—even Amanda and Chance—had their hands on the coffin, eyes closed.

"Godspeed, Levi Verbosa," said Eddie.

The circle broke apart. Everyone smiled, wiped tears from their faces. The men crowded Stefy, anxious to introduce them-selves and their wives. Eddie walked to Chance, patted him on the shoulder.

"I'll wait for you by the car," he said. "Amanda, God bless you and your sister. Y'all know where to find me."

"Thank you, Eddie," said Amanda.

Eddie gave her another wink before he turned and started back towards the parking lot. Chance took Amanda's hand and walked her away from Lee's grave. With each step, his slacks drew higher above his worn, scraped-up boots. Amanda's dress trailed behind them, lapping at the small patches of grass and piles of freshly turned dirt.

"I made a promise to Father Dunne," said Chance. "I'm leav-ing, going to see my folks. I owe them—I owe you an apology, Amanda. That night with Georgie, I shouldn't have gone back there . . . I should've just shut up and listened to Stefy."

"That makes two of us."

Chance held Amanda in his arms. When they kissed, the wind kicked back up and threatened to lift Amanda's dress. Nei-ther said good-bye. Neither told the other what would happen next. They broke apart in a dance. Both knowing they had to turn away, not look back—those were the next steps. Together, the sisters watched Chance and Eddie drive away. As the Buick turned onto the street, Eddie honked twice and waved out his window. Stefy lit a Parliament, pulled a silver flask from her bag.

"Really, Stefy?—here?" asked Amanda.

"It was Lee's—had to have one last drink with him."

Stefy uncapped the flask, offered it to Amanda.

"I can't," said Amanda, pointing to her belly.

"Did you tell him?"

Amanda smiled and caressed her stomach, her hand still warm from Chance's touch. She turned from Stefy, shut her eyes tight from the blinding white. She didn't answer the question. She was already into the next month, the following year. Every single day—no matter the time or weather—Amanda saw herself standing alone, her voice pounding with her big heart. There were doctor's appointments to keep. Paperwork that needed to be filled out. She saw herself waking up in her own apartment, rising from her own bed, and standing at her own window. The city—her cold city—stretched to the horizon, clutched the freezing lake, and drew the black water close. For all she'd ever done—all she'd seen—swam back to her in the black currents. The ashes of Pap, Caroline's body floating in her satin gown, her father's ghost flew across the beach like a lost bird whistled home. She tapped at her stomach, sent a new message in love.

I won't leave you. You will be the exception to my life.

Even after all these years, the rooms looked the same. The scratched-up steel table was bolted to the floor in the center of the room. Suspect street names, gangs, and area codes covered the top, scrawled in frantic scratches— likely etched in with a pin of a belt buckle or a contraband set of keys. The chairs hadn't changed either; they were the same hard yellow plastic hand-me-downs from City Hall and the school district. Paul remembered Norman bringing in throw pillows from home because the seats killed his back, burst his hemor- rhoids when he sat too long. Norman's file boxes covered the table and filled the back wall of the interrogation room. Paul sipped from his Styrofoam cup of coffee while Terry flipped page after page.

"What the hell do I do with all this, Paul?"

"I don't know, Terry. You're the commander."

Paul leaned back, stretched his cuffed hands behind him. Terry closed the folder and pulled a soft pack of Marlboros from his pocket.

"You want one?" he asked, shaking a cigarette out.

"I thought you quit," said Paul.

"It would've been eleven years today. I bought a pack on my way in—didn't even think about it. The words came out of my mouth at the gas station, and all of a sudden, I was stubbing my second one out in the parking lot."

"We all got hang-ups, Terry."

"What's yours?"

Paul rubbed the stubble on his chin. The left side of his face was still bruised a deep purple and scarred black, and his body ached from sleeping on the air mattress in his holding cell.

"Old Style magnums, those Entenmann's crullers—I can't get enough of them."

"Those'll kill you on their own," said Terry.

"That's what Norman used to say. He'd bring over cake do-nuts with no icing. He always thought they were better."

"They are . . . a little."

Terry slid a file folder back into the box with the others and closed the top.

"Fuckin' Norman—he was thorough. I'll give him that. Some of this reads like a training manual."

"That's 'cause Norman didn't think he was doing anything wrong," said Paul. "He thought it was the best way to do the job. He wanted people to know."

"Bullshit," said Terry. "He knew what he was doing."

"Did he? . . . Did I? Did you?"

"I never did anything like this," said Terry, pointing to the files.

"You're gonna sit there and tell me you never roughed up anyone in one of these rooms? You never gave an extra shove, tightened the cuffs a bit too much, belted a perp with your baton? C'mon, Terry, you watched just like me, and you didn't stop him."

"That's not the same, and you know it."

"How you figure that?"

"Busting a guy in the jaw because he took a shot at you ain't the same as taking a cattle prod to his nuts. Sorry, you're not gonna convince me of that."

Terry put his cigarette out on the table and pulled another from the pack. Fresh tobacco and ash sprinkled onto the floor. He got up and stared into the two-way mirror behind Paul. His stained, scratched-up reflection stared back.

"It's a murder charge, Paul. You killed Norman. We have the gun. We have your prints."

"I know."

"If you were me, what would you do?"

"I'm not you."

"Quit the crap."

"I'll tell you what I'd like to do, Terry, and you can take it or leave it. I'd like to go home, kiss Sheila, take a long hot shower and cry. I'd eat. I'd breathe, probably have a couple of beers. Then I'd go claim Norman's body down at the morgue and make all the arrangements to have my best friend of thirty years buried next to his son and wife. I'd probably cry some more, drink some more, and go to sleep . . . Basically, I'd try to hold my shit together for two weeks."

"What's in two weeks?"

"Before all this crap, me and Sheila got tickets for a cruise— one of them Alaskan whale-watching things—"

Two quiet knocks came at the door before it opened. The

same young detective, Nick Weiss, came in carrying a box at his chest. He set it on the table, opened it, and pulled out two tall stacks of old VHS tapes.

"Take her to Paris," said Terry. "Sheila brought these in this morning. They were left on your doorstep."

"What's on them?" asked Paul.

"About 400 hours of victim testimony of police brutality—that man, Levi, was just as thorough as Norman. Paired with Norman's files, they destroy the department for the foreseeable future. The number of overturned cases and lawsuits would be in numbers that no one has ever seen. "

"Chicago problems—Chicago solutions," said Paul quietly.

"What's that?" asked Terry.

"Ah, nothing. Just something Norman used to say."

Terry took a long drag. The cigarette burned bright at his mouth. He dropped it on the ground, half-smoked, and let the burning cherry slowly fill the room. He took the box of video tapes off the table and stacked them with Norman's files on the back wall. He unlocked Paul's cuffs and went to the door.

"I always liked you, Paul. I hated Norman—God rest his soul. But you I always liked."

Terry walked out, left the door open. The thick cigarette smoke drifted out of the interrogation room and was replaced by the ringing of electronic telephones and the sound of police officers in the middle of their day. Paul slowly got up. His legs ached. His chest caved in the center, curved his once strong shoulders and bent his once sturdy back. His gut swayed back and forth as he shuffled through the precinct offices. No eyes looked up.

Conversations continued. Officers laughed. When they released him into the lobby, he met eyes with all that he had left. Sheila embraced him, let him hide his face in her shoulder. As he collapsed in her arms, tears spilled over his face. He was ashamed. He was broken. He was invisible—just another victim of assault, a balding retiree with no children and partial loss of sight.

Printed in the United States
by Baker & Taylor Publisher Services